Acclaim for the
SCOTT

"Terrific...A white-knuckle fun machine."
—*Stephen King*

"Impressive...inventive...immensely enjoyable."
—*Wall Street Journal*

"Highly entertaining."
—*Publishers Weekly*

"A wildly inventive fantasia spiced with frequent revelations."
—*Kirkus Reviews*

"Wonderful, intricate and satisfying...Von Doviak has done an incredible job."
—*The Crime Review*

"A riveting tale...worthy of Dashiell Hammett in his prime."
—*Ernie Cline*

"Breathtakingly clever...Scott Von Doviak [is] a storyteller of the first order."
—*Criminal Element*

"The sort of canny, witty crime novel that doesn't come along often enough...The crew at Hard Case Crime has found another gem!"
—*Owen King*

"An amazing sense of place and time...Can't imagine it not making the Best Of lists next year."
—*Thomas Sniegoski*

Sheriff Giddings went inside. Tables were overturned, windows were broken—along with many glasses and pitchers—and the floor was slick with beer and blood.

The bartender looked like she'd gone a few rounds with George Foreman. He showed her the photo.

"Yeah, they were here." She grinned, revealing a cracked tooth in an otherwise brilliant smile. "That's Dean, the foxy one. His cousin Chuck I didn't meet."

"How long ago did they leave?"

"Maybe an hour ago? Why, they in some kind of trouble?"

"They killed a police officer in cold blood."

"Oh, I don't believe it. Chuck, maybe. Like I said, I didn't meet him. But Dean, he's just as sweet as pie."

"Do you know where they were going?"

"Dean said something about Evel Knievel. I guess he's doing some big jump this weekend."

"Do you know if they were planning on stopping for the night?"

"Not really. They left in a hurry. If you're trying to catch them, I don't think you're alone. They pissed off a bunch of bikers too, and they're headed for the same place."

Giddings called the motel and canceled his room for the night. Too many other people were after the Melville boys, and he wasn't about to let any of them beat him to the punch...

SOME OTHER HARD CASE CRIME BOOKS YOU WILL ENJOY:

Lowdown ROAD

by **Scott Von Doviak**

A HARD CASE CRIME BOOK
(HCC-159)
First Hard Case Crime edition: July 2023

Published by

Titan Books
A division of Titan Publishing Group Ltd
144 Southwark Street
London SE1 0UP

in collaboration with Winterfall LLC

Print edition ISBN 978-1-80336-413-1
E-book ISBN 978-1-80336-412-4

Design direction by Max Phillips
www.maxphillips.net

Typeset by Swordsmith Productions

Printed and bound in the United States of America by LSC Communications, Harrisonburg

Visit us on the web at www.HardCaseCrime.com

LOWDOWN ROAD

ONE

Chuck Melville managed to stay out of trouble for six months following his release from the Texas state prison in Huntsville. That's what folks would say later over coffee at the Buttered Biscuit, although it would be more accurate to point out that Chuck got into a great deal of trouble during those six months—he just managed to evade the attention of law enforcement while he was doing it.

That lucky streak ended on a sticky late summer night in 1974 when Chuck pulled into the parking lot of the shopping plaza at North and Hutchison and spotted Gary Foulke getting out of his Ford F250. It was Gary who got Chuck sent to Huntsville in the first place, or at least that's how Chuck saw it. The way he told it to his lawyer, it was Gary who beat the Sac 'n Pac cashier with a tire iron while Chuck helped himself to the contents of the register. But when the judge read the verdict, it was Chuck who got a five-year stretch in Huntsville for aggravated assault, while Gary got away with six months in the county jail.

Watching Gary make his way from his truck to Discount Liquors, Chuck figured his old pal could use a lesson in aggravated assault. He hit the gas and the Magnum V8 engine under the hood of the 1970 Dodge Challenger jumped to life. Gary heard it and glanced back over his shoulder, and Chuck saw his eyes go wide as the Grand Canyon just before he managed to dive out of the way. The plate-glass window bearing the Discount Liquors logo and the neatly arranged displays of cut-rate gin and bourbon behind it all exploded at once as Chuck plowed through the storefront.

Chuck shook it off and threw it into reverse as Discount Liquors proprietor Rob "Rooster" Reubens charged at him, arms waving, face redder than a Hill Country sunset. Chuck skidded and slammed into a VW Beetle, crumpling its hood like tissue paper. He glimpsed Gary hot-footing it back to his truck and slammed on the gas pedal again, forgetting he was still in reverse. He pancaked the Beetle into the Olds 88 parked behind it, shifted into forward gear, and clipped Rooster just as he'd reached the passenger side door. He heard Rooster holler and saw him roll to the pavement clutching his ankle in the rear-view.

He'd missed his shot. Gary's truck was already squealing out of the lot, heading west on Hutchison. At least he'd put a scare into his old pal. He spotted a frantic woman screaming into the pay phone in front of the check-cashing place and decided he'd shop for his liquor elsewhere. He pulled the Challenger out of the lot and drove it like he stole it. Technically, he *did* steal it, but that was another story.

Chuck headed south until he crossed the county line. He was thirsty and remembered a place somewhere out on Route 46 where he could wet his whistle and maybe hustle up a game of pool. The trees thinned out ahead and he spotted the neon beer signs. It was nearly midnight and Sonny's Icehouse was hopping.

The Challenger's tires crunched over the gravel and bottlecaps that made up the parking lot. He found a place to park around back, which was perfect since he didn't want the Challenger attracting undue attention. The events at the shopping plaza earlier might have made the radio news by now.

Once upon a time in Texas, icehouses had been just that—places where you could pick up blocks of ice to keep your food from spoiling in the days before home refrigeration. Having all that ice on hand made them the coolest spots in town to hang out, and the proprietors soon realized they could keep beer nice and cold, too. Sonny's typified the modern Texas icehouse: a dozen or so picnic tables outside, crowded with happy drinkers laughing and whooping it up; a jukebox inside playing Jerry Reed's "Lord, Mr. Ford"; a couple of cowboys shooting pool and a bunch more crowded around watching; a jar of pickled eggs on the bar. Most surprising of all to Chuck, an attractive woman seated alone at the bar, unbothered by anyone.

Chuck pretended to study the jukebox selections, but his eyes kept wandering over to that woman. She was blonde, probably not naturally, and looked to be about thirty years old. She wore cutoff dungaree shorts and a tank top that barely restrained the gifts God gave her. A pack of Virginia Slims sat on the bar in front of her, minus the one she was smoking. She took an occasional sip from a bottle of Lone Star. A bar full of men, all of them ignoring her.

Chuck put a nickel in the jukebox and selected Merle Haggard's "Mama Tried." He considered it to be his theme song. He unrolled the pack of Winstons from his left sleeve, popped one in his mouth, and lit it. He walked over and leaned on the bar next to the woman, playing it cool, signaling to the barkeep.

"Lone Star longneck," he said.

The man nodded and set a cold one in front of him. "Fifty cents."

Chuck set a dollar on the bar. "Might as well give me another. This one ain't gonna last."

True to his word, Chuck chugged down half the bottle in one go. Licking his lips, he turned his attention to the woman next to him. "Maybe you can help me understand something."

"Maybe I can," she said, lighting another smoke.

"How is it that such a gorgeous woman as yourself can sit here alone at the bar, and not one of these red-blooded Texans in here even seems to know you're alive?"

"Oh, they know I'm alive. Only reason they ain't drooling all over me like you is they're afraid of my husband."

Chuck laughed and crushed his cigarette in the ashtray. "Perks of being from out of town, I guess. I don't know your husband, and I damn sure ain't afraid of him."

The woman looked him over. "Well, that's a refreshing change. What's your name, stranger?"

"Charles Melville III. But you can call me Chuck."

"I'd rather call you Charles, honestly."

"That'll work. And your name is…?"

"Gwen Harlan. See, everyone else in here knows that."

"And now I know it. Buy you another round, Gwen?"

"I was hoping."

He did so, and they clinked bottles and drank.

"So what do you do, Charles?"

"Well now, that is a complicated question."

"Didn't sound complicated when it left my lips, but I guess we're just getting to know each other."

"What I mean is, I had a job. Working at a car wash. I quit it this morning. Had a little disagreement with my boss. He was under the impression that I stole some quarters out of the ashtray of this Buick station wagon while I was vacuuming it. Now, we're talking about maybe six to eight quarters, so that's two dollars at most. How the hell am I gonna risk losing my job over a lousy two bucks?"

"But it sounds like you did lose it."

"No, ma'am. Like I said, I quit that job. Just the very suggestion that I would do such a thing was too much for me to bear.

And anyway, I could tell he was gearing up to fire me, and no way was I gonna give him the satisfaction. Turns out it was the best thing I could have done, because I ran into an old associate of mine this afternoon and we discussed a new business opportunity."

Chuck didn't feel it was the right moment to mention that the associate in question was also a former inmate of the state prison in Huntsville. The particulars of the business opportunity were criminal in nature, and Chuck and his friend had discussed them while snorting crank and shooting at empty beer cans. Nor did Chuck think the time was right to disclose that he'd later tried to run over another old associate of his. Maybe once they'd gotten to know each other a little better.

"So where is this husband of yours everyone is so scared of?" he said by way of changing the subject. "You expecting him tonight?"

"No, he's working the night shift."

The overhead fluorescents flashed, signaling last call. "So that means your place is free for the rest of the evening?"

She looked him over again: his bushy muttonchop sideburns, his prominent chin, the gleam of a gold tooth in his smile. She'd seen worse. "You've got a lot of confidence, Charles."

"I'm a man who knows what he likes. And what I'd like right now is to get a six-pack to go, take you out to my car, and drive you back to your place. At that point, we can just see where the night takes us."

"My car is here."

"And I'm sure it will be safe here until the morning. But I've got a Dodge Challenger parked out there, and you would not believe what that baby can do on these back roads."

"Charles, I think you talked me into it."

*

When Gwen climbed into the passenger seat, her foot hit an object on the floorboard. She picked it up. "What do we have here?"

"That's my Saturday night special," said Chuck. He'd been using the .25 semi-automatic pistol for target practice earlier in the day, after which he'd stuffed it under the passenger seat. He figured it must have gotten kicked loose while he was barrel-assing around the shopping plaza parking lot. "Why don't you be a doll and stuff that back under your seat for me."

She squinted and aimed the pistol toward Sonny's front door. "Next one out is a dead man."

"Come on, now. That ain't funny."

She shrugged and stuffed the gun back under her seat. "I thought it was."

Chuck started the car. "Which way we headed?"

"Turn right out of the parking lot and show me what this thing can do."

Chuck cracked open a Lone Star and peeled out of the lot. He gunned it when he hit the blacktop and ten seconds later the speedometer hit eighty. It was a winding Hill Country road, and the car hugged every turn.

"It straightens out up here for a couple miles," said Gwen, sipping her beer. "Bet you can't hit 120."

"Shit, I can get 'er to 130 without breaking a sweat."

The engine revved and the speedometer climbed. The stars hung low in the Texas night sky, zipping by like comets. Gwen ran her fingers along Chuck's leg. The Challenger hit 120 as it squealed past the police cruiser hidden by a mesquite tree just off the road.

Gwen spotted the red and blue flashing lights in her side-view mirror first. "Better hit it or quit it."

Chuck had no intention of quitting it. He pushed the

tachometer into the red as the Challenger neared 130 miles per hour. Whatever their pursuer had under the hood, there was no way he could catch them. Except the stretch of straightaway had come to an end and the road started winding again. At eighty, Chuck could still hug the curves. At 130, no chance. "Keep it between the ditches," his Daddy always told him, the golden rule. The Challenger spun out as Chuck hit the brakes and did three full donuts before leaving the road entirely.

The car came to a rest gently enough under the circumstances. Chuck surveyed their surroundings. Running wasn't an option, as the wide-open plain they found themselves in afforded no cover. The cruiser rolled to a stop behind them.

"You just let me handle this," said Chuck. Gwen turned her head and stared out the passenger-side window.

The beam of a flashlight filled Chuck's window. The cop knocked and Chuck rolled it down.

"License and registration, please."

Chuck handed them over. The cop examined them for a moment. "Now, you'll have to help me out here, sir. Your driver's license says Charles Melville, but this here vehicle is registered to a Dean Melville."

"He's my cousin."

"Does he know you have his car?"

"He'll figure it out."

The cop leaned down and peered into the car. As Chuck's eyes adjusted, he could see he was dealing with a sheriff's deputy. He had a calm demeanor and an ingratiating smile, as if they were just neighbors chatting over a fence. His nametag read "Harlan," and that sounded familiar.

"This woman in the car with you," said Deputy Harlan. "Is that your wife?"

"Nothing so formal as that," said Chuck.

"Ma'am, I'm going to need to see your face."

Gwen turned to face the deputy and gave a little wave.

"See, this is exactly what I thought," said Deputy Harlan. "She couldn't be your wife, because she's my wife."

"Gwen Harlan," Chuck muttered.

"That's right. And I'm Beau Harlan."

"Listen, deputy, this is all a misunderstanding. She didn't say nothin' about being married."

"No, I believe I did," said Gwen. "I distinctly remember telling you that no one else in that bar was talking to me because they're all afraid of my husband."

"I'm going to have to ask you both to step out of the vehicle now."

"Deputy, I think we can settle this up real simple," said Chuck. "Why don't you just take her with you, and I'll be on my way? After all, I was simply giving the woman a ride home with no bad intentions, and now there's no need for me to do that."

"Get out of the car. Now."

Chuck sighed, pushed open his door, and climbed out.

"Put your hands on the hood and spread your legs, please."

Chuck complied. "Listen, I'm gonna be completely straight with you. I am on parole. Anything you could do in the way of letting me off with a warning would be greatly appreciated."

Deputy Harlan patted him down. "I guess I don't even need to ask if you've been drinking tonight, judging from the empty containers in your vehicle. Well, your cousin's vehicle, I mean to say."

"Beau!"

Chuck and the deputy both looked in the direction of the outburst. Both saw Gwen standing there, holding Chuck's Saturday night special, but Deputy Harlan didn't see her for long. She squeezed off three shots. The deputy shuddered and stumbled backward, his face transformed into a mask of shock. He touched his chest, and his hand came away covered in blood. He collapsed to the ground.

"Holy shit!" said Chuck. "Are you crazy?" He knelt down to confirm what he already knew. The deputy was gone. "Jesus Christ. I mean, yeah, you got us out of our immediate predicament, but this is really bad. He must have called in the license plate before he got out of his car, searching for wants and warrants and what-have-yous."

"Your cousin's license plate."

"Well, yeah. I see what you're saying, but it's not going to take long for anyone investigating this here crime to learn that you and I were together at Sonny's Icehouse tonight and that we left together. Maybe even an eyewitness saw us leaving in this car."

"Stand up, Charles. I need you to explain something to me."

Chuck did as she asked, nice and slow. "What is it, dollface?"

"Two questions. First, is my husband dead?"

"Oh yes. He's really most sincerely dead."

"Second question. How could you kill my husband like that? In cold blood?" She pointed the gun at him.

"Now, let's think about this, Gwen. I get what's going through your head. You want to pin this on me, and that makes sense from your point of view. That is my gun, although I should tell you it is not a registered weapon. I bought it at a flea market, paid cash. But here's the most important thing. If you shoot me with the same gun that killed your husband, well, it's not gonna take Columbo to figure out you're the one who pulled the trigger on both of us."

"Step away from my husband's body."

Chuck did so. Gwen took a few steps toward the corpse.

"What's the plan here, Gwen?"

"What you say is true. I can't shoot you with this gun. But if I shoot you with my husband's gun, it looks like you shot each other. And I'll just be the grieving widow they find on the scene. I'll tell them how you made me leave Sonny's with you at gunpoint. How you drove like a maniac with me as your terrified prisoner. It's all gonna work out for me."

"It does sound that way, except for one minor detail," he said as she leaned down beside her dead husband. He watched as she reached for his holster and found it empty. He raised Deputy Harlan's .38 and took aim. "You see, I already liberated this from your husband while I was checking his vitals. Not that I knew right away what you had planned. I ain't that clever. But seeing what you had just done to your husband did make me kinda wonder what you'd do to a man you just met tonight."

Gwen stood up, hands raised. "Now, listen, Charles. We can work this out another way. We can get back in your car and drive all the way to Mexico."

"No, I don't believe that will work. Like I said, this car is already burnt. He called in the plates, so if we try to cross the border, they'll have the number and we'll be in cuffs. Here's how I see it. They're gonna find you and your husband here, both shot dead with separate guns. Some kind of lovers' quarrel, who knows. They'll find his patrol car, but they won't find that Challenger. No one's ever gonna see it again. Now, my cousin Dean is gonna be pissed about that, but to be honest, that's the least of my worries at the moment."

"You're not going to kill me, Charles." She turned and started running back toward the road.

Chuck didn't want to shoot her in the back, but the way he saw it, she hadn't left him much choice. He kept squeezing the trigger until the gun had nothing left.

TWO

Dean Melville wished he felt as cool as he knew he looked. His mane of jet-black hair just touched his shoulders; his mustache had not a hair out of place; his Lynyrd Skynyrd t-shirt clung to his pecs and biceps; his Levi's hugged his crotch; his Aviators were tinted just the right shade of light brown. But he was standing in Antoine Lynch's office at the salvage yard, and Antoine had given no indication he'd even noticed yet. He just ran a pick through his afro, occasionally flipping the pages of the *Sports Illustrated* issue on the desk in front of him.

Dean kept chewing his gum and pretending to study the posters of muscle cars and women with power tools on the walls. He'd seen them all before and was particularly enamored of the blonde in the pink bikini wielding a Makita drill like she was James Bond, but today his nerves were on fire. He didn't think Antoine had called him in for a friendly chat.

Finally, Antoine shook his head and held up the magazine so Dean could see the cover. "I swear, you white people crack me up sometimes. Y'all just love this crazy shitkicker, don't you?"

Dean squinted at the cover. A man in a form-fitting white jumpsuit with blue star-spangled stripes held a cane and sneered into the distance in front of a pastoral scene.

"You don't like Evel Knievel?" said Dean.

"This Elvis-looking peckerwood is gonna strap his ass to a firecracker and blow himself to Kingdom Gone, and y'all act like he's some kind of real-life superhero. Like the Six Million Dollar Man or some shit."

"They say he's broken every bone in his body. That's kind of like the Six Million Dollar Man, right?"

"This redneck motherfucker ain't bionic, that's for shit sure. I tell you what, you ain't never gonna see a brother get up to this kind of nonsense. For real, think about all them little white kids all across America with their wind-up Evel Knievel stunt-cycles. They're all gonna be bawling their eyes out when they scrape this fool off the side of the canyon."

"What if he makes it?"

"Then he'll try something even more stupid down the line. Try to jump the Grand Canyon in a go-cart or some shit. I'm telling you, he's got a death wish. You got a death wish, Dean?"

"No way. Life is good." Dean blew a bubble and it popped. He sucked the gum back into his mouth and continued to chew.

"Well, it can be. If everything works the way it's supposed to work. Take you and me, for instance. We've got a pretty good working arrangement, don't we?"

"Absolutely."

"You buy the product from me at my price, you sell it at your price, and everybody's happy. It's pretty basic capitalism. I don't know if it's the best system, but it's the one we have. Only last week you ran into a bit of pickle, and we switched things up. And I was happy to do it, because you've been so reliable. So you got the product on consignment with the understanding that you'd be paying me the usual price plus ten percent when we met today. Now, are you prepared to do that?"

"Look, I'm not gonna bullshit you, Antoine. The fact is that I don't have the money right now as we speak. See, there was a little shakeup at work, and Gonzo gave my spot to his brother who just moved back to town. So now I'm out at the medical center, and that's not exactly a good fit for, you know, what we do."

Gonzo was Emilio Gonzales, owner of three Gonzo Taco trucks in the San Marcos area. For the past six months, Dean had operated the taco truck parked outside Cheatham Street

Warehouse, a honky-tonk just a stone's throw from Southwest Texas State University. It was the perfect location to sell tacos, and even more perfect for the other business Dean conducted through the truck: selling weed. He bought the product in bulk from Antoine and sold it in joints to trusted customers who knew the password.

It was all good until Gonzo's brother showed up and claimed the spot, sending Dean to another truck near the medical center, greatly reducing his walk-up traffic. He was doing less than a third of his former business in the new location. Compounding his problems, a costly transmission repair to his beloved Dodge Challenger had put him in the hole. Now he was in debt to Antoine, and worst of all, he had no idea where the Challenger was. He had a pretty good idea who had it, though.

Antoine owned not only the salvage yard, but the land behind it, including a landing strip where small planes from Mexico could touch down just long enough to unload their cargo. Antoine was the wholesaler and Dean was one of his retailers—one of how many, he didn't know. This was a business, yes, but an illegal one with its own set of rules.

"You don't have my money today, the penalty goes up to twenty percent. You can't sell the product out of your truck, find somewhere else to sell it. But you're going to get my money or else I'm going to take your car."

"Come on, Antoine. You know I love that car."

"I know you do. And I assume you also love having the use of both your legs. Do we understand each other?"

"We do."

"Piece of advice, though. Learn how to fix your own car. You take it to a garage, you're just begging them to empty out your wallet. Come out here, find the parts you need in the yard, and I'll charge you a fair price. You can fix it here using our tools, gratis. Now, that assumes you bring me my money and get to keep the car."

"That's solid advice, Antoine."

"Best believe it. While I got you here, let me ask you something. You know what onomastics is?"

"A fancy word for jerking off?"

"No, that's onanism. Onomastics is the study of names. See, I find names fascinating. For instance, my last name is Lynch. Kind of ironic, seeing as how lynching is what your people used to do to my people. Hell, still do when they can get away with it."

"I never thought of it that way. But I was always told we never had any slaveowners in our family tree."

"Oh, I'm sure you were. But what about Klan?"

"Well...my Uncle Red was Klan, true. I think he was all talk and no action, but who knows."

"Now, your family name, Melville. You share that with one of the greats of American literature. You ever read *Moby Dick*?"

"The classic comics version, in high school."

"I thought you went to college?"

"One year. Well, almost one year." Dean had attended the University of Texas at Austin, but in truth he had mostly attended Barton Springs and the Armadillo World Headquarters. There was too much fun to be had in Austin, and classes just got in the way.

"Well, your loss. But *Moby Dick* might be a little too deep for you. I got another fish story here might be more your speed." Antoine dug a hardcover book out of a drawer and tossed it on the desk. Dean picked it up.

"*Jaws* by Peter Benchley. I think I heard about this."

"They're making a movie out of it. How the hell they're gonna train a shark to do all the shit it does in that book, I have no idea. Anyway, take that and read it. And when you're done, bring it back to the library at Southwest Texas. I'm serious about that. I don't do business with any triflin' motherfucker would steal from a library."

"Will do. Anything else?"

"Get my money, Dean."

"I will." He knew he had to do it. He just had no clue how.

THREE

One thing Sheriff Edwin Giddings couldn't stand was having a screamer in one of the cells, especially when he was trying to do his crossword. There were three jail cells in the Ivor County Sheriff's Department, only one of which was occupied at the time. That occupant, one Randall Jennings, age twenty-two, had been caught with a baseball bat outside his ex-girlfriend's house, where he failed to come up with a plausible explanation for all the dents and broken windows in the Buick LeSabre parked in the driveway that would dissuade the responding deputy from taking him in. Now he was hollering about a stomach ailment, which Sheriff Giddings aimed to make much worse for him once he'd puzzled out a seven-letter word meaning "dessert in a tall glass."

It had already been a long night. Giddings would have been home in bed hours earlier if he hadn't received an emergency call from the Twilight Ranch. Miss Mona, the madam of the aforementioned house of ill repute, had caught Giddings just as he was leaving the office for the day.

"I need you out here right away, Bud."

"Dammit, Miss Mona. I was just heading home to get some dinner and watch the ballgame."

"Bud, unless you want me to call your wife and tell her a couple things about a thing or two, you'd best get your ass out here pronto. I have a situation. Code Red."

"What the hell is Code Red supposed to mean?"

"Use your imagination, Bud. Just hightail it out here, toot sweet."

Giddings hung up, rubbed his eyelids, and cursed his heritage.

There had been a Sheriff Giddings in Ivor County since the 1920s. His grandfather held the job first, and his father took over when he returned from beating the Nazis. There was never any question that the job would be his one day. He never had any say in the matter. Now he had to deal with shit like this.

To get to the Twilight Ranch, you had to know it was there. It wasn't down on any map, and the Chamber of Commerce for sure didn't have it listed on their pamphlet of notable attractions. Like a real ranch—the kind with cattle—it was separated from the main road by a gate and a long dirt entrance. It was just after 7:30 P.M. when Giddings arrived and stepped through the front door into the parlor.

No one was ever going to write a musical about the Twilight Ranch. The parlor housed a couple of stained, ripped couches and a ratty loveseat currently occupied by a sad-eyed redhead with runny makeup who kept checking her watch. The bar consisted of a half-empty bottle of cheap tequila and a couple of shot glasses that looked like they hadn't been washed since Lyndon Johnson was president. The radio was broadcasting a station from San Antonio it could barely pick up; Giddings couldn't identify the music buried in the static.

When Miss Mona entered the room, Giddings' first thought was that she'd put on thirty pounds since he last saw her. Not that he had much room to talk, with his gut hanging low over his Texas belt buckle, but then, he wasn't in the sex trade. Well, that wasn't strictly true, as he took monthly payoffs from the Twilight Ranch to turn a blind eye to its illegal activities. He supposed that made him a silent partner of sorts, but at least no one was paying to see him naked. Still, if you lived in Ivor County, you couldn't afford to be picky. The Twilight Ranch was your only option if you didn't want to drive more than fifty miles.

"What am I doing here, Miss Mona?"

"Come with me." She led him up the stairs, past one bedroom, from which a variety of unpleasant grunts and moans echoed through the thin walls, to another at the end of the hall. Once they were inside the room, she closed the door behind them and gestured to the bed. The man lying there was naked except for the nylon stocking wrapped tightly around his neck.

"Jesus, Mary, and Joseph," said Giddings. "Is that Freddy McElroy?"

"It is."

"Is he dead?"

"He looks dead to me, but I ain't touching him. That's why I called you."

"What exactly happened here?"

"He had a date with Marie tonight. His usual."

"Marie is the sad clown downstairs?"

"She is. Freddy likes her because she'll indulge in the kind of horseplay he enjoys."

"Horseplay? You mean strangling him with her stocking?"

"That's part of it. He likes spankings too. And some other stuff with his rear end, but you probably don't want to hear about that."

Giddings winced. Freddy McElroy was a county commissioner and a bank president. If Ivor County had any upstanding citizens, he was one. Or so Giddings had always thought.

"So…this was an accident?"

"Well, that's what Marie says. But she's had dozens of dates with Freddy where they've done this exact same thing, and somehow it never went wrong before."

"What are you telling me? You think she killed him?"

"I don't know. But I do know he liked filthy talk in addition to the horseplay, and sometimes Marie didn't appreciate that as much. Especially when he was the one doing the talking."

Giddings nodded and started formulating a plan. His thought

process was derailed when Freddy launched into a coughing fit.

"Oh, shit!" said Miss Mona. "He's alive!"

Giddings walked over to the bed and loosened the stocking around Freddy's neck. "You all right, Freddy?"

Freddy coughed some more.

"Well, don't just stand there," said Giddings. "Run and get this man a glass of water!"

Miss Mona hurried out of the room. Giddings helped Freddy sit up.

"Sheriff," Freddy managed once the coughing subsided. "I want you to arrest that crazy bitch who tried to kill me. I want you to arrest Miss Mona too, and I want you to close this place down forever. I want you to burn it to the ground!"

"Now, Freddy, you're a little excited. It's understandable. Why don't you just relax a moment and—"

"I am not going to relax until that bitch is in jail and this place is gone for good!"

"You don't mean that, Freddy. The Twilight Ranch is an Ivor County institution."

"A mental institution, more like. Listen to me, Sheriff. I know you're on the take here and a dozen other places besides. You better do as I say or there's going to be big trouble coming your way."

"I tell you what, Freddy. I'm getting just a little bit tired of people threatening me this evening." Giddings picked up a pillow from the bed and pressed it down over Freddy's face. Freddy struggled, but he was no match for the iron strength of the county sheriff. Giddings held the pillow in place until Freddy stopped moving and kept holding it until Miss Mona returned with the glass of water, which promptly fell from her hand and shattered on the floor.

"What have you done, Bud?"

"I didn't do anything. He was dead when I got here, remember? Now who else knows about this besides you and Marie?"

"Nobody."

"Who is that carrying on in the other bedroom?"

"That's Jerry Hunsicker with Charlene. But he got here before Freddy, so they don't know he's here."

"All right." Giddings wrapped the naked corpse up in the bedclothes. "Go through his pants and find his keys. He and I are gonna take a ride, and you're gonna follow in my cruiser."

"Where are we going?"

"You'll find out."

In the morning, an accident scene would be discovered, and an upstanding citizen of the county would be mourned. Giddings would never lose any sleep over it. The only thing that bothered him was that a pervert like Freddy had been a county commissioner in the first place. Once he'd set it all up, he drove Miss Mona back to the Twilight Ranch in his cruiser. She asked if he wanted a bubble bath in her clawfoot tub, and he thought that sounded like a fine idea. She scrubbed his back and offered to do more, but he had an ugly rash on his scrotum he didn't want her to see, so he declined. Besides, Miss Mona didn't really do it for him anymore. He got his kicks elsewhere these days.

Afterward he was too wired to go home, so he headed back to the office. He poured himself some bourbon and got to work on the crossword, but that's when Randall Jennings started hollering in his cell. Giddings tried to block out the sound, but eventually he gave up and walked to the back room.

"Maybe you can help me," he said to Randall, who was flummoxed enough to stop howling for a moment. "I'm looking for a seven-letter word for a dessert served in a tall glass. The fourth letter is F, and the last letter is T."

"Please," said Randall. "It's my stomach. I need a doctor. Please, call a doctor. The pain, it's more than I can stand."

Giddings nodded and unlocked the cell. He motioned for Randall to come out. Randall took two tentative steps forward before Giddings wound up and punched him as hard as he could right in the gut. Randall crumpled to the floor and his hollering turned to whimpering.

"That's a little better," said Giddings, locking the cell. "You just rest up and we'll call the doc in the morning."

He returned to his desk and got back to work on the puzzle. He solved fourteen down and got the first letter for the word meaning dessert in a tall glass. "I'll be goddamned. It's 'parfait.'"

The phone rang. He sighed and answered it. "Sheriff's office."

"Is this Sheriff Giddings?"

"Who's asking?"

"This is Officer Perez with the Department of Public Safety. I'm afraid I've got some bad news for you. Your deputy, Beau Harlan, he's dead."

"What the hell are you talking about?"

"He's been shot. And not just him. His wife, too."

"What did you just say?" Giddings felt like he was the one who'd taken the gut punch. "Gwen Harlan has been shot? Is she okay?"

"She's dead too. I think you're gonna want to come out here right away."

Officer Perez gave him the mile marker and Giddings wrote it down with a shaky hand. He put on his Stetson and headed back to his cruiser, hoping there had been some kind of mistake.

FOUR

Dean was forty-five minutes into his shift when Gonzo pulled up in his purple 1957 Cadillac Eldorado convertible. Since he'd opened the truck for business, Dean had sold a grand total of three breakfast tacos and none of his other, more profitable commodity.

He knew there was nothing wrong with the food. Dean wasn't a particularly good cook, let alone a master of Mexican cuisine, but that didn't matter. All the food prep was done at Gonzo's brick-and-mortar location just off the interstate. The truck had warmer bins full of scrambled eggs, bacon, chorizo, refried beans, and home fries, all awaiting his meager morning trade. When lunchtime rolled around, all Dean had to do was reach down into the refrigerator and pull out the picadillo or the carnitas or the achiote chicken and toss a handful onto the countertop griddle. The corn tortillas were made fresh each morning, and he kept a pile on the prep station to heat up as needed. The most taxing thing he ever had to do was remember to open the exhaust hood whenever he threw a batch of chips into the fryer.

No, the problem was location, location, location. The truck was parked in the lot farthest from the main entrance to the medical center, and the foot traffic was nearly nonexistent. He had a few loyal customers from his old spot who made the trek, but most of his clientele had found alternate sources of illegal mind expansion closer to campus.

All of which was at the top of his mind as Gonzo approached the takeout window. Gonzo wore black chinos and a white t-shirt, a cigarette pack tucked into one rolled-up sleeve. He had a wallet chain and a pompadour piled up to the heavens. In Gonzo's world, it was always 1957. He told anyone who would listen for more than two minutes that he went to high school with Buddy Holly and played drums in his first band. He claimed they'd made plans to reunite right before the Day the Music Died. Dean once flipped through a biography of Buddy Holly at the library and checked the index, where he found no listing for Emilio Gonzales. He never mentioned it to Gonzo, though.

When he reached the window, Gonzo checked the squeeze bottles of homemade hot sauce in the rack beneath it. They were arranged in order of spiciness, from Gringo to Gonzo, the latter being the hottest habanero sauce in town. He squeezed a drop of his namesake sauce onto his fingertip, touched it to his tongue, and whistled.

"Como te va, Dino?"

"Not too bueno, jefe. This location, man. I mean, what the hell?"

"My amigo in the parking office here, he arranged this for me. Gratis."

"But nobody knows we're here. Just the few people who park this far out, and it's hardly worth opening for them."

"Word of mouth, Dino. It's gonna spread like wildfire through this place. You wait, the lunchtime rush is gonna start soon and it will be bigger than yesterday. And tomorrow will be bigger still."

"I don't know, Gonzo. I feel like I'm being punished out here."

"No, no, that ain't it at all, Dino. It's mi hermano, you know, he's been down there in Nuevo Laredo for six years and he just got back. Now, he can't go and get a job just any old place, so I had to take him on."

"So why not start him out here? Ease him into it?"

"Because he won't do shit out here. You, on the other hand, you built that location at Cheatham Street up from nothing.

You got more business there than I ever dreamed. He's gonna have to work his ass off. Meanwhile, you're out here, building up the next big thing."

Dean stared out at the desolate parking lot and shook his head. "I don't know, jefe. There must be somewhere else we can try this."

"What do you care anyway, Dino? You get paid just the same either way, right?"

"Well...yeah, but the tips were better over at Cheatham."

"Oh yeah? The tips from college students were good, huh?"

Dean raised his hands in surrender. "Whatever, Gonzo. I'll make it work somehow."

"That's what I want to hear. You know, when Buddy and I were starting out in Lubbock, we had no hope of ever getting on the local radio, let alone having national hit records. And look what happened."

Yeah, thought Dean. He did it without you and died in a plane crash at twenty-two. But what he said was, "Rock on, Gonzo."

Gonzo high-fived him and headed back to his Caddy. When he pulled out of the lot, he hit the horn and cranked up "Not Fade Away" on the stereo.

Dean took a seat on the prep counter and cracked open the book Antoine had given him. He'd already read the first chapter, in which a skinny-dipper got eaten alive by a shark. He'd just started chapter two, where the police chief investigates the woman's disappearance, when the passenger-side door banged open and his cousin Chuck stumbled inside.

"Jesus Christ," he said. "I thought he'd never leave."

"Where the fuck did you come from?"

"Wasn't easy finding you. Now we gotta go."

"Fuck you talking about, Chuck? I'm working."

"Cuz, shut it down, get your ass behind the wheel, and get us the fuck out of here. I'm serious. The cops are looking for you."

"The cops are—?" Dean laughed. "Fuck you, cuz. The cops'll be looking for you when I report my car stolen, which I should have done already."

"You really should have, but it's too late for that now. Look, I don't have time to explain this at the moment. We gotta roll."

"Roll where?"

"Not your place. Anywhere else."

"Fuck you, Chuckles. I'm tired of your shit. You been out of prison for six months, it feels like six years already."

"I will make it worth your while. And you owe me, cuz. I saved your life."

Dean rolled his eyes. "For the rest of my life I'm gonna hear this."

"Yeah, that's how it works. I saved your life, so you owe the rest of it to me. Now let's fucking roll!"

Dean sighed, tossed the book aside, and hopped down off the prep counter. He killed the griddle and shut down the propane tank, shoved every loose utensil and food tub into a cabinet, and locked it. He climbed behind the wheel and started up the truck.

"Where the hell are we going?"

"If all goes well, a long fucking way from here."

"Where's my car, Chuck?"

They were on Route 12 headed northwest. Chuck thought it would be a great idea for them to drop by and see his friend Double H in Wimberley. Double H was Hank Hendricks, Chuck's friend from prison with whom he'd done some target-shooting and crank-snorting the day before. Hank had a business opportunity Chuck wanted Dean to hear about.

Chuck had already explained the events of earlier that morning—his visit to Sonny's Icehouse, his joyride with Gwen Harlan, who he shot and killed shortly after she'd shot and killed her husband, Deputy Beau Harlan. Dean took it all in without a great deal of surprise, but for him, the most important question had yet to be answered. "What the fuck did you do with my Challenger?"

"Dean, have you ever heard of Crane's Mill, Texas?"

"No, I never have."

"Well, Crane's Mill was a little cattle town, not too far from here. I believe it was founded in the 1850s, and it never got very big—never even close to a hundred inhabitants—but it had a post office and a church, and it even had a bowling alley for a while."

"Why the fuck are you telling me this?"

"Just hold your horses, cuz. See, long about 1958, the Army Corps of Engineers started work on the Canyon Lake Dam. This was for flood control on the Guadalupe River, and obviously it wasn't called the Canyon Lake Dam when they were building it, because it ended up creating Canyon Lake. I'm sure you're familiar with it. But what you may not know is that the few remaining residents of Crane's Mill had to evacuate when the dam was built, because it ended up flooding the whole town. And to this day, the remains of the town of Crane's Mill are down there, a hundred feet beneath the surface of Canyon Lake."

"One more time, cuz. Why are you telling me this?"

"Because you asked me where your car is. And what I'm telling you is, your car is in the town of Crane's Mill, Texas."

Dean considered his response carefully. "Cousin, could you let me know if you see a gas station?"

"Why? We low on gas?"

"No. I just need a place to pull over so I can drag you in the back and shove your face in the deep fryer."

"I did it for your own good. I mean, would you rather I left it there at the crime scene?"

"I'd rather you never stole it from me at all."

"I borrowed it. You left the keys on your kitchen counter."

"I just had a new transmission put in it. And while I was at it, I got a tune-up and four brand-new tires. And that's why I'm now in debt to Antoine for more than two grand. So, since I can't give him my car, I'm gonna give him you. And I'm gonna say, 'Here's my cousin Chuck. Do whatever the fuck you want with him. Feed his dick to your dogs. Scoop out his eyeballs and play ping-pong with 'em. I don't give a shit.'"

"I understand that car meant a lot to you, but I'm urging you to see the big picture here."

"The big picture."

"I'll let Double H explain it. But I'll just say this. We're gonna be rich. This can't miss. And when you hear what he has to say, you're gonna thank me. And you're never gonna think about that car again."

"You better hope so. Otherwise, you're gonna get real familiar with the bottom of Canyon Lake."

FIVE

"Cripes, what a mess," said Deputy Curtis Winslow. He was referring to the puke and blood he was busy mopping up in the cell formerly occupied by Randall Jennings, who was now in the hospital undergoing emergency surgery. But as far as Sheriff Bud Giddings was concerned, Curtis might as well have been describing the last twelve hours of his life.

He'd arrived at the crime scene at quarter to four that morning. The DPS officer, Perez, led him through it. "Your deputy's cruiser, right there where we found it," said Perez, gesturing to the car with his flashlight. It was in the middle of an open field, about fifty yards from the road. "The lightbar was still flashing, which is how our witness saw it."

"Who's the witness?"

"Ramon Cruz, bartender at Sonny's Icehouse. He was driving home when he saw the lights. But he also saw one of the victims, the deputy's wife, leaving Sonny's with another man at closing time. In fact, he says they were sitting together at the bar for a while, so he got a pretty good look at the guy."

"So what happened here?"

Perez aimed his flashlight down at the evidence markers on the ground. "Number one, that's the wife, Gwen Harlan. Where her body fell, I mean. Two bullets in her back, one in the back of her skull. She was running away from whoever shot her, back towards the road. Number two, that's your deputy. Three shots to the chest. He was shot by a cheap semi-auto .25, which we found next to her body, She was shot by your deputy's .38, which we found next to him. Absent any other evidence, it looks like she shot him and ran, and he managed to get off a few shots before he died."

"But there is other evidence."

"There is." Perez swung his flashlight beam along the ground. "A second set of treads in the grass here. Now, at about quarter after one, your deputy radioed a license plate into us, a Dodge Challenger he was pursuing. But that's the last we heard from him. He never answered our return calls."

"So the Challenger is the second vehicle."

"Looks like it. Now, the Challenger is registered to a Dean Melville, 36 Hancock Court, San Marcos. But the driver's license photo we have on file for Melville doesn't match the description Ramon Cruz gave us. On top of that, this same vehicle was reported as hitting the owner of a liquor store in San Marcos earlier tonight. He ended up with a broken ankle and there was a ton of property damage besides. Anyway, we've got a car on the way to Melville's address. And, of course, we put out an APB on the Challenger."

"Anything else?"

"The dead woman, your deputy's wife. She had bruising on her lower back and torso. Unrelated to the gunshots, looked to be a few days old."

Giddings stepped away for a moment and took a couple of deep breaths before he returned. "I want to talk to this Melville."

"We'll keep you in the loop. But let's be clear, Sheriff. This is a DPS investigation. You find Melville in Ivor County, we expect a call. But San Marcos is in Hays County, and I think we can both agree that's outside your jurisdiction. We've got it under control."

Giddings didn't like that one bit, but he chose not to argue the point in the moment. Now, watching his only surviving deputy wring blood and guts out of a mop, he felt bile rise in his throat.

"Jeepers, this stinks."

"Curtis, do me a fuckin' favor. Either swear or don't. You ain't fooling anyone with this 'cripes' and 'jeepers' bullshit. You think you're outsmarting the Almighty? You think he doesn't know you mean 'Christ' and 'Jesus'?"

"Well…no, I guess I never thought of it that way."

"So you don't think God is a dumbass."

"No, course not."

"All right then."

Silence prevailed for nearly five minutes before the phone rang. "Get that for me, would you, Curtis?"

Curtis put down the mop and grabbed the phone. "Sheriff's office, Deputy Winslow speaking…Yes…Oh no! That's terrible news…Yes, I'll let the sheriff know right away." He hung up.

"Well?" said Giddings.

"It's Freddy McElroy. He got in a car accident last night or early this morning. He's dead."

"I'll be damned."

"Sweet Moses, what a night."

Giddings stood and grabbed his Stetson. "Curtis, I'm gonna need you to hold down the fort here. I gotta see Doc Hastings, and then I'm taking a ride up to San Marcos."

"San Marcos? But that's in Hays—"

"I know where it is. But I'll be damned if I'm gonna let DPS bigfoot this investigation. That's my deputy they found murdered, and I mean to dispense a little old-fashioned Texas justice to whoever took out my best man. No offense."

"Oh. None tak—"

"Just try not to burn the place down before I get back."

The morgue at Ivor County General had no vacancies. Three bodies were laid out, covered with sheets, but Giddings was only interested in one of them. His already foul mood was not improved by the strong disinfectant smell and the flickering of one of the overhead fluorescents. It got even worse when Hastings, the coroner, pulled the sheet covering Gwen Harlan's corpse down to her navel.

"Jesus," said Giddings, covering his mouth. Gwen's torso was black and blue in three different places. A wound on her side had been hastily stitched with thick black thread. Her beautiful face had a sickly gray pallor.

"One of the bullets went through," said Hastings. "I dug out the other two and sent them to forensics. There's no question about the cause of death for either her or Beau. Now, Freddy McElroy, on the other hand—"

"Could you please step out for a moment?"

"But Sheriff, I still have to—"

"Would you get the fuck out of here, Doc?"

Hastings saw something in Giddings' eyes he'd never seen before. If he didn't know better, he could have sworn they were tears. He nodded and quickly exited the room.

Giddings ran his fingers over the bruising on Gwen's body. Beau had beaten her, no question about it. Maybe she'd finally told him something he didn't want to hear. Giddings wished his deputy would come back to life just so he could kill him. Choke the life out of him and tell him what had been going on behind his back.

Until he met Gwen, Giddings was just going through the motions, following the course that had been plotted for him before he was even born. He'd been in Ivor County all his life, except for two years in the Marines after high school. When he returned from service, he married his high school sweetheart and began the job that was waiting for him as his father's deputy.

Giddings took over as sheriff in July 1967—the Summer of Love. It was the worst possible timing. Watching the new freedoms blossom around him, he felt the uniform squeezing like a straitjacket. He couldn't picture himself as a hippie—in fact, he took great pleasure in beating on them—but he did envy their ability to opt out of society, to ignore all the rules he was meant to enforce.

Gwen offered a way out. Beau Harlan had been his deputy for over a year before Giddings finally caved to Megan's wishes and invited Beau and his wife over for dinner. He was smitten right away. But what of it? There was no path forward. He added Gwen to the list of delights he'd be denied in this life.

But then Beau went on a three-day fishing trip with his brothers at Lake Buchanan. That Friday afternoon Gwen called the station to report a break-in and asked that the sheriff respond personally. He sucked in his gut when she answered the front door.

"Did they take anything?" he said.

She leaned in and whispered in his ear. "Sheriff, my favorite panties are missing."

She invited him inside. She gave him a glass of iced tea. She told him she didn't love her husband, and that he could stop holding in his stomach because she didn't care about his beer belly. She led him upstairs. He didn't put up a fight.

"Let's get away," she said afterward. "I've made a two-night reservation at the Driskill Hotel in Austin."

"You made it before I even got here?"

She tweaked his nose. "I just had a good feeling things were gonna go my way."

"What am I gonna tell my wife?"

"Tell her you're consulting with the APD. Tell her whatever you want. She'll never question what you say, will she?"

Giddings knew she wouldn't. He and Gwen went to Austin. He'd never been there before, and he'd never seen anything like it. There was no dividing line between the hippies and the rednecks. They went straight from seeing a rock band at the Soap Creek Saloon to two-stepping at the Broken Spoke. They hiked the Greenbelt and went swimming at Barton Springs. Nobody knew him. He didn't have to be anyone but Gwen's man. He knew this was the life he'd always wanted, and he meant to have it. Over Beau Harlan's dead body if necessary.

Now that dead body was on a table four feet away, but it was no victory. Giddings ran his hand along Gwen's cheek. She was cold to the touch. Someone was going to pay.

Giddings knocked on the door of the postwar split-level house at 36 Hancock Court in San Marcos. A thirtyish woman with a tangle of mousy brown hair and a wary expression answered it.

"Ma'am, Sheriff Giddings to see Dean Melville."

"He's not here, and I already talked to the cops. Y'all woke me up at four o'clock this morning."

"Well, ma'am, that was DPS. Department of Public Safety. And like I said, I'm the Sheriff."

"And like I said, Dean isn't here. I haven't seen him in three days."

"Are you his wife?"

"I'm his girlfriend. Or ex-girlfriend. Loretta Starr."

"Is this your house?"

"Yes. My husband and I bought this as a starter home. Then he got killed in Vietnam, so we never started a thing. To make ends meet, I had to rent out a room upstairs. Dean was my tenant, and then one thing led to another. But if I'd known how many other girlfriends he had, I never would have fallen in love with him."

"I'm going to need a list of those other girlfriends."

"I don't know all their names. Like I told the cops this morning, the only one I know is Missy Sanderson."

"How do you know her?"

"Because this is why Dean and I broke up. Three nights ago, he brought Missy over here. Got it in his head that we could have what the French call a mélange de trois. You know, a threesome. Why he thought I'd go along with that—well, I *know* why he thought it. Because he's so damn charming and good-looking, he thinks he can get away with anything. But he's a piece of shit too, and I told him so. Anyway, if you're looking for Dean, I suggest you start with Missy Sanderson."

"And where do I find her?"

"I don't know where she lives, but she's a waitress at the Buttered Biscuit Diner."

"Mr. Melville's room is upstairs?"

"Like I said, but you can't go up there without a warrant."

"Is that what you told the DPS cops?"

"Yes."

"And they left without searching his room?"

"Yes, they did."

Giddings sneered. "Pussies." He moved Loretta aside like she weighed nothing at all and headed for the staircase.

"Hey! You can't do that! I'm gonna call—"

"Call whoever the fuck you want."

It wasn't hard to find Dean Melville's room. It was the one that looked like it had been decorated by a college freshman. Posters of the Rolling Stones and Roger Staubach, a pinned-up *Playboy* centerfold of Claudia Jennings, a Nerf basketball hoop over the garbage can, an unmade bed. Dirty laundry piled everywhere. A stack of hot rod magazines and porn on the nightstand.

In front of the window was a wooden desk with an ashtray, a small pipe, and a baggie with about half an ounce of marijuana in it. On top of a Led Zeppelin sleeve with no record in it, he found a Polaroid photo of two shirtless young men with their arms around each other's shoulders, each raising a bottle of Lone Star to the camera. He took it downstairs.

"I called the cops," she said.

"Good for you. Might want to flush the weed upstairs before they get here."

"That's not mine and you know it."

"Don't give a shit. Take a look at this here. Which one of these boys is Dean Melville?" He showed her the Polaroid.

"The good-looking one. Like I said."

"And who's the other one?"

"That's his cousin Chuck. This was taken right after Chuck got out of prison a few months ago. A bunch of us went tubing on the Guadalupe to celebrate. Dean was happy to see him at first. That wore off pretty quick."

Giddings pocketed the photo. For the first time, Loretta got a good look at his badge. "Ivor County? What the hell are you doing up here anyway?"

"You've been a great deal of help, Loretta. When them DPS boys come back with their warrant, you give 'em my best."

SIX

Dean turned down a dirt road as directed by Chuck. The entrance was marked by signs reading KEEP OUT, PRIVATE PROPERTY, NO TRESPASSING, and most puzzling to Dean, HENDRICKS SNAKE FARM.

"Not very welcoming," he said.

"Double H knows we're coming." Chuck drummed on the dashboard to the beat of Grand Funk Railroad's "Shinin' On" as it crackled through the radio.

"I mean if there really is a snake farm down here, they're not doing a whole lot to attract the tourists."

"Hank's daddy ran the snake farm up until about two years ago. That's when he started going senile and couldn't keep it up no more. Hank was up in Huntsville with me, so he couldn't do it, and his sisters moved away years ago and want nothing to do with their daddy or his snakes."

"So the snakes are still here?"

"Sure, some of 'em are. Hank's daddy let 'em all go when he closed the place down, but the older ones didn't wander too far from home."

"Great. This day just gets better and better."

"Might want to put on the brakes. That's barbed wire in the road up ahead. We go on foot from here."

Dean shut down the truck and they climbed out, stepping carefully over the strips of barbed wire stretched across the road. "You sure he knows we're coming?"

"I told you, cuz. This whole thing was his idea."

The road grew steep heading down to the Blanco River. A

ramshackle house came into view. The yard was strewn with junk—old tires, soiled mattresses, a washing machine stripped for parts. As they neared the river, Dean spotted a bulky figure swaying in a hammock. A shotgun leaned against the tree closest to the figure's head.

"Why don't you go wake him up?" Dean whispered.

Chuck laughed, picked up a beer can with a bullet hole in it, and chucked it at the figure's head.

"What the—" Double H twisted and fell out of the hammock. He reached for his shotgun.

"You ain't gonna need that, Double H!"

Double H, wearing only a dirty pair of overalls, struggled to his feet. "Goddammit, Chuck. I told you, it's Triple H now. Huntsville Hank Hendricks."

"This here is my cousin Dean I was telling you about."

Triple H offered a greasy hand Dean reluctantly shook. "So Chuck tells me you're in the marijuana trade."

Dean shot a dirty look at his cousin. "Oh, did he now? What else did he tell you?"

"Well, he told me you might be interested in making a shitload of money."

"I might be." Dean's train of thought was derailed by something long and white slithering through the grass near his feet. "What in the fuck is that?"

"Oh, that's just Sammy. He's an albino Burmese python."

"Is it poisonous?" The snake was now slithering directly over Dean's foot.

"Nah, he's non-venomous."

"Is he a vegetarian?"

Triple H laughed. "Afraid not. But he generally swallows his prey whole, so you're probably all right. He's just hunting up a squirrel or a possum for a snack."

After what seemed like forever, the tail end of the snake finally passed over Dean's boot. "Jesus Christ. You got any poisonous ones out here?"

"Sure, we got rattlesnakes, cottonmouths, copperheads. But that's just Texas, man. Not much for the outdoors, are ya?"

"I tried the Boy Scouts when I was a kid. You know the problem with the Boy Scouts? No girls. It wasn't for me."

"Anyway," said Chuck. "Let's talk turkey."

"Sure, let's sit out here on the porch," said Triple H. He grabbed a cold beer for each of them out of a cooler and they sat on wicker chairs facing the water. Dean watched the river flow and sipped his beer, trying to feel better about his life.

"Okay, here's the deal," said Triple H. "Up in Huntsville—this was before your time, Chuck—I got to know this fella named Bob Dillon. Not the singer, obviously. Spelled his name different. Bob was in for a bank job in Archer City. But he'd grown up in Butte, Montana with this fella Bob Knievel. In fact, it was Bob Dillon who hung the name Evel on Bob Knievel, or so he claimed. Figured they couldn't both be Bob, and he wanted to keep the name. Anyway, he and Evel used to rob liquor stores together when they were in high school. But when Bob went into the Army, they lost track of each other. And then Bob got locked up in Texas, but when he got out, about six or seven years ago, he and Evel got back in touch. By now Evel was doing his stunt shows, and he hired Bob on as a roadie. Bob moved up from there and, long story short, he's the event manager for this jump Evel is gonna do up in Idaho."

"Snake River Canyon," said Dean.

"That's right. Now, I talked to Bob the other night, and he's saying this thing is gonna be big. He says, 'picture a redneck Woodstock,' and that's when I got dollar signs in my eyes. And so did he, because Bob's still got the heart of a criminal. Now,

Bob is hiring all the vendors, overseeing all the concessions. In other words, he's got his hand in the till. So he's thinking, what would a redneck Woodstock be without a marijuana concession? Now, Bob figures he can sell at least a hundred pounds of pot over the weekend leading up to this jump, but he's got no connection. And this is where you guys come in."

Dean was barely listening anymore, as his eyes were fixed on a fearsome creature flopping out of the river onto the dock. "Cousin, does the Blanco River have alligators in it?"

"Not to my knowledge."

Dean pointed down to the dock.

"Oh, that's just Roy," said Triple H, standing up and heading down to the river. "It's his lunchtime."

Dean scooted his legs up onto the wicker chair. "And what does Roy have for lunch?"

Triple H picked up a bucket on a rock down near the water's edge and tossed its contents into the river. Roy dove back in and swam over to the spot where blood and guts were now churning to the surface. "Just a bunch of trash fish I cut up for him," said Triple H, making his way back to the porch. "Roy's not native to the area. My daddy bought him in Louisiana when he was just a baby."

Dean watched Roy's teeth gnashing as he consumed his midday meal. "Roy can't find his own lunch in that river?"

"Sure he can, but why would he bother when he knows we'll feed him?"

"Makes sense, I guess. Any other non-native creatures around here we should be aware of?"

"Well, we used to have a spider monkey named Mr. Jitters. One day he was sunning himself out on the dock and Roy caught up to him. That was sad." Triple H took his seat. "Now where were we?"

"Bob's marijuana concession," said Chuck.

"Right. So Chuck here tells me you've got a marijuana concession of your own over in San Marcos."

"Look, I've got a little weight to unload, and maybe we can work something out. But we're talking about a couple of pounds. Not a hundred."

"What my cousin is saying is we don't have it on us," said Chuck. "But we can get it."

"Is that what I'm saying, Chuck?"

"For the sake of argument, let's say we can. How is this gonna work?"

"The jump is scheduled for this Sunday, the eighth, so you would need to get up there with the goods by Friday morning, which is when Bob figures the crowds will start showing up."

"Hold on a second," said Dean. "So in this scenario, we are transporting a hundred pounds of weed across state lines—several state lines—all the way up to fuckin' Idaho? And what is your part in this grand scheme?"

"Well, I would get a finder's fee for bringing y'all together. Of course, I can't take part in the actual transportation, what with having to stay here and take care of my daddy and Roy and all."

"It's cool, Triple H," said Chuck. "Once we get our hands on the weight, we'll be in touch to discuss your compensation."

Dean stood. "Yes, my cousin and I have much to discuss. And we have another appointment. Let's go, cuz."

"I'll await your call," said Triple H as they headed out.

All the way up the hill, Dean kept glancing back over his shoulder, just in case Roy decided he was still hungry.

SEVEN

Antoine Lynch was enjoying a cup of coffee at the counter of the Buttered Biscuit when the pig walked in the door. He wore tan khakis, a white Stetson hat, and a crisp white shirt with a badge pinned to it. His arms were well-muscled, but he had a beer belly drooping down over his belt. There were three empty stools at the counter, but he deliberately took the one right next to Antoine.

"What's good here?" he said, picking up a paper menu. Now that he was close, Antoine could see that he'd sweated through his shirt at the armpits. Sweating like a pig, Antoine thought.

"Biscuits and gravy," said Antoine. "Or the pecan waffles. Whatever you get, you're gonna want a side of the cheesy hash browns."

Sandy walked over and topped off Antoine's coffee. She raised the pot toward the pig. "Coffee?"

"Yes, please."

She filled his cup. "Cream?"

"Just sugar, thanks." He picked up the shaker from the table and poured what looked like a pound of sugar into his coffee.

"Something to eat?"

"Maybe. I was wondering if Missy Sanderson is working today."

"Should be in by noon." Sandy checked the clock. "Twenty minutes or so."

"I'll just study the menu a bit, then."

Sandy nodded and walked off to tend to other customers.

"What about for lunch?"

Antoine looked up from his coffee. "Say again?"

"You mentioned some breakfast items, but I already had my breakfast. What's good for lunch?"

"Tuna melt. Bowl of chili."

The pig nodded as if considering the options. "Funny how times change, ain't it?"

"Not sure I follow you."

"Just to say that when I first started as a lawman, if I'd come in that door and seen you sitting here at the counter, I'd have dragged you off that stool and thrown you out in the street. But now here we are, having a nice, civilized conversation."

Antoine felt his ears burning. He checked out the pig's badge. "Well, Sheriff, that was then, and this is now. As it happens, I have a good lawyer. So if you were to try that today, here in Hays County, I'd have a pretty juicy police brutality case to pursue. You dig?"

Sheriff Giddings laughed. "Yes, indeed. Times have definitely changed."

"What the fuck, cousin?" Dean was hauling ass down Route 12 back to San Marcos.

"Lighten up, leadfoot. You get pulled over, we're both going to jail."

Dean slowed to the speed limit. "You must be out of your damn mind. Even if I wanted to get involved in this crazy shit, I don't have anywhere near that kind of weight."

"But Antoine Lynch does."

"Yeah, I'm sure Antoine is just gonna hand me a few bales of Acapulco Gold and wish me luck."

"I know it's not my business, but I just can't see how any self-respecting white man can work for someone like Antoine."

"Now that's your daddy talking. That's Uncle Red the Grand Wizard."

"He never was a Grand Wizard."

"But he was Klan. He's still a stone hateful racist. Like it or not, Antoine calls the shots. And I already owe him money."

"And if we do this, you'll be able to pay him back. Hell, he'll get rich right along with us."

They crossed the town line, back into San Marcos. "He'll never go along with it."

"He doesn't have to know until it's over."

Dean looked at his cousin like he was speaking Portuguese. "What are you saying?"

"When those planes come in with the Acapulco Gold, and they get unloaded, where do the bales go?"

"They go in the equipment shed out…oh, no. Nope. Just forget it."

"We wouldn't be stealing it. Antoine is going to get his cut."

"Oh, I see. So we should just leave him a note. 'Hey, Antoine, we're taking your whole supply up to Idaho to sell it to a bunch of redneck freaks. Back with your cut in a week or two.'"

"Well, no, I wouldn't actually advise that. Think about it, cousin. What choice do we really have? By now our pictures are probably hanging in the post office. We've got to get out of town, way out of town. And Idaho is way the fuck out of town."

Dean pulled into the parking lot of the Buttered Biscuit Diner and shut down the engine.

"What the hell are we doing here?" said Chuck.

"I gotta see Missy. We got in a fight last night and she threw me out, but I still have some stuff at her place."

"Wait, *Missy* threw you out? I thought you were shacked up with Loretta Starr."

"She threw me out three nights ago."

"Christ, you sure can pick 'em."

"You're saying that to me? What happened to the last woman you picked up?"

"Cuz, we gotta get out of here."

"There she is," said Dean, pointing to the woman in a waitress uniform getting out of a Chevy Vega.

"Forget her. Look." Chuck pointed at the police cruiser with the IVOR COUNTY SHERIFF banner on the side, parked right next to the Vega.

"Fuck."

At two minutes past twelve, Giddings glanced up from his chili and out the diner's plate-glass window. Parked in the lot, he saw a panel truck with a colorful GONZO TACO logo painted on the side. A Chevy Vega pulled up in front next to his car and a woman in a waitress uniform got out of it and hurried inside.

"Sorry I'm late," she said as she hustled over to the counter.

"This gentleman wants to talk to you," said Sandy, gesturing at Giddings.

Missy rolled her eyes. "I already talked to the cops. That's why I'm running late."

"Let me guess," said Giddings. "They asked you about Dean Melville."

Antoine Lynch's ears perked up at that.

"Yes, and I told them I threw him out on his ass last night because he's a cheating dog."

"I assumed you already knew that about him, seeing as how he was with Loretta Starr when you started fooling around with him."

"Do we have to discuss my personal business here in front of my co-workers and customers?"

Giddings pulled the Polaroid out of his pocket and showed it to her. "What about his cousin here?"

"No, sir. I never messed with him."

"Do you know where he lives?"

"He's been staying with his daddy since he got out of prison. Charles Melville, Jr., but everyone calls him Red."

"And do you know where I could find Dean Melville now?"

"He should be at work. Making tacos."

"Where?"

"I think he's out at the medical center now. The Gonzo Taco truck."

Giddings looked back out the window. The truck was gone. He grabbed his hat and ran out the door.

"Hey!" Sandy called. "You didn't pay for your chili!"

"It's on me," said Antoine, setting a five-dollar bill on the counter. "I gotta be running along, too."

EIGHT

After a stop at the hardware store to pick up a few supplies, Dean and Chuck were parked behind the Church of Christ out on Montgomery Lane. Among other things, Chuck had grabbed a half-dozen cans of black spray paint.

"We're just a little conspicuous in this vehicle," he said. "We're making it way too easy for the cops to find us."

"We and us," said Dean.

"Excuse me?"

"You keep saying we and us, like we're outlaws on the run together. Butch and Sundance. But here's the thing, cousin. I didn't do anything. You stole my car and used it in the commission of a crime—several crimes. I mean, you killed a woman for Chrissakes!"

"She left me no choice, cuz. I explained that. She was trying to frame me for murdering her husband. A cop. They would have found me hanging in an Ivor County jail cell this morning if I hadn't done what I did."

"Nevertheless, it has nothing to do with me. You made your choices. The sensible thing for me to do would be to walk right into the police station downtown and tell them the whole story. Instead, here I am, an accessory to you. Give me one good reason."

"I saved your life, cousin. You owe me."

Dean rubbed his eyes. What Chuck said was true. Ten years earlier, when Dean was sixteen and Chuck was eighteen, they had gone canoeing on the Blanco River, just a few miles from the Hendricks snake farm. They hit some whitewater rapids, the canoe flipped, and Dean went headfirst into a rock. The way Chuck told it, Dean was seconds away from being sucked under and drowning or being torn apart on the rocks in the rapids, or some combination of the two, when Chuck grabbed him and pulled him to safety on the shore. Having been knocked unconscious, Dean couldn't confirm Chuck's account of events, but he knew he was alive, which probably wouldn't have been the case if Chuck had let him float away.

"Chuck, if I go along with this, it's the last time you get to play that card. I don't ever want to hear about you saving my life again. You read me?"

"Loud and clear, cuz. Now let's go over the details. What exactly is standing between us and the weed in that equipment shed?"

"Number one, we have to break into the salvage yard. Then we gotta get past Maalik and Cerberus."

"Who are they?"

"Antoine's Dobermans. If they don't kill us, the night watchman will."

"Who's the night watchman?"

"Antoine rotates them. Think it might be a guy called T.J. this week. But whoever it is will be carrying a M16."

"All right. What's next?"

"Well, we get past all that, we still have to get inside the locked shed."

"What's the shed made out of?"

'I dunno, it's metal."

"What kind of metal? Can we cut through it?"

"I don't know, Chuck, I never examined the shed with the idea of cutting through it. I've never even been inside it."

"All right. We'll just be prepared. That's the Boy Scout motto, right? Oh, I guess you wouldn't know, since you didn't last a week."

"Hey, I got my first aid merit badge."

"Well, let's hope we don't need that."

Giddings had a busy afternoon. He drove out to the medical center and asked where he could find the taco truck, but when he got to the north parking lot, the truck wasn't there. That made it even more likely that the Gonzo Taco truck he'd spotted at the Buttered Biscuit was in the possession of Dean Melville, possibly with his cousin Chuck aboard. He had missed them by minutes.

His next stop was the address for Charles Melville, Jr. It was a ranch house in need of a decent paint job, with a Confederate flag mounted beside the front door. Giddings rang the bell. The man who answered looked to be in his early sixties and half in the bag.

"More cops," he sneered.

"Yes, I'm sure you already talked to my friends at DPS. Save me the trouble of asking you any questions and just tell me what you said to them."

"Last time I saw Chuck was breakfast yesterday morning. It ain't no surprise to me if he got into some trouble since then. He's been gettin' into trouble since he could walk."

"Did he mention any plans he might have?"

"He said he was going to hang out with his prison buddy. Hank Hendricks. I used to know his daddy. We belonged to the same…lodge, I guess you could say."

"You know where I can find Hank?"

"Nope. His daddy used to own a snake farm in Wimberley, on the Blanco River. Far as I know, it's closed, but you might give it a shot."

"All right. If Chuck comes home, I'd appreciate you giving me a call." Giddings handed him a business card.

"The other cops already gave me one of these."

"Can I see it?"

Melville fished around in his pocket and handed a card to Giddings. OFFICER MARTIN PEREZ, DEPARTMENT OF PUBLIC SAFETY. Giddings tore up the card and threw the pieces over his shoulder. "You have a good day, now."

His next stop was back in his home territory. Sonny's Icehouse would be open by now, and he wanted to talk to the bartender. It was a forty-five-minute drive, at no point during which did Giddings notice the black Pontiac Firebird Trans Am tailing him.

"Buenos dias, Ramon," he said, entering the icehouse.

"What can I get you, Sheriff?" said Ramon Cruz as Giddings took a seat at the bar.

"I never drink on duty. Then again, I haven't officially been on duty all day. So I guess I'll have a Jack and Coke."

Ramon poured the drink. "I guess you want to know about that fella Mrs. Harlan left here with last night."

Giddings pulled the Polaroid out of his pocket and showed it to Ramon.

"Yep, that's him," said Ramon. "The one on the left."

"Describe their behavior when they were sitting here at the bar. I mean, were they friendly? Did she leave with him willingly or under duress?"

"Yeah, they were friendly. I mean, they weren't kissing or nothin' like that. Just talking."

"Did you hear any of what they were talking about?"

"Let's see, he said something about quitting his job, but he wasn't worried about it because he'd met with an old friend about a business opportunity."

"Any details on that?"

"No, that was about it."

"Now, Ramon. When them DPS fellas were questioning you, you didn't mention anything to them about Mrs. Harlan's private life, did you? Like any secrets you might be privy to?"

"Course not. I mean, I ain't saying I know anything, but if I did, I sure wouldn't be telling it to them."

"That's good. See, we want to handle this in-house. Those state boys don't need to be lookin' in our drawers."

"I agree."

"Thought you might." Giddings finished off his drink, slammed the glass on the bar, and stood. "All right, Ramon. I'll be back first of the month to pick up my usual envelope. I expect it won't be light this time."

"No, Sheriff. You'll have it in full."

"That's good. Hasta la vista, Ramon."

Giddings headed out. When he was sure the sheriff was gone, Ramon made an obscene gesture toward the doorway.

A minute later, a tall black man with a bushy afro and a neat beard walked in through the door. "How you doing today?" he said.

"I'm good," said Ramon. "You need a drink?"

"Nah, I was just curious." Antoine Lynch set a fifty-dollar bill on the bar. "Wondering if you could tell me what you and the sheriff were talking about."

NINE

It was nearly sundown by the time Dean and Chuck finished spray-painting the taco truck jet-black.

"Let's check into a motel and rest up," said Chuck. "We want to wait 'til the dead of night to make our move, and I figure that's about three in the morning."

"They know me at most of the motels in town."

"All right, so we'll head out of town. How 'bout we go out by the Austin airport, check into one of the hotels there? You ain't been doing a lot of jet-setting, have you?"

"Who's paying for this?"

"I've got a little cash in my pocket."

"Do I want to know how you got it?"

"I sincerely doubt it."

Antoine was saying goodnight to Maalik and Cerberus when T.J. approached the fence.

"Hey, boss, you hear about Dean?"

"First of all, don't call me boss. Boss is what our people had to call their white overseers on the plantation. Second, yes, I did hear the news on the radio."

When Antoine heard Dean Melville's name come out of the sheriff's mouth at the diner, all the gears in his head started turning. Could Dean, who was in debt to him and in danger of losing his car or his legs, have turned against him and cut a deal with law enforcement? Antoine thought it was possible, though he couldn't figure why or how Dean would make such a deal with the Ivor County Sheriff.

He tailed the sheriff all afternoon, from the medical center to a residence and finally down to a bar in Ivor County. The bartender at Sonny's proved to be a talkative guy, fueled by a burning hatred of Sheriff Bud Giddings. Antoine learned an awful lot about the sheriff, little of it flattering, and though he couldn't picture that information coming in handy down the road, he'd been surprised before.

He also learned the nature of the sheriff's interest in Dean Melville, confirmed by a news report he heard on the radio during his drive home. Dean and his cousin Chuck were wanted by the law for their possible involvement in a double murder in Ivor County. Antoine strongly doubted Dean was actually involved, but that cousin of his was another story. He was a stone-cold peckerwood degenerate as far as Antoine was concerned. Still, if Dean was captured by the law and facing a prison stretch, he might try to deal. And Antoine was the biggest fish he could serve up.

"Sounds like Dean's in big trouble," said T.J.

"He'll keep his mouth shut," said Antoine. But his own words sounded unconvincing.

Just before three in the morning, the taco truck came to a stop a block and a half from the salvage yard. "We walk from here," said Dean. "Anything looks even a little funky, we bail on this caper."

"Fair enough," said Chuck, slinging a duffel bag over his shoulder as he climbed out of the truck. The street ahead was poorly lit, dead-ending at a ten-foot chain-link fence topped with barbed wire, beyond which could be glimpsed stacks of junked cars. Dean and Chuck followed the fence along until they were out of sight from the street. Chuck dropped the duffel bag and unzipped it. He pulled out a pair of bolt cutters.

"This is the easy part," he whispered. "Where are those dogs gonna be?"

"Could be anywhere. Antoine lets 'em roam around the yard at night. They hear us or smell us, they'll be coming fast."

Chuck nodded and got to work with the bolt cutters, snapping the chain links in a circle pattern. After each snap, he paused, and they listened for Maalik and Cerberus. After a couple of minutes, he had done enough cutting to allow him to push in the circular section of fence, which was just big enough for them to crawl through. Chuck shoved the duffel bag through first, then dragged himself on his elbows and knees until he reached the other side of the fence. Dean followed.

Chuck unzipped the duffel again and removed two Tupperware containers, which he handed to Dean. "You're in charge of these," he whispered.

"If this doesn't work, we're in for a world of hurt."

"One thing at a time. Which way to the shed?"

Dean gestured to a narrow alley between two long stacks of cars that quickly faded into darkness. Chuck set off in that direction, followed by Dean. They crept quietly between the stacks, with only the starry skies above providing light. Whenever the wind blew, the stacks creaked, and Dean's heart jumped into his throat. They were halfway along the path when Dean heard a loud clunk followed by Chuck swearing.

"What was that?"

"Muffler laying in the path."

The dogs heard it. They were barking, and the sound was getting closer. "Set the trap and climb," said Chuck, who was already moving up the stack, using car hoods as ladder steps.

Dean popped the top off the carnitas container and set it down. He heard the dogs loud and clear now, heard their tags jangling as they ran. His fingers slipped on the cover of the second container.

"Move it!" said Chuck.

Dean fumbled the container open and set down the picadillo just as Maalik and Cerberus rounded the corner and charged at him. He scrambled up the car hoods, pulling his feet up just in time to hear a set of jaws snap shut beneath them. He was already out of breath, but he was also out of reach. He looked up at Chuck, who had made it to the top of the stack.

"Look," said Chuck, pointing down.

The dogs were chowing down on Gonzo's delicious taco filling, which Chuck had seasoned earlier in the evening with the contents of numerous Benadryl capsules.

"How do you know how much to use?" Dean had asked.

"When I was a kid, whenever we'd go on a long car trip, my mother used to put this stuff in my peanut butter sandwich. I was knocked out in five minutes or less. I figure those Dobermans each weigh about twice as much as I did then, so I'm doubling the amount and adding a little for good luck."

The dogs finished up the food and went right back to barking and jumping and scratching at the cars. By now Chuck and Dean had another problem, as the night watchman couldn't help but hear the commotion the dogs were causing.

"Maalik! Cerberus! Where are you?" It was T.J.'s voice, not too far off.

The dogs' energy began to lag. The barking died down.

"Maalik! Cerberus!"

The dogs didn't respond. In another minute, they were snoring. Just as Dean climbed down, T.J. appeared in the alley entrance, flashlight in one hand, machine gun in the other.

"Hello? Who's down there? Answer me before I start shooting."

Dean cleared his throat and did his best to turn on the charm. "T.J.? That you?"

T.J. began walking toward him. "Dean? The fuck you doing here, boy? You know you're in some deep shit, right?"

"Don't I know it! But you gotta believe me, Teej, I'm an innocent man. That cousin of mine, he's crazier than a circus clown in a barrel full of monkeys."

T.J. kept coming. "That may be, but it don't answer my question. What the fuck are you doing here? And why ain't them dogs busy rippin' your throat out?"

T.J. tilted the beam of his flashlight down to where Maalik and Cerberus were snoozing comfortably. In that moment, Chuck dropped from the top of the stack, tackling T.J. to the ground. A burst of automatic gunfire. Dean pressed against the stack and squeezed his eyes shut. When he opened them again, he saw that Chuck had wrestled the M16 away from T.J.

"Don't kill him, Chuck!"

Chuck raised the gun and struck T.J. in the head twice with the butt of it. T.J. crumpled to the ground next to the slumbering Dobermans.

"Make yourself useful and grab the rope and the duct tape from my duffel bag," said Chuck.

"Make myself useful? I'm dodging hellhounds and bullets over here." Dean pulled the requested items out of the duffel.

"Hand me the rope. You can tape up his mouth."

"Just love giving orders, don't you?" Dean peeled back the end of the tape, stuck it to T.J.'s cheek, and proceeded to wrap the roll three times around his head, completely sealing off his mouth. Chuck tied T.J.'s arms behind his back and got to work on his legs.

"Crazier than a circus clown in a barrel full of monkeys, huh?"

"It was the nicest thing I could think to say about you in the moment. How long are these dogs gonna be out?"

"Hard to say. Couple hours at least."

"I just don't want them waking up angry and mauling T.J. to death."

"Sounded like they have a pretty good working relationship. I wouldn't sweat it." Chuck tested the ropes. "All right, he's secure. Let's go."

Chuck shoved the M16 into his duffel as they made their way out the other end of the alley. The shed was directly ahead, near the rear of the main building. They jogged over to it, and Chuck gave it the once-over.

"Looks to be about eighteen by twenty-four feet." He rapped on the metal wall. "I don't know what gauge this is, but probably in the low twenties. That's the heavy kind."

"All right, I didn't come here for your construction class. Can you get through it?"

"I don't have anything with me that can cut through that. Looks to be built on a concrete pad, so we can't go under it."

"What about the lock?"

"Let's check it out."

They walked around to the door. Chuck ran his fingers over the padlock. "I've seen these before. Heavy-duty. This is a two-pounder, I'd say. Got an anti-drill plate, as I recall. And these metal covers here protect the shackle, so we can't cut through that."

"Can you pick the lock?"

"I probably could. But I don't think I need to." Chuck reached into his breast pocket and pulled out a key, which he displayed with a grin. He stuck it in the padlock and turned it. The lock popped open.

"Where the hell—?"

"From your buddy T.J., of course. Found it in his pocket and knew right away it was a padlock key."

"Shit, this is gonna be easier than we thought."

Chuck opened the door. Dean stepped inside, felt for the light switch, and flipped it on. Chuck came in behind him. They both stood and stared for a moment.

"Uh, cousin?" said Chuck. "Where the fuck is the weed?"

TEN

The inside walls of the shed were lined with metal pegboards holding wrenches, hammers, screwdrivers, ratchet sets, sockets, and power tools. A couple of large workbenches were stacked with automotive parts, cans of oil, work gloves, and tubs of grease. Other parts were stacked in boxes on the floor, along with a couple of axle stands and an industrial dolly leaning near the door. All the sorts of things you would expect to find in an equipment shed at a salvage yard, and nothing Dean and Chuck were looking for.

"I know this is it," said Dean. "I was here once when the plane landed, I saw them load the weed in here."

"You saw this happen once. You ever think maybe they switch it up? Are there any other sheds out here?"

"No, this is it!"

"Well, maybe he's already gone through his supply and he's waiting on another load."

"No way. I heard them talking about it in the office yesterday, they just got the resupply."

"Look around you, cousin. There ain't no weed in here. What the fuck are we gonna do now? Your buddy T.J. knows we were here. We're not gonna get a second chance at this."

Dean sighed and looked down at his boots. He stared down for a long moment, but when he looked back up at Chuck, he was grinning.

"Step off the rug, would you?"

Chuck took a few steps back and Dean kneeled down. There was indeed a twenty-by-forty-inch Navajo rug on the concrete floor. Dean rolled it up, revealing the door of a vault embedded in the floor. He tapped it with his fist. It felt as solid as Fort Knox.

"I don't suppose T.J. has the key to this, too?"

"I'll run and check," said Chuck.

Dean slumped against the wall, took a pack of gum out of his pocket, and stuck a fresh stick of Wrigley's in his mouth. He badly wanted a cold beer but chewing gum would have to do for now.

After five minutes, Chuck returned. "No such luck," he said.

"Didn't figure Antoine would trust him with that. So can you pick this one?"

Chuck squatted down and examined the lock. "I'm sure as hell gonna try."

He got back up, pulled a bobby pin out of his pocket, and took two sets of pliers from one of the pegboards. He stood at a workbench and carefully twisted the ends of the bobby pin with one set of pliers while holding it steady with the other. When he was done, he returned to the vault door, pressed the ends of the bobby pin together, and slid them down into the lock. He started twisting and wriggling the pin. As the seconds passed, his expression evolved from confident to determined to pissed off.

"How's it going there, cuz?"

"Just let me concentrate, will ya?" Chuck pulled out the bobby pin, wiped it on his shirt, and stuck it back in the lock. His twisting and wriggling grew more aggressive. Dean considered speaking up again but thought better of it. He chewed his gum and studied his fingernails. After another minute or so, he heard a snap.

"Goddammit!" said Chuck. He pulled the pin out of the lock. Half of it remained there, broken off.

"You got another one?"

"It don't matter, the fucking thing broke off in there!"

Dean blew a bubble. It popped and he sucked it back in. "So we're screwed?"

Chuck was distracted, his eyes darting back and forth around the shed. Dean stood up.

"Well, cuz, we tried," he said. "I'm gonna turn myself in to the cops, and I suggest you hightail it to Mexico."

Chuck jumped to his feet. "Find me the biggest drill bit in this place," he said.

"You're going to drill through that door? How thick is it?"

"Probably three or four inches. But that don't matter. I'm gonna drill through the lock." Chuck picked up a device from the workbench that looked to Dean like a cross between a chainsaw and a weed-whacker. "This baby should do it."

Dean rummaged through the boxes on the floor. "Do you know how to do this?"

"I've seen it done."

"Where have you seen it done?"

"Well, I've heard stories about it being done. I got a pretty good idea about it."

"What if it has an anti-drill plate like that padlock?"

"I suspect it does, but I can avoid it if I go in at the right angle."

Dean popped open a plastic case. Paydirt. A rack of drill bits. He tossed the largest one to Chuck. "What if you go in at the wrong angle?"

Chuck screwed the bit onto the industrial drill. "It'll probably kick back and go right up my nose."

"There's a welding mask on the wall over there."

Chuck went down on a knee in front of the vault door. "I got this. But go ahead and stand back. If I manage to kill myself, you can blame me for everything."

"Already planning on it."

Chuck angled the drill and fired it up. Sparks flew as he pushed it forward. Dean couldn't watch. He stood in the open doorway and stared up at the starry night sky until he heard a loud, metallic thump.

"Got it," said Chuck, shutting down the drill and flipping open the vault door. He braced his arms on either side of the opening and lowered his legs into the darkness below. "Here goes nothing," he said, and dropped down.

"You alright?" said Dean.

"Oh, I've never been better."

Dean followed him down. It was about an eight-foot drop. The space he found himself in was cool and dank and stacked with greenery.

"Is this a humidor?" he said.

"I guess. But for us, it's a gold mine." He picked up one of the plastic-wrapped, vacuum-sealed bales stacked in the small room. "What do you figure these are, twenty pounds?"

"They're twenty-five. I've heard Antoine mention it."

Chuck whistled. "There's ten of 'em down here."

"Well, we only need four."

"What the hell are you talking about?"

"I know math was never your strong suit, cuz, but twenty-five times four is one hundred pounds, which is how much that Bob Dillon guy wants to buy."

"That's the least he's willing to buy. He's gonna go nuts for this. Two hundred and fifty pounds!"

"You're getting greedy, Chuck."

"Dean, we're all in. We're doing this thing. We've come this far. What the fuck is the point of leaving six bales behind? You think Antoine is gonna be less mad at you?"

"Fine. Let's just get it out of here. If we can even climb out of this place."

Chuck pushed a stack of three bales under the opening above. "Give me a boost."

Dean laced his fingers together and Chuck used them as a step to climb up onto the shaky stack. He reached up. His fingers were inches short of the floor above. He started sinking into the top bale. "Another boost!"

Dean grabbed him around the ankles. "On three. One… two…three!"

Dean hoisted and Chuck jumped. He grabbed the edges of the opening and hauled himself up. "All right, toss them bad boys up here."

"How am I getting out?"

"Hang on, I saw a stepladder in here somewhere."

Chuck found it and lowered it down. Dean set it up and started passing the bales up to his cousin. When they were all out of the vault, Dean climbed to the top step and Chuck dragged him back into the shed.

"Let's use the dolly. We can get this done in two trips."

Outside the dogs were still snoozing, but T.J. was awake and kicking, trying to free himself as they passed by.

"Sorry about this, T.J.," said Dean. "Just let Antoine know it's cool, he's going to get his cut. This is going to work out for all of us."

Judging from the way T.J. thrashed and strained against the ropes, he didn't take much comfort from Dean's words.

On the second trip through, Cerberus was starting to stir.

"Hold up," said Chuck. "We need one more thing."

"What now?"

Chuck rifled through his duffel bag until he came up with a screwdriver. "We've got to change the license plate on the taco truck. The cops will definitely have the number by now."

"Get it and let's go."

"Hang on, I gotta find one from this century."

As Chuck surveyed the stacks, Cerberus licked his lips. His eyes rolled open.

"It's time to go, Chuck. We can grab one later."

"This one will work." Chuck got to work with the screwdriver. Cerberus lifted his head and looked around like a drunk waking up on his own front lawn.

"I'll meet you at the truck," said Dean.

"I've got it," said Chuck, pulling the plate loose. "Let's go."

Cerberus tried to stand, wobbled, and fell over as Dean and Chuck hustled out of the salvage yard. By four A.M., they had the truck loaded and the license plate changed. Dean climbed behind the wheel as Chuck settled into the passenger seat.

"Damn, that's pungent," said Chuck. "I can smell it even through the plastic."

"I told you, that's the good stuff. That's why I can sell it for three bucks a joint."

"And what's Antoine's cut of that?"

"I pay him by the pound. Two grand."

"Okay, so that's..." Chuck started counting on his fingers.

"Are you seriously trying to do math again? If you're trying to figure out his share of two hundred and fifty pounds, it's half a million."

"Christ on his throne. All right, then. I'm gonna call Triple H and tell him this Bob Dillon needs to come up with a cool million in cash for what we've got in this truck, or we take our business elsewhere."

"Elsewhere? Where's elsewhere?"

"It's a negotiation tactic. Like *The Godfather*, an offer he can't refuse."

"But he *can* refuse it."

"He won't. Cousin, we are fixin' to be rich."

*

When Antoine arrived at the office in the morning, he could hear Maalik and Cerberus barking outside. He went out into the yard and tracked the sound. The dogs ran to him as soon as they saw him, and he kneeled to scratch them behind the ears.

"What's going on, boys? What's the matter?"

The dogs took off down an alley between two rows of junked cars, and he followed them. They stopped in front of a limp figure lying in the path.

"T.J.?"

The figure stirred. When Antoine reached him, he crouched down and started unpeeling the duct tape. "Okay, this is gonna hurt." He ripped the last strip loose and T.J. howled, fully awake.

"What the fuck happened here, brother?"

T.J. gathered his breath. "Dean…it was Dean…and his…his fucking cousin."

"Fuck." Antoine abandoned all pretense of tending to T.J. and sprinted for the shed. He saw the door wide open. He ran inside, where he found the door to the vault also open. He didn't have to look down into it.

He slow-walked back to T.J., who was still bound with rope and flat on his back. Antoine sighed and leaned down to untie him. "Come on, man. Get your ass up."

Antoine offered a hand and pulled T.J. to his feet. They walked to the office. Antoine took a seat behind his desk and gestured to the couch. T.J. sat down gingerly, rubbing his wrists.

"You alright?" said Antoine.

"Yeah, boss—I mean, yes. I'm good."

"I'm gonna need you to tell me everything that happened. But first, did they say anything to you?"

"Yeah. Dean said you shouldn't worry because you're gonna get your cut."

"Oh, I see. That certainly sets my mind at ease."

"They took it all. I don't know where they think they're gonna sell it. Anyone around here is gonna know that's your shit. No way they're gonna cross you for these two fugitives."

"I doubt they're planning to sell it around here."

"Where are they gonna sell it, then?"

Antoine's eyes settled on the *Sports Illustrated* cover on his desk. "Well, I know where I'd go."

ELEVEN

Dean and Chuck drove to Fredericksburg, a Hill Country town about seventy miles northwest of San Marcos. They parked two blocks from Main Street and snoozed for a couple of hours in the truck. At around seven-thirty, the glare of morning sun through the windshield woke Dean. He got out and walked down to the Walgreens, where he bought a cup of coffee and the morning edition of the *Austin American-Statesman*. His driver's license photo and his cousin's mugshot were plastered above the fold on the front page. The headline read COUSINS SOUGHT IN DOUBLE HOMICIDE.

When he got back to the truck, he woke Chuck up and showed it to him.

"Well, the good news is, we don't look like this no more. You're a baby-face there, short hair, no 'stache. Me, I had a crewcut, no sexy sideburns."

"Nevertheless, I suggest we hit the happy highway posthaste."

"I gotta make a call first."

"Triple H?"

"Yep. Be right back."

Chuck hopped out and walked down to a payphone on the corner. He put in his dime and dialed.

"Hello?"

"It's Chuck. We've got it. A lot of it."

"What's a lot?"

"Two hundred and fifty."

"Pounds?"

"You think he'll go for it?"

"I don't want to speak for him, but I don't see why not."

"Well, you give him a call. Tell him he can have it for a million in cash."

Silence.

"You there, buddy?"

"Yeah, I just…I guess I wasn't thinking of that kind of money."

"It's time to start thinking about it. Especially with your ten percent finder's fee."

"Sheeyit. All right. I'll call him right away. Get back with me when you can."

"Will do." Chuck hung up. He put another dime in the phone and dialed a number he knew by heart.

"Yeah?"

"Hey, Daddy."

"Chuck? Where the fuck is my mad money?"

"Oh, you mean it's not in the jar you keep under the bathroom sink?"

"You little shit. I'm gonna pull your teeth out through your asshole."

"No, I don't believe you will, you miserable old snake. You're never gonna see that money again and you're never gonna see me again. But don't worry, I'll come back someday to piss on your grave."

Chuck hung up and headed back to the truck.

Red Melville stared at the phone receiver for a long minute before he hung it up. He went into the garage, inching through the narrow passage between piles of broken appliances and the beer can collection he still planned to display whenever he got around to building the shelves. On top of a dresser with no intact drawer knobs rested a stack of Yellow Pages. Every year when the new one came, Red brought the old one out and dropped it on top of the stack. Now he set aside the first couple and flipped through the 1971 directory. He was pretty sure the Hendricks Snake Farm was still open then, and sure enough, he found the number. He went inside and dialed it.

"Hello?"

"Is that Hank?"

"Who's this?"

"It's Red Melville. We met before. I'm Chuck's daddy."

"Oh, I see. How are you, sir?"

"Well, I'm not too good, Hank. I don't know if you've heard, but my boy is in trouble with the law. It's got me worried. Now, I know he came out to see you yesterday. He told me all about the plan you two cooked up."

"He told you?"

"Of course. He tells me everything. Except now I'm wondering if it's really such a good idea."

"Huh. Well, I ain't sure what kind of trouble he's in, but if it's local, I reckon he'll be a hell of a lot better off up there in Idaho than hanging around here. Don't you think?"

"Yeah, I guess you got a point there. All right, Hank, I appreciate you letting me bend your ear."

Red hung up the phone. He went to the refrigerator and took down a business card that had been held there by a magnet. He went back to the phone and dialed the number on the card.

"Sheriff's office."

"Give me Sheriff Giddings."

"May I ask who's calling?"

"This is Charles Melville, Jr. He asked me to call him if I had any information about my son. I think he'll want to hear what I have to say."

*

"Idaho?" said Giddings. "What the hell's in Idaho?"

"I'm sure I don't know, Sheriff," said Cora at the switchboard. She'd caught him at home, in the middle of shaving. "Mr. Melville said that's all the information he had."

"All right. Thanks, Cora." Giddings wiped a blob of shaving cream off the telephone receiver before hanging it up. He finished shaving and put on his work clothes. As he walked downstairs, he could smell the breakfast Megan was burning.

"I'm making pancakes," she sang as he entered the kitchen.

"Don't I know it."

She pecked him on the cheek. He tolerated it. He sipped from the cup of coffee she'd made him and set it back down.

"Can you pack me a lunch? I'm gonna be on the road today."

"Chasing down those boys who killed poor Beau?"

"Can't talk about it."

"Just tell me you'll be careful. Those boys must have the mark of Satan on them to do what they done. Beau was such a sweet man."

"Yeah. Real sweetheart. Tell you what, forget the lunch. I'll grab something on the road."

"What about your pancakes?"

"No time, I'm afraid. More for you."

Dean and Chuck spent the morning clearing everything out of the truck's cabinets and bins, as well as the fridge. Dean felt a little bad about trashing Gonzo's truck, but not too bad; after all, if Gonzo hadn't taken away his prime location, he never would have been in trouble with Antoine in the first place. They managed to tuck all ten bales out of sight. The truck would pass a cursory once-over if they got pulled over, but nothing more in-depth than that. Dean fired up the griddle and threw some bacon on it in hopes of killing the dank, herbal funk in the air.

Chuck ate his breakfast in the front seat, wiping bacon grease on the pages of the road atlas he'd bought at Walgreens. "Today's Tuesday, right?"

"All day."

"The jump is on Sunday, but we want to get up there by Thursday night. Friday morning at the latest. No need to make a race out of it. We can stick to the back roads, keep to the speed limits, not draw any attention."

"Listen to you, talking sense for once."

"Of course, once we're up there, we're gonna want to stick around and see the jump."

"What the hell are you talking about?"

"What do you think? Evel Knievel jumping the Snake River Canyon. This is going to be one of the great American triumphs of our time."

Dean cackled. "If he even makes it. Antoine thinks he's gonna get smeared all over that canyon. Some triumph."

Chuck set down the atlas, an indignant look on his face. "What the fuck does Antoine know? No way, cuz. Evel is gonna make it. He's the hero this country needs right now. I mean, look at what's going on. We're getting our ass kicked in Vietnam. OPEC has us by the short and curlies. Hell, the fuckin' president of the United States just resigned in disgrace! We need someone to lift us out of this quicksand we're sinking in, and Evel Knievel is the man to do it."

"He's not Superman, Chuck. I mean, you've seen the film of him trying to jump that fountain in Vegas, right? Reminded me of the time you threw that wooden puppet off the back of your daddy's truck."

Chuck howled. "Oh, yeah! That was fuckin' cool, cuz."

"Anyway, we need to get rolling. What's the first leg of this trip look like?"

Chuck picked up the atlas and flipped through the pages. "All right. Looks like Route 83 from here. When we hit Ballinger, we'll peel off to 153 to avoid Abilene."

Dean climbed into the driver's seat and started up the truck. For the first time since this insane mission started, he had a feeling it might actually work out. Like Evel Knievel jumping the Snake River Canyon.

TWELVE

Antoine couldn't believe his eyes. Parked in front of the Old German Bakery on Main Street in Fredericksburg was a police cruiser marked IVOR COUNTY SHERIFF. He pulled over, climbed out of the Trans Am, stretched, and headed into the bakery. Giddings was sitting alone at the counter. Antoine took the stool beside him.

"We meet again. This is starting to feel like fate."

Giddings looked up from his pancakes. "No, I don't believe so."

"You don't believe in fate?"

"I didn't say that. I just don't believe it's my fate to encounter you again."

"Well, I don't think it's purely coincidence that you and I both find ourselves out this way. In fact, I think we're pursuing similar ends."

"Don't think I caught your name."

"Antoine Lynch. How are those pancakes?"

"Hell of a lot better than my wife's."

Antoine ordered coffee and a short stack. "I'm sure she has her good qualities too."

"Excuse me?"

"Your wife, I mean."

"Boy, you'd best not be talking about my wife. I don't want to hear her name come out of your mouth."

"I don't know her name, so you have no concerns on that front."

"You gettin' smart with me?"

"Sheriff, we have met twice now, yesterday in San Marcos and again here today in Fredericksburg. Neither municipality being under your jurisdiction. Now, difficult as it may be for you to constrain your racist impulses, I am sitting at this counter as your equal. And I do believe we have something in common besides eating pancakes."

"Do tell."

"Dean and Chuck Melville."

Giddings folded his arms. "What's your connection to them?"

"Chuck I don't know at all. Just by reputation. But Dean, he works for me. And he and his cousin stole something from me."

"Was this before or after they killed my deputy?"

"After, though it's my guess Chuck did the killing on his own. Point I'm trying to make, though, is there's no need for you to trouble yourself trying to track them down. See, I know exactly where they're going. And I'm going to find them there, or somewhere between here and there, and I'm going to get back what's mine. And punishment will be meted out, you can rely on that. So Sheriff, I'd advise you to enjoy the rest of your breakfast and head on back to Ivor County."

Giddings got up from his stool and loomed over Antoine. Looming was one of the things he did best. "Now, you listen to me, Mr. Lynch. Jurisdiction don't mean a damn thing to me. God is on my side for this one. An eye for an eye, like the good book says. Justice will be done for my deputy, and no man will get in my way."

"Come on, now, Sheriff. We both know you don't give a good goddamn about your deputy. Now, his wife on the other hand—"

Giddings put his hands under Antoine's arms and lifted him into the air. He threw him across the counter and watched him crash through a stack of clean plates before coming to a landing on the floor. Giddings leaned over the counter and pointed down at him.

"Don't cross my path again. I see you anywhere or anytime between here and Armageddon, I will put your lights out for good."

Giddings threw a fiver on the counter and stormed out as a waitress helped Antoine to his feet.

"What's his problem?" she asked.

"I think he's got more than one."

"Goddamn, there ain't nothin' out here but tumbleweeds and Christian radio." Chuck had been fumbling with the dial for five minutes without finding anything satisfactory on the airwaves.

"I've got a box of eight-tracks back there," said Dean, hooking a thumb over his shoulder. "Bring it on up and find us something to listen to."

Chuck found the box and brought it to the front. He flipped through the eight-track tapes: Pink Floyd, *Dark Side of the Moon*; *Led Zeppelin IV*; The Who, *Quadrophenia*; David Bowie, *Ziggy Stardust*.

"This'll work," he said, sticking Little Feat's *Sailin' Shoes* into the player. Chuck drummed his bare feet on the dashboard and hung his arm out the window. A sign by the side of the highway said SWEETWATER 8 MILES. "How are we on gas?"

"We could use some."

"Let's fill up in Sweetwater. I gotta call Triple H back anyway."

"How far were you thinking we'd go today?"

"I guess we can figure that out at the gas station."

"Yeah. Well, I was thinking we'd probably get to Amarillo around six. There's someone I'd like to look up there."

Chuck winced. "Someone you want to look up?"

"A girl I knew once."

"For real, cousin? We're on the run and you're lookin' to get laid? Don't you think this girl has seen you on the news by now?"

"I doubt it. We're big news back home, but out here? They got their own problems. Besides, how often do I get to Amarillo?"

"Oh, here we go." Chuck cranked up the volume on the eight-track and started bellowing along with Lowell George. "And I been from Tucson to Tucumcari..."

Seventy-five miles to the south in San Angelo, Antoine was on the phone with T.J.

"Any news since this morning?"

"Just heard it on the radio. Gonzo reported one of his taco trucks stolen. Definitely the one Dean was working yesterday. Plus, a clerk at the True Value says he sold a bunch of black spray paint to someone matching Chuck's description yesterday, so the cops think—"

"They painted the truck black. Good, now I know what I'm looking for. Anything else?"

"Rico came by to pick up his resupply. I just told him what you said. There's been a delay due to cartel trouble down in Sinaloa. Sit tight."

"I'm guessing he was not happy to hear this."

"Not at all. He got a little mouthy about it. Said Manny Diaz down in San Antonio would be happy to take him on if you can't come through for him. I told him shit is dry all over, but I don't know how long that's gonna hold him."

"I'm hoping to wrap this up sooner than later. Only problem is not knowing what route they're taking. Well, no, that ain't my *only* problem. I got a pig problem, too. That sheriff from Ivor County I was telling you about. He might get in my way."

"And then what?"

"It's not gonna go well for him."

*

While Dean gassed up the truck, Chuck found a payphone and called Triple H. "Did you talk to him?"

"Yeah, I did. He won't go a million. He says he'll pay seven-fifty."

"Call him back and counter-offer with nine hundred thousand. He'll go up to eight, then you meet him in the middle at eight-fifty. But that's the rock-bottom price. He won't pay that, we'll drive this load to California. Them rock stars will pay top dollar for this shit."

"I'll tell him. Call me back tonight. Oh, and Chuck. Your daddy called me."

"Red called you? Why?"

"Said he was concerned about you. Said you got in some kinda trouble. What's that about?"

"Don't you worry about it. What did you say to him?"

"Nothing. Why did you tell him about our plan?"

"What? I didn't tell him shit. Hank, what did you say to him?"

A pause. "Chuck, I think I might have fucked up."

When Chuck got back to the truck, he was carrying a six-pack of Lone Star and a box marked BEARCAT.

"Whatcha got there?" said Dean.

"CB radio. I'll hook it up tonight."

"What for?"

"This is how the truckers talk to each other. We can get all sorts of good information on here about speed traps, police checkpoints, road conditions."

"Don't they talk in code?"

"How hard can it be to figure out? These are truck drivers, not CIA agents."

They got back in the truck. Chuck pulled a can of Lone Star from the six-pack ring and tossed it to Dean, then grabbed one for himself and pulled off the tab.

"So this young lady I mentioned—"

"Oh, here we go."

"Last I knew, she worked at this place called the Silver Dollar just outside Amarillo."

"Whorehouse?"

"No, it ain't no whorehouse. It's just a roadhouse. Somewhere we can grab a chicken-fried steak and a cold one, and if she happens to be working, well…"

"I guess we gotta eat somewhere."

"That's the spirit." Dean started up the truck and they got back on the road. Chuck found ZZ Top's *Tres Hombres* in the box of tapes and stuck it in the eight-track player. He cranked up the volume and Billy Gibbons' nasty opening riff of "Waitin' for the Bus" blasted them on down the road.

THIRTEEN

Giddings called the office and got the same news update from Deputy Winslow as Antoine had gotten from T.J.

"That checks out. I'm at a truck stop in Sweetwater. Showed the Polaroid to the clerk, he said the guy on the left bought some beer and a CB radio less than two hours ago. So far, I'm on the right route. If I get lucky, I might catch up with them tonight."

"All right, but Sheriff…"

"What is it, Winslow?"

"What are you planning to do if you do catch them?"

"That's a question you shouldn't be asking me, deputy. Do me a favor, call Megan and tell her I won't be home for dinner. Oh, and I'm gonna need you to call Judge Harper, too."

As Dean drove into the Panhandle, the land flattened out until the arid plains of the Llano Estacado stretched as far as the eye could see in every direction. Pink Floyd's "Brain Damage" blasted from the truck's speakers.

"Never been up this far," said Chuck. "Sure ain't much to look at."

"I like to think it has a kind of rugged beauty," said Dean, sipping his beer.

"There's no shortage of Texas, that's for damn sure. You know, except for a road trip to New Orleans when I turned eighteen, I've never been out of this fuckin' state."

"I'm not feeling the Texan pride from you right now."

"Pride in what? Things that happened a hundred years ago

that I had nothing to do with? You want me to remember the Alamo? I couldn't even tell you what happened there."

"Well, back in 1836, Santa Anna—"

"My point is, I don't care. It's just a tourist trap now, right?"

"It's a piece of history, and I happen to think Texas history is pretty fuckin' interesting. The one subject in eighth grade I got an A in. I mean, look out there. Can't you just imagine a cattle drive heading up from the Rio Grande? Maybe they encounter a Comanche war party. There's a bloody battle."

"And now somewhere there's just a plaque."

In a nowhere spot on the map called Ralls, they intersected with Route 62 heading west toward Lubbock.

"Gonzo is from Lubbock," said Dean. "He swears he was in a band with Buddy Holly in high school. I'd halfway like to take a detour there and ask if anyone ever heard of him."

"Why? Let him have it. You already took the man's taco truck, now you want to take Buddy Holly away from him too?"

"Shit. I'm still pissed off at him for kicking me out of my primo spot. You know, when I saw him yesterday, I halfway got the feeling he knew what I was up to, as far as selling contraband out of this truck."

"Maybe that's the problem. Maybe he expected you to kick a piece up to him in return for him letting you keep operating at your primo spot."

"If that's the case, I wish he'd just come out and said it. Well, he'll get his truck back eventually."

Chuck had nothing to say about that.

Antoine was thirty miles from Lubbock when the red and blue flashers filled his rear-view.

"Motherfuck," he said, though this was not an entirely unexpected development. A black man driving alone through the

Texas panhandle in a flashy car was going to attract the attention of law enforcement early and often. He wasn't speeding and had a clean record, but he doubted that was going to help him much.

He pulled off onto the shoulder and shut down the engine. The cruiser stopped behind him. For a long moment, nothing happened. The lights kept flashing. No cars passed. Trying to make me sweat, Antoine thought.

After two long minutes, an officer stepped out of the cruiser. Antoine noted with some alarm that he had his weapon drawn.

The officer approached the Trans Am and tapped the driver's side window with the business end of his sidearm. Antoine rolled down the window, doing his best to offer a pleasant smile. The officer kept the gun trained at his head. His eyes were lost behind mirrored shades.

"License and registration, slow as you please. I won't need half a reason to blow your head off."

"No problem, officer," said Antoine. He narrated his progress. "I'm slowly reaching into my pants pocket for my wallet. I have produced the wallet and I am now removing my driver's license from it. I am handing you the license. Now I am slowly opening my glove compartment and reaching inside for my registration. I have the registration in hand. Here it is."

As the officer looked over the documents, Antoine realized with a shudder that he was a sheriff's deputy.

"Do you know why I pulled you over today, Mr. Lynch?"

"I'm starting to get an idea."

"There is a warrant for your arrest out of Ivor County. You are wanted on suspicion of involvement with a double homicide there two nights ago. Please step out of the vehicle and keep your hands where I can see them."

The deputy backed away, still holding the gun on Antoine as

he pushed open the door and slowly stood. "Sir, I need to inform you that this is nothing but a personal vendetta on the part of the Sheriff of Ivor County. I was not in Ivor County on the night in question. I have witnesses who will—"

"We have a saying around here," said the deputy as he holstered his weapon and patted Antoine down. "Tell it to the judge."

Antoine considered his options. In seconds he would be in cuffs. There was a very good chance he would be turned over to Sheriff Giddings, soon after which he would no doubt be shot dead while "trying to escape." He decided he had no options.

It was karate time.

Lightning-quick, he spun and ducked, swinging out his right arm, palm flat and stiff. He connected with the soft tissue under the deputy's rib cage, causing him to stumble back a step. Antoine followed up with two palm strikes to the face, the first catching the deputy in the jaw, the second producing a satisfying crack that let Antoine know he'd broken the man's nose. This was no time to let up, however. His next move was nothing fancy, just a solid groin kick that doubled over the deputy, allowing Antoine to spin behind him and grab him by the wrists.

As Antoine twisted the deputy's arms upward, his captive hollered an epithet Antoine didn't like to hear from any white man.

"You get one of those for free," he hissed into the deputy's ear. "Next one gets you a broken arm."

"You're a dead man."

"Sounds like wishful thinking to me." Antoine ripped the handcuffs from the deputy's belt and shackled his arms behind his back. He pulled the Smith & Wesson Model 39 out of the deputy's holster and tossed it onto the driver's seat of the Trans Am. He marched the deputy back to his cruiser, opened the back door, and pushed him down onto the seat.

"I expect someone will come along for you eventually. For what it's worth, I was telling the truth earlier. Sheriff Giddings is bad news. You cross his path, tread lightly."

Antoine slammed the door and hustled back to his car. He had to ditch it as soon as possible, which was a shame. He'd grown rather fond of the Firebird.

"This is it, cousin," said Dean. "The original Route 66."

Chuck was aware of the cultural significance, but the road didn't look like anything special to him. Per the song, he knew they'd hit Kingman, Barstow, and San Bernadino if they stayed on it long enough, but that wasn't the plan.

Dean couldn't recall the exact location, but he knew the Silver Dollar was on Route 66, just west of Amarillo. That's where he'd met Marla May Perkins the previous summer. This was before he'd started working for either Gonzo or Antoine. Though he'd never told Chuck this, he'd been getting pretty steady work as a male model up in Dallas. He'd done ads for jeans, boots, a line of western shirts, and most embarrassing of all, designer underwear. On that last shoot, the photographer asked him if he'd ever consider posing nude, and that was the end of his modeling career. He figured it was only one step from *Playgirl* magazine to hardcore pornography, and he didn't trust himself not to take that step.

Flush with designer underwear money, he planned a road trip out to California along the legendary Route 66. He got no further than the Silver Dollar. He was smitten with Marla May from the minute he walked inside, and he proceeded to charm the pants off her, quite literally. He stayed with her for a week, all the while calling Loretta back in San Marcos and updating her on his trip to the coast. He'd hang out at the Silver Dollar while Marla May was working, and afterward they'd go back to her place and ball 'til daylight. He never wanted to leave, but as always happened, the money ran out. He told Marla May he'd be back soon, but he hadn't so much as called her since. He wasn't going to call now, either. Better to surprise her.

"What in the jiminy fuck is that?" said Chuck, pointing to something on the roadside ahead.

Dean squinted. "Looks like…cars? Sticking out of the ground?"

"What on earth happened here? Pull over, cuz."

Dean did so and they climbed out of the truck. Chuck counted ten cars lined up like dominos, their hoods buried in the ground, their tail-ends sticking out at forty-five-degree angles. Sitting on a lawn chair in front of this display was a man dressed in a spangled orange Nudie suit and smoking a cigar. He stood as Dean and Chuck approached.

"Welcome to the Cadillac Ranch!" He shook their hands.

"This wasn't here last year," said Dean.

"No, indeed. My associates and I just put the finishing touches on this installation days ago."

"They're all Cadillacs," said Chuck.

"Indeed, they are. Starting at the far end, that is a 1948 Club Coupe. We move along through the years, all the way up to this 1963 sedan right here."

"The tail fins are different on all of 'em," said Dean.

"Exactly so! That's American ingenuity for you. Planned obsolescence. See, if you're a rich Texas cattleman, you want everyone to know you're driving the latest Caddy. You can't be seen with last year's tail fin, so you've got to buy yourself a new one every year."

"Is that what you've done here?" said Chuck. "You buy a new one every year and dump the old ones here?"

The man laughed. "Mercy, no. These were all found in junk-yards or bought in private sales for under two hundred dollars."

"So what is the point of this?"

"It's art, son! Art!"

"Oh, I get it," said Dean. "It's like a social comment or something."

"If you want it to be. Personally, I think Amarillo needs a lot more of this kind of stuff. We're basically known for two things: beefsteak and the Pantex Plant."

"What's that?" said Chuck.

"That's where they make the nukes. Just a few miles northeast of here is the largest facility dedicated to the manufacture of nuclear weapons in this country. It's what put us on the map. And by that, I mean the map of American cities the Soviet Union will target first in the event of a nuclear war. That's no shit, people around here are actually proud of that. Dallas, Houston, San Antonio, they're way down the list. Every day I wake up in Amarillo is a day Pantex didn't have the kind of major accident that would make us all glow in the dark. So that makes it a good day. Now, there's nothing I can do to close that place down, so I put my energy into more positive pursuits."

"Positive?" said Chuck. "This has got to be the biggest waste of time and money I've ever seen in my life."

"Don't listen to him," said Dean. "I think it's pretty cool. He was just complaining how there's nothing to see up here in the Panhandle. Well, now there is something to see."

"Well, I appreciate that. I appreciate both points of view, actually. Now, if you'll excuse me, it looks like I have more guests."

Dean looked back and saw two other cars pulling off behind the taco truck. "I guess we better get a move on, Chuck."

"Fine by me. That's ten minutes of my life I'm never gonna get back."

FOURTEEN

Giddings arrived on the scene just as the medic finished patching up Deputy Pruitt's nose. They exchanged terse greetings.

"He told me to tread lightly around you. The sumbitch who broke my nose said that."

"Antoine Lynch."

"Yessir. He said he wasn't in Ivor County that night and had witnesses to prove it, but guess what I told him?"

"Tell it to the judge."

"That's right. He said you have a personal vendetta against him."

"Consider the source. This man is an accomplice to a double murder. My deputy is dead."

"I know. Makes you wonder why he didn't kill me. I mean, they can only fry him once, right?"

"What about the other two? The white boys in the black truck?"

"Never saw them. Never heard from anyone who did."

"Might have bypassed this area. Might be on another route entirely."

"They make it out of Texas, you might not get the level of cooperation like you got from me."

"That had crossed my mind."

The east side was Lubbock's black neighborhood, and that's where Antoine cruised the streets, block by block, until he saw what he was looking for. It was a puke green El Camino, just about the ugliest car Antoine had ever seen, but it had a FOR SALE sign in the back window. It was parked in front of a small house where a shirtless black man was mowing his small lawn.

"This your El Camino, brother?" Antoine said, leaning out his window. The man stopped pushing the mower, wiped his brow, and nodded.

"I know she ain't much to look at," the man said. "But she runs good."

"What's the year and the mileage?"

"She's a '68. Got just about eighty-five thousand miles on her."

Antoine was in no position to haggle. "Tell you what. I'll trade you straight up. This 1973 Firebird Trans Am for your '68 El Camino. We exchange pink slips, we go our separate ways."

At first the man just stared as if Antoine had sprouted an asshole in the middle of his forehead. Seconds later, he was laughing like Antoine was Richard Pryor. "You crazy, man. Get on your way."

"I'm dead serious. You can take it for a spin around the neighborhood if you want. I'll even finish cutting your grass for you." Antoine stepped out of the car and tossed the man his keys. "My name is Antoine Lynch. Yours?"

"Russell Wayne." He gave Antoine a hard look. "Is it stolen?"

"It's mine, free and clear. Here." Antoine took out his wallet. "Here's my driver's license. And here's the title for the Firebird. As you can see, they both say Antoine Lynch."

Russell looked them over and handed them back. "This ain't that *Candid Camera* shit, is it? Because I'll whip your ass if it is."

"Take it for a ride, Russell."

Russell shrugged and climbed into the Trans Am. He started it up and peeled away from the curb. Antoine pushed the mower through the grass for a few minutes before the Trans Am rounded the corner and pulled up in front of the El Camino. Russell got out of it.

"Nothing wrong with it that I can tell."

"Not a thing. Do we have a deal?"

Russell thought it over. Antoine could tell he was trying to come up with a reason to say no.

In the end, he said, "Pink slip's in the house. I'll go get it."

"There it is," said Dean.

It was hard to miss. Breaking up the monotony of sunbaked earth and yellowed grass stretching to the horizon was a barn-like structure with a neon sign reading SILVER DOLLAR. On either side of the dirt entrance, a wooden fence was festooned with plastic banners: COLD BEER ON TAP; FRIDAY NIGHT IS LADIES NIGHT; LIVE MUSIC EVERY SATURDAY; FINISH OUR 72 OUNCE STEAK AND ITS FREE.

"Park around back," said Chuck.

"No shit," said Dean. The dirt lot sprawled around the building, and it looked to be getting crowded early. Near the front entrance, a dozen Harley Davidsons were lined up in a row. Dean drove past a highly competitive game of horseshoes and found a spot between two pickup trucks in the back.

"You head on in," said Chuck as they got out of the truck. "I'm gonna call Triple H and make sure this thing is nailed down."

Chuck walked around front to the phone booth he'd spotted when they pulled in. He dialed Triple H's number for what he hoped was the last time.

"Hello?"

"It's me. Do we have a deal?"

"He says it's a deal at eight-fifty. He says when you get up there to follow the signs for concessions check-in. Whoever you find there, just tell 'em the Texas boys are here to see Bob Dillon. He'll come get you to make the exchange."

"Sounds like a plan."

"And I know you won't forget me, but just to be clear, we agreed on ten percent as my finder's fee. So that's eighty-five grand for me."

"All yours as soon as we get back." Chuck hung up, straightened his shirt, and headed inside.

While Chuck made his call, Dean took a seat at the bar. The Silver Dollar was just as he remembered it: a cavernous space with dining tables, pinball machines and billiards, a stage with a dance floor in front of it, and plenty of customers who were either drunk or well on their way. The walls were decorated with license plates, big game trophies, and photos of the owner with various luminaries who had passed through. The bartender was a pretty blonde who offered him a gleaming smile.

"What can I getcha, honey?"

"Do you know if Marla May is working tonight?"

"I don't believe so, but I can find out."

"Oh, that's all right. Can I ask your name?"

"I'm Hannah. And who are you?"

"Hannah, my name is Dean. I would like a cold Lone Star and a cheeseburger with fries when you get a chance."

"My pleasure." She set a coaster in front of him and pulled a Lone Star from the tap. "Not from around here, are ya, Dean?"

"No, ma'am. I'm from San Marcos, just outside Austin."

Her eyes lit up as she set the beer in front of him. "Oh, Austin! I've always wanted to get down there. My cousin Roberta lives down there, and she's always talking about this place, the... Sarsaparilla?"

"The Armadillo World Headquarters."

"That's it! She saw Willie Nelson play there, and ZZ Top. Oh, and Frank Zappa. Too weird for me, but she had fun. Well, let me get that cheeseburger going for you, Dean. And then you can tell me all about Austin."

"Be happy to oblige."

When Chuck walked in, he saw Dean was already busy chatting up a pretty young thing at the bar. No surprise there. He wondered if she was this Marla May he was so intent on seeing, or if he'd already moved it on down the line. He decided to give Dean his space and grabbed a table near the dance floor. After a moment, an older, sadder-looking waitress approached.

"Welcome to the Silver Dollar. What can I get you?"

"I'm pretty hungry. Tell me about this 72-ounce steak deal."

"It's twenty dollars up front, refunded if you complete the meal within one hour. You must eat all of the steak, plus the salad, roll, and baked potato to get it for free. You cannot get up from the table while you're eating or allow anyone else to sit with you. If you become sick, we ask that you use the provided container. If you finish in time, your picture goes up on our Wall of Fame."

"How many have finished in time?"

"Since we started in '66, nine people have completed the meal within an hour."

"What the hell, let's try to make it ten. And keep the cold Lone Star coming."

"It's almost time for Chicken Shit Bingo," said Hannah.

"Chicken Shit Bingo? That a band?" said Dean, his mouth full of cheeseburger.

"No, it's not a band. I've got my break in five minutes. If you want, we can go out back and I'll show you."

"Hannah, I would love for you to show me this Chicken Shit Bingo."

She flashed him the dazzling smile again. Something caught her attention and she tapped him on the shoulder. "Look, someone's going for the steak challenge."

Dean glanced over his shoulder. He saw a small crowd gathered around a table where Chuck was cutting pieces off a gigantic sirloin and shoveling them in his mouth. He turned back to Hannah, shaking his head. "That's my cousin Chuck. Soon to be my cousin Upchuck, I'm guessing."

"We could watch him instead if you want."

"No. Let's head out back."

Twenty minutes into the challenge, Chuck was feeling queasy. He'd finished off the salad and the roll, but he still had half a baked potato and what looked to be almost three pounds of meat sitting in front of him. He'd attracted a cheering section, however, so he wasn't about to quit.

"You got this in the bag!" hollered a hulking man in a leather vest with DEMON RIDERS stenciled on the back.

"No, don't get it in the bag," a cowboy joked. "Get it down your gullet."

The biker flashed the cowboy a dirty look. The cowboy decided to find a game of pool.

Chuck felt his jaw getting sore as he kept chewing. He hoped his prison dental work would hold up.

"Thirty minutes to go!" another spectator cried.

Chuck kept eating.

Behind the Silver Dollar, Dean saw a line of people waiting to buy a ticket from a man seated at a table. Next to him was a large, empty chicken coop. Hannah took him by the arm and they got in line.

"Here's how it works," she said. "Woodrow sells you a ticket for fifty cents. The ticket has a number on it. There's a grid laid out at the bottom of the chicken coop, like a bingo card. At seven o'clock, Woodrow fetches Big Bertha from her holding pen where she's been stuffing her face with feed. He drops her in the coop, and if she poops on your number, you win a prize."

"Sounds like there's not a lot of skill involved in this contest. For Bertha, maybe, but for me it sounds like random chance."

"Feeling lucky?"

Dean was feeling lucky, as a matter of fact. When he reached the front of the line, he handed Woodrow two quarters. Woodrow tore him off a ticket.

"Number sixteen. If Bertha hits your number, you win the grand prize of fifteen dollars. If she poops on the line between your square and another, you split the pot."

"Sounds fair to me."

Hannah checked her watch as they left the line. "Almost seven."

"You know, Hannah, fascinating as it would be to watch ol' Bertha pop a squat, and much as I'd love to win that fifteen-dollar prize, I was wondering if you'd have time for a quick tour of my truck. It's parked right over there."

Hannah's eyes lit up and a grin spread across her face. "Yes, I believe I have just enough time for that."

The first shooting pain through Chuck's gut arrived when he had about twelve ounces of steak left and five minutes on the clock.

"You can do it!"

"Mind over matter!"

"Too close to quit now!"

Chuck cut a small piece and forked it into his mouth. The meat was now cold, the texture gummy, the flavor nonexistent.

All his teeth hurt. His throat was raw. He chewed. He swallowed. They cheered.

Another piece. Another.

"Two minutes!"

Reverting to his most primal state. he picked up what remained of the steak with one hand and gnawed it. He felt pressure on his chest and sweat pouring down his face and something evil growing deep inside his belly. He chewed. He swallowed.

"Thirty seconds!"

He shoved the last bit of it into his mouth and forced his jaws up and down.

"Ten seconds!"

He swallowed. He opened his mouth and stuck out his tongue. The crowd went wild. He tried to stand up.

Top that, Evel Knievel, he thought as he tumbled to the floor.

FIFTEEN

With everything that went down in Lubbock, Antoine figured he had some time to make up. It was possible that the Melville boys planned to drive through the night, but he had a feeling they would stop to party along the way. It didn't matter so much that he didn't know what route they were taking. He knew their final destination, and if he could get there before they did, he'd be in a better position to reclaim what was his.

He took Route 84 the rest of the way through Texas, past desolate towns with names like Shallowater and Muleshoe. Outposts of civilization grew even more sparse when he crossed into New Mexico. The El Camino had nothing but an AM radio to keep him company, and he spent about an hour listening to a show that seemed to be broadcasting from the 1950s through a crack in time—a lone voice ranting about communism and the Satanic plot to mind-warp the children of America known as rock 'n roll.

At Santa Rosa, he picked up Interstate 40. He caught himself yawning several times, and his eyelids grew heavy. When he hit Albuquerque at just after eleven P.M., he decided he could use a pick-me-up. He saw a sign reading HILTON at the top of a tall building downtown and took the nearest exit. He parked near the hotel bar and went inside.

"I'll have an Irish coffee," he told the bartender, a heavyset man with an enormous gray beard.

"Funny. You don't look Irish." The bartender smiled at his own joke and started fixing the drink. Antoine ignored him and looked around the dimly lit room. He saw guys who looked like traveling salesmen, tourist couples, and one woman at the other end of the bar who had to be on the clock. He wasn't being judgmental, as he felt both sex work and the marijuana trade should be legalized, but he didn't want to be bothered. It looked like that was going to happen anyway.

"Buy me a drink?" she said, settling on the stool beside him. Her lipstick and eyeshadow were too heavy, and her platinum blonde wig was askew.

"I will, but that's the only transaction taking place here tonight."

She nodded to the bartender, who got to work on a regular order he clearly knew by heart.

"I'm not sure I like what you're implying," she said.

"If I've made a mistake, I apologize. I'm just trying to make it clear that I'm not interested."

"Interested in what?"

He turned to face her. "In a woman."

"You don't look like a holy roller to me," she said, "or a man who denies himself the finer things." When he didn't respond, she went on, a touch of hurt in her voice now. "Is it something about me? Or don't you like girls?"

And maybe she saw something back of his eyes, because the hurt look was replaced with a sly, rueful smile. "I see. Well, friend, let me recommend a place that might be more your speed." She took a matchbook out of a bowl on the bar. "Dennis? Grab me a pen, wouldja?"

The biker who'd cheered him on reached down and pulled Chuck to his feet.

"You all right, buddy?"

Chuck looked down at his distended belly. He could swear he saw something trying to fight its way out. "Yeah. Couldn't be better."

"Congratulations," said the waitress, approaching with two items in her hands. "It is my honor to present you with a certificate of achievement, as well as a Silver Dollar commemorative steak knife. We'd like to take your photograph right over there in front of Billy the Steer."

She handed him the certificate and a leather sheath marked with the Silver Dollar logo. He took them and allowed himself to be led over to the stuffed steer in the corner. His legs shaking, he held up his winnings and forced a smile for the camera.

"Be sure to sign our guestbook before you leave," said the waitress. "Oh, and here's your twenty dollars back."

Chuck folded the certificate around the sheath and the twenty and shoved them into his front pocket.

"Buddy, you gotta let me buy you a shot," said the biker.

Chuck was about to refuse, but on second thought decided that a shot of liquor might be just the thing to settle his stomach. He and the biker made their way to the bar, where Chuck slowly lowered himself onto a stool.

"Two shots of Cuervo Gold!" the biker shouted in the general direction of the bartender. "I'm Uptown Mike, by the way." He extended his hand.

"Chuck." His hand disappeared inside Uptown Mike's iron grip. "Is there a Downtown Mike?"

"There used to be. He got pancaked by a semi on the Fourth of July. Come to think of it, I guess I don't have to go by Uptown Mike anymore, since I'm the only Mike left in the M.C. But I dunno, I kind of like it."

Uptown Mike released Chuck's hand as the tequila shots arrived. The biker raised his shot and downed it. Chuck did the same. It felt warm going down. Maybe everything was going to be okay.

"Two more!" said Uptown Mike.

"Uh…sure, why not. You come here often, Uptown Mike?"

"First time. Me and my boys—you see 'em over there playing darts and pool—we're from Dallas. We're on a road trip. Heading up to Snake River Canyon."

"Oh yeah? You guys big Evel Knievel fans?"

Uptown Mike sneered. "Fuck, no. And he's no fan of ours. He thinks clubs like the Demon Riders and Hell's Angels give motorcycles a bad name. Hell, at least we know how to take care of our bikes. We don't crash 'em into buses and shit like that. Well, except for Downtown Mike, but that wasn't really his fault. The truck driver was high on mescaline. So was Downtown Mike, but it was the truck driver who crossed the line."

"So why are y'all going up there?"

"It's gonna be a great fuckin' party, that's why. We're meeting up with clubs from all over the country. And we're all gonna cheer when that sumbitch tumbles ass over teakettle down that canyon."

"I bet you ten bucks he makes it."

"I'd take that bet, but how am I gonna collect when you lose?"

"I'm heading up there too. Me and my cousin."

"No shit? All right, you're on. Let's drink to it."

They threw back their second shots of tequila. Chuck's head began to spin. He felt bile in his throat and a rumbling down below.

A salad, a roll, a baked potato, seventy-two ounces of meat, six Lone Stars, and two shots of Cuervo Gold. It all came spewing forth like a volcanic eruption. All over Uptown Mike.

It wasn't the first time Dean had dirty laundry sex. One night in the dorm at UT, his roommate's friend had passed out in Dean's bed, so when Dean returned with a girl he'd met at the tailgate, he dumped out the hamper and made a bed of dirty clothes on the floor for them to screw on. In the back of Gonzo's taco truck, he and Hannah made a bed of their own clothing and got down to business.

"That was kind of nasty," she said as he helped her out of the truck afterward. "But I like it nasty."

"Oh, I can get a hell of a lot nastier than that. I'd love to show you."

"Well, maybe you can stop back here on your way home from Idaho."

He leaned in for a kiss.

"Hannah? *Dean?*"

Dean looked up to see a woman he recognized striding across the parking lot toward him. She was the woman he'd come to see.

"Marla May!" He pasted a shit-eating grin on his face. "I was hoping you'd show up."

"Oh, were you?" Marla May folded her arms and turned to Hannah. "Did you fuck him yet?"

"Just finished," said Hannah. "What do you care? You've got a boyfriend."

"So do you, bitch!"

Hannah grabbed Dean by the arm. "Come on, Dean. Let's go inside. A little too trashy out here, don't you think?"

As she dragged him toward the door, Dean glanced back over his shoulder and offered Marla May a sheepish shrug. He'd learned to always keep his options open.

When Chuck came to his senses, he realized he was on the floor of the bar with Uptown Mike's hands around his neck. At first, he thought Uptown Mike had puked ali over him, but then he remembered he had puked all over Uptown Mike, and it was therefore his own puke that was now dripping down onto his face.

He thought he should try to explain this to Uptown Mike, but he found it hard to speak with the big biker's hands squeezing his throat. It seemed as though Uptown Mike was trying to tell him something, but Chuck couldn't make any sense of it.

What happened next, Dean would have to explain to him later.

"So Hannah pulls me back inside, I guess to show me off," he would tell Chuck, having detailed his evening up to that point. "But Marla May is right behind us, and she's pissed off. She comes up behind Hannah and gives her a big shove, right into this cowboy who's walking back to his table with a full pitcher of beer. Well, that pitcher goes flying and crashes down right on the head of that biker dude who's got you by the throat. That's when all hell broke loose."

All Chuck knew in the moment was that Uptown Mike had released him and was up on his feet again. Chuck coughed and wheezed and tried to stand. By the time he got his bearings, the bar had erupted into a full-on brawl. He saw a cowboy break a pool cue over a biker's head. He saw a biker flip a cowboy onto the green felt of a pool table and pile-drive his fist into the cowboy's teeth. He saw two women, who he would later learn were Hannah and Marla May, wrestling in a pool of beer on the floor. He saw his cousin Dean pop a stick of gum into his mouth and grin at the mayhem erupting all around them.

"Cousin!" Chuck shouted, pulling himself to his feet. "Time to go!"

It wasn't quite time to go yet, however, as Uptown Mike—fresh from lifting up the cowboy who'd inadvertently shattered a pitcher of beer on his head and mounting him onto the horns of Billy the Steer—took notice of the fact that Chuck was standing again.

"Nobody ever puked on me and lived," he snarled.

"That happen to you a lot, Uptown Mike?"

Uptown Mike charged Chuck. Dean charged Uptown Mike from behind. Dean jumped onto Uptown Mike's back and wrapped his arms around his neck. Chuck lowered his shoulder and drove it into Uptown Mike's solar plexus. All three of them crashed to the floor.

As Uptown Mike struggled to catch his breath, Chuck reached into his pocket, popped open the sheath, and drew the steak knife. He placed it to Uptown Mike's neck.

"One flick of the wrist and you're bleeding out all over this floor. So do yourself and us a favor and stay down until we clear the back door."

Chuck nicked Uptown Mike's neck, no deeper than a shaving cut, just to show he meant business. He nodded to Dean, and they scrambled for the back door. Dean caught sight of Marla May tossing Hannah across the bar.

"See you next time!" he hollered as they made their escape.

"Clip that bike in front," said Chuck as Dean turned into the front lot. Dean timed it just right, pushing open his door as they passed and hitting the handlebars of the first motorcycle in the line. He pulled it shut as that bike tumbled into the one behind it and on down the line.

"That's gonna leave a mark," said Dean. "But fuck it, I can fix this truck up good as new before I give it back to Gonzo."

Chuck had nothing to say about that.

SIXTEEN

Sheriff Giddings could have quit for the night. He'd checked into a room at the Route 66 Motel, but he wasn't quite ready to watch Johnny Carson and turn in yet. He sat in his patrol car eating a bag of Fritos and listening to the local police band. That's how he learned about the disturbance at the Silver Dollar roadhouse, just a few miles west of the motel. He had no reason to believe the Melville boys were involved, but he couldn't see the harm in checking it out.

The local cops were already on the scene when he arrived, and a little mystified by his presence.

"Long way from home, Sheriff," said Officer Briggs.

"This is personal for me. I'm on the track of two fugitives responsible for the death of my deputy. I'd like to show this picture around." He held up the Polaroid.

"Be my guest. Our drunk tank's already full for the night, so there's nothing left for us to do here."

Giddings went inside. Tables were overturned, windows were broken—along with many glasses and pitchers—and the floor was slick with beer and blood. It never got this bad at Sonny's, Giddings thought. Not as long as he'd had his badge anyway.

The bartender named Hannah looked like she'd gone a few rounds with George Foreman. He showed her the photo.

"Yeah, they were here." She grinned, revealing a cracked tooth in an otherwise brilliant smile. "That's Dean, the foxy one. His cousin Chuck I didn't meet, but he did finish off the 72-ounce steak dinner in under an hour."

"Quite an accomplishment. How long ago did they leave?"

"Maybe an hour ago? Why, they in some kind of trouble?"

"They killed a police officer in cold blood."

"Oh, I don't believe it. Chuck, maybe. Like I said, I didn't meet him. But Dean, he's just as sweet as pie."

"Do you know where they were going?"

"Dean said something about Evel Knievel. I guess he's doing some big jump this weekend."

"Snake River Canyon."

"If you say so."

"Do you know if they were planning on stopping for the night?"

"Not really. They left in a hurry, and I was kind of busy at the time. If you're trying to catch them, I don't think you're alone. They pissed off a bunch of bikers too, and they're headed for the same place."

"All right, ma'am. Appreciate your help."

"Oh, Sheriff?" Hannah reached into her bra and pulled out a ten and a five. "If you run into Dean, could you give him this?"

He took the cash. "What for?"

"That's his winnings from Chicken Shit Bingo tonight. That Dean is a lucky boy."

"Yeah. I guess we'll see about that."

Giddings called the motel and canceled his room for the night. Too many other people were after the Melville boys, and he wasn't about to let any of them beat him to the punch.

Antoine found the address the woman at the Hilton bar had given him. It wasn't much to look at—a concrete bunker with a single red lightbulb posted beside the front door. The door was locked. He pressed the buzzer.

After a moment, a heavily muscled man in a leather vest opened the door a crack. He looked at Antoine expectantly, saying nothing. Antoine glanced at the matchbook, where the woman had written one word under the address.

"Ambergris," he said.

The man nodded and opened the door for Antoine, who stepped inside. Every eye in the place turned toward him, except for the two belonging to a dapper young brother sitting alone at the bar reading a book. As expected, the place was populated exclusively by men. It was bathed in blue light, with leather booths and Al Green on the stereo. Once the denizens had got an eyeful of him, they went back to what they were doing, whether it be talking, dancing, or messing around.

"What are you reading?" Antoine asked, taking a seat next to the young brother, who held up the book cover for him to see. "'Politically cunning, shockingly violent, and horrifyingly possible,'" Antoine read. "'Blyden Jackson, *Operation Burning Candle*.' Sounds heavy."

"It's pulp, but it's powerful."

"Tell me about it."

For the first time, the young brother peered at Antoine over his reading glasses. "I haven't seen you in here before."

"I'm not from around here. Name's Antoine."

"I'm Julian. Buy me a drink and I'll tell you about the book."

Antoine signaled for the bartender. Julian ordered a pina colada. Antoine paid for it and a club soda for himself. "All right, Julian. Cheers."

They clinked glasses and drank. "Okay," said Julian. "These black soldiers in Vietnam, all presumed dead, come back to America and form their own revolutionary army. They do battle against the forces of the white establishment, culminating in a bloody attack on the Democratic National Convention."

"Sounds a little like *The Spook Who Sat by the Door*."

Julian looked pleased by the reference. "If you liked that, you'll love this. But you better get your hands on it soon. Books like this have a way of going out of print forever. And the author just might meet a mysterious demise. Too dangerous to the powers that be. Anything about dismantling white supremacy or the police state or any of the systems that keep us down, you've got to read it when you can."

"Dismantling the police, now that sounds like a fine idea to me. I would have had a much easier time today, for example."

Julian set the book down and sipped his cocktail. "You were hassled by the pigs today?"

"Indeed, I was. Not for the first time, of course, but this was part of a personal vendetta. I may have made things worse for myself in the long run."

"Do we really have the luxury of thinking about the long run? Brothers like you and me?"

Antoine knew what he meant. It was hard enough being a black man in Texas. Being a gay black man in Texas was a near impossibility. He couldn't play white and wouldn't want to, but he could play it straight. Wear the right clothes. *Sports Illustrated* on the desk. He pursued his desires exclusively in Austin, in the sort of clubs not found in San Marcos. Julian reminded Antoine of himself a decade earlier. Thoughtful, studious, and not quite effeminate, but definitely possessed of a lightness Antoine no longer allowed himself.

"Are you a student?" he asked.

"Yes, I'll be starting my junior year at UNM in a week or so."

"Do you live in the dorm?"

"No, I took an apartment in town with two other guys. They're seniors."

"Do you have your own bedroom?"

"Yes."

"Is it nearby? I have one hour."

"It's just around the corner."

*

"We've got to get off Route 66 as soon as possible," said Chuck, consulting the atlas. "We can catch Route 385 in a couple miles and keep heading north. It's not the most direct route, but it will get us out of Texas by midnight. All that shit tonight was way too public. We've gotta stay out of sight. No more towns with more than one traffic light."

"Fine with me. But we're definitely stopping back there on the way home. If I play my cards right, I think I can pull off a threesome."

Chuck threw the atlas to the floor. "Christ, will you snap out of it?"

"Out of what?"

"We're not going home, Dean. Ever. We can't go back. We're fugitives. We're on the run. We're gonna do this deal in Idaho, then we're heading for Canada. We're gonna be right next to Oregon at Snake River anyway, so we just shoot up through there and Washington, and cross the border. We'll get new identities, we'll go our separate ways, and that's that. We'll have all the money we'll ever need. Antoine isn't getting his cut. Triple H isn't getting his finder's fee. Gonzo isn't getting his truck back. And you ain't having no goddamn threesome at the Silver Dollar. There's no going back. We cross the state line and Texas is behind us forever."

Dean was silent for a moment. Chuck expected a battle, but when Dean finally spoke, he was cool. "Everything you just said made perfect sense. That may be a first. But Chuck, what the fuck do we know about Canada? We're Texans to the bone. The idea of never coming back here..."

"I know, it's a lot to take in. But think about it. What do you really have here that's worth coming back for, even if you could? A couple chicks who threw you out on your ass? A job selling tacos? Think of this as a fresh start. And hell, it's not like we're digging a hole to China. Canada is right next door. They speak English there, mostly."

"You think they have Lone Star in Canada?"

"I seriously doubt it. They got Molson. Labatt's. You'll be fine."

"I guess. I'll say this much—if this was our last night in Texas, we did it up right."

Chuck laughed. "Hell yeah, we did. We left our mark. Let's enjoy this next couple hours before we cross into Oklahoma."

"Two more hours in Texas. Goddamn." Dean stuck Willie Nelson's *Shotgun Willie* into the eight-track player. He and Chuck sang along with the title track and "Whiskey River" and "Sad Songs and Waltzes." Outside, the grasslands of the high plains stretched out into the darkness. They passed fewer and fewer cars as the clock ticked toward midnight. Houses were scarce, hidden from sight by small clusters of juniper or cedar oak trees.

Willie was singing about bubbles in his beer when the left rear tire blew.

SEVENTEEN

"How in the hell do you not have a spare tire?"

"Goddammit, it ain't my truck. It's Gonzo's, and he never intended for it to be driven halfway across the country. Mostly these things just sit in one spot. The only reason I was driving it around in the first place is that my own car mysteriously went missing. Remember that, Chuck?"

"Alright, let's not relive the past here. We have immediate concerns to deal with. Can you patch it?"

Dean wondered if Chuck could possibly be serious. Someone driving ahead of them had lost their muffler and not bothered to pick it up or even move it out of the road. Distracted by singing along with Willie, Dean hadn't seen it until it was too late. He managed to swerve the front tire out of the way, but that just lined it up perfectly for the back one. Fortunately, he'd been driving under the speed limit and was able to bring the truck to a halt, though not before leaving the pavement entirely.

Dean shined the flashlight on the shredded tire again. "Does it look like I can patch it? We're stuck here until someone comes along."

"When's the last time you remember seeing another car out here?"

"So we're stuck here until morning. Not the worst thing in the world. We've got time."

"What if those bikers come along? We're way out in the open here. We'd be sitting ducks."

"Why would they come this way? Don't you think they'll stick to the main highway?"

"There was a house about a mile or so back. I'm pretty sure I saw a light on."

"I'm sorry, was this a house or a tire shop?"

"You know how country people are. They've probably got a bunch of tires lying around. Something that will get us to the next town at least. That's thirty miles from here."

"I dunno, Chuck. Leaving the truck unattended? Our whole future depends on what's in there."

"Look, you can wait here with the truck if you want. Take a nap, I don't care. I still have about four pounds of meat in my belly to walk off, so I'm gonna go."

"Do what you want. Just be back here by sunup."

"Why wouldn't I be?"

"I want to come with you," said Julian.

Antoine's first instinct was to say hell no. He was on a mission and didn't need any distractions. On the other hand, having Julian along for the ride could have its advantages. Not just the sex, which was surprisingly passionate and enthusiastic, but the lively conversation as well. Antoine didn't know many people who could keep up with him in San Marcos, but Julian was quick-witted and knowledgeable on a variety of subjects. It might also be advantageous to have him along in case the cops were on the lookout for a black man driving alone. He'd already opened up to Julian about where he was going and why; he'd only left out the part about what he planned to do with the Melville boys once he caught up to them.

"Don't you have school starting up?"

"Not until Tuesday. And the first day is just introductory bullshit I can skip anyway."

"Why do you want to come with me?"

"I want to see more of the country. I want to be present for this absurd event in the history of white nonsense. I feel this is something I could write about, put my own perspective on. And I want to get to know you better."

"Can you drive a stick shift?"

"Absolutely."

"Get dressed and pack whatever you need. I'll be browsing your bookshelves."

Chuck was beginning to think he'd hallucinated the light he'd seen peeking through a cluster of trees off the side of the road. He figured he'd already walked more than a mile back the way they came, and had yet to pass a single tree, let alone a house surrounded by them. He decided to give it fifteen more minutes before turning back.

Ten minutes later, a faint flicker in the distance. Chuck quickened his pace. He reached a gravel driveway branching off from the main road and started down it. In his haste to depart, he'd left the flashlight in the truck. As the trees grew thicker, the starlight dimmed, and his path got darker. He passed under a high wooden arch carved with words he couldn't make out. The crunch of gravel beneath his feet was the only sound in the still night. Chuck thought about Antoine's guard dogs and wondered if he might be making a big mistake.

As he got closer, he could see that the light he'd spotted was coming not from the rambling farmhouse he was nearing, but from another building behind it. He started down a stone path that circled around the main house, but his footsteps sounded impossibly loud. He paused to gather his thoughts. Now that he'd stopped walking, he could hear someone puttering around in the barn or garage, whatever it was.

He'd taken two steps toward it when something solid struck the back of his skull.

*

Dean couldn't get comfortable enough to doze off. The night was too hot and sticky, and no matter how he adjusted the driver's seat, he kept cramping up. He decided to sit on the hood and read *Jaws* by flashlight. He was enjoying the book, but it had been a while since the last shark attack, and now the police chief's wife was screwing around with the oceanographer from the mainland. Dean had no interest in this romantic subplot at all, and he wondered why the writer had included it. He figured maybe Peter Benchley had to write a certain number of pages and there were only so many shark attacks he could describe before it got old. Dean usually stuck to men's adventure novels, like the *Executioner* series about Mack Bolan, or the *Destroyer* books about Remo Williams. They were short, full of nonstop action, and any romance was strictly of the wham-bam-thank-you-ma'am variety.

He felt the call of nature. He set the book down and walked into the high plains. He stared up at the night sky as he urinated. A million diamonds spread across a blue-black blanket. "The stars at night are big and bright," he sang. "Deep in the heart of..." He choked back a sob. His last night in Texas. He wondered what the night sky looked like in Canada.

He heard an engine.

Quickly zipping his fly, he sprinted back toward the road. He saw headlights approaching from the north. He stepped onto the blacktop and started waving his arms and jumping up and down.

"Hey! Traveler in distress here! Hey, pull over!"

The blare of a horn drowned out his words. Blinded by the headlights, Dean stumbled back onto the grass. A Ford pickup blew past him without slowing down. Dean charged back onto the road and lifted both of his middle fingers in salute.

"Fuck you, asshole!"

He saw brake lights illuminate as the pickup slowed, about a hundred yards further up the road. The truck came to a halt.

Dean stood still, waiting for the pickup to back up. It didn't move.

"Okay. What the fuck, guy?"

Dean started walking toward the pickup. When he was halfway there, he heard the engine rev. The truck peeled out and did a 180-degree turn. The headlights faced Dean.

"Oh, shit."

The pickup squealed toward him.

Chuck never completely lost consciousness, but he was dazed enough that he didn't put up a fight as he was dragged into the barn and dropped onto the dirt floor. When his head and vision cleared, he saw a man in a Texas tuxedo holding a shotgun on him.

"Can't you read?"

"Dunno," said Chuck. "Used to could, before you walloped me upside the head."

"That wasn't me. That was my brother Noah." The man in denim jerked his head toward his left shoulder. Chuck saw another man who must have been Noah standing near the open barn door. He was dressed identically to his brother down to the matching bolo ties, but otherwise they bore little resemblance. Noah was built like a circus strongman and had a vacancy behind his eyes. The left side of his face was raw hamburger.

"What happened to him?" said Chuck.

"I ask the questions here."

"Yeah, you asked one and I answered it. Why did you ask if I could read?"

"Because there is a No Trespassing sign posted in plain sight at the end of the driveway."

"Well, it may be in plain sight during the day, but in case you haven't noticed, it's dark as a dungeon out there."

"What are you doing here?"

"Now we're getting somewhere. You mind if I stand up?"

"I do mind. Answer my question."

"My tire blew out about a mile and a half north of here. I was hoping y'all could help me out."

"I don't know as we can. Not now that you've seen it."

"Seen what?"

"That." The man pointed the shotgun to Chuck's right. Chuck turned and saw an eight-foot-tall structure of tarnished copper. It had a barrel shape, a temperature gauge, and a coil snaking out of the top and leading to another container. Next to that he saw two rows of oak barrels stacked three high. He could guess what was in them.

"Shitfire, pardner, I had not seen that until you just drew my attention to it. And now that I've seen it, I really don't give a shit. I ain't no snitch."

"I know who you are."

"How's that?"

"I was down in Austin yesterday on business. Left this morning. And you were all over the morning news. You're that cop killer."

Chuck laughed. "Buddy, you got the wrong guy. I'm just a fella with a flat tire looking for some help."

"It was you and another dude. Your cousin. Where's he?"

"Only cousin I got's a girl, and she married and moved to California years ago."

"You're a liar. And I ain't quite sure what to do with you. Noah, I need you to go up to the house and get Daddy. He'll know."

*

Dean sprinted into the grasslands as the pickup screamed past him. He turned and saw it come to a stop next to the taco truck.

"Oh, fuck this." Dean ran back toward the truck. He saw a figure get out of the pickup. "Hey! Hey, what the fuck, dude?"

Caught in the beam of Dean's flashlight, the figure raised a hand. "Can you get that thing out of my eyes?"

It was a female voice, which made sense, as Dean could now see that the figure belonged to a woman. He lowered the beam. "What's the idea, trying to run me over?"

"I wasn't trying to run you over. I didn't see you until it was too late, so I turned around to come back."

Now that he was only a few feet away, he could see that the woman was in her early thirties, wearing tiny cutoffs and a barely buttoned shirt tied off around her midriff. She was a little more rugged than his usual type, but she had his attention. "Well, I appreciate it. We ran into a bit of trouble here."

"Yeah, your tire is Swiss cheese. Who's we?"

"Excuse me?"

"You said we ran into a little trouble, but you're the only one here."

"Yeah, well, my cousin Chuck got a little impatient and headed back that way. He thought he saw a light about a mile away."

"More like a mile and a half. Yeah, that's my house."

This was getting better and better. "Any chance you could help us out of this mess?"

"Why don't you ride back with me? I'm pretty sure we've got a tire that will fit."

"We?"

"Excuse me?"

"You said we've got a tire that will fit."

"Me and my family. My brothers and our daddy."

"Great. Can't wait to meet them."

EIGHTEEN

When Noah returned, he was pushing an old man in a wheelchair. The man was dressed in an immaculate white suit that appeared to have been tailored for someone eighty pounds heavier. The way it hung off his emaciated frame reminded Chuck of a scarecrow he'd seen earlier in the day, its oversized clothes flapping in the breeze. The man had a cigar in one hand and in the other an oxygen mask attached to a tank on the side of his chair. A blackish-green tumor sprouting from his neck looked to Chuck like an avocado going bad. When he spoke, it was in a thin, papery voice that commanded Chuck's full attention, as if the rest of the world had gone silent just so he could be heard.

"What is he doing here, Elijah?" he said to the man with the shotgun.

"Trespassing, Daddy."

The old man took a puff of his cigar, followed by a hit of oxygen. "Why didn't you just scare him off?"

"Well, he's seen the still. Plus he might be valuable to us. He's a fugitive from down Austin way, and we might could turn him in for a big reward."

The old man shook his head and fixed his gaze on Chuck. "Allow me to apologize for my son. Both of them, actually. My name is Amos Farrell, and I did not raise my boys to cooperate with the gubmint, reward or no reward."

"I appreciate that, sir. See, this is all a case of mistaken ident—"

"He's lying, Daddy! He killed a cop and his wife in cold blood."

"Be quiet, Elijah. Grown folks are talking." Farrell took

another puff and another hit and turned back to Chuck. "Rest assured, stranger. Whatever you may have done to rile up the law, it's none of my concern. One less cop in the world certainly don't trouble my mind. But I would like to know how you came to be trespassing on my property."

"As I explained to Elijah here, I got a flat tire shortly after passing by your place. I remembered seeing a light, so I walked back here in hopes y'all could help me out."

"Hell, we got plenty of tires stacked up around here. Nothing brand new, but I'm sure we could find something to get you as far as Stratford. That's the closest town, about thirty miles north."

"Well, I sure would appreciate that. And you can rest assured, Mr. Farrell, I won't never say a word about your…operation here."

"It's funny you mention that. See, one thing Elijah said that made sense—and it don't happen too often, so when it does, I take notice—he said you might be valuable to us. And I do believe you might."

As a pair of headlights washed over them, Elijah glanced out the door to see a truck pulling into the driveway. "Ruthie's back," he said.

"Close that door. We don't need her poking into our business down here."

The pickup driver introduced herself as Ruth. She was listening to a late-night call-in show on an AM station out of Albuquerque. The topic was UFOs.

"You know about Roswell?" she asked.

Dean rubbed his chin. "Nope. Is he the host?"

"Roswell is a place, not a person. In New Mexico, about three or four hours from here. That's where they have the aliens."

"That's where who has the aliens?"

"The government. A UFO crashed at a ranch near Roswell in 1947. A flying saucer, as they used to call 'em. Of course, they changed their story right away and said it was a weather balloon, but by then the word was out. They've got little green men on ice at the Air Force base there. Or little gray men, I'm not sure. I've seen 'em. UFOs, not aliens. But my brother Elijah, he was abducted. He'll tell you all about it. Well, here we are."

She pulled off onto a gravel driveway leading to a ramshackle farmhouse. They passed under a wooden arch with FARRELL FARMS carved into it. Dean could see a light coming from a building behind the house, but as Ruth pulled to a stop, the light disappeared. When they got out of the truck, Dean noticed a lumpy tarp in the Ford's flatbed.

"What's that? Aliens?"

Ruth laughed. "No, silly. That's hogs." She lifted the tarp so Dean could see the two dead beasts. "Feral ones. They run wild around here, and they got a habit of getting hit by cars. People leave 'em by the side of the road, but that's a waste of good meat. You can help me field dress 'em."

"Uh, dress them how?"

Ruth laughed. "You know, skin 'em. Butcher 'em. We make our own sausage and sell it to the restaurants in Stratford."

"Roadkill sausage? Does it say that on the menu?"

"Course not. They don't know it's roadkill. But it don't much matter how the animal dies. Once it's sausage, it's all the same."

Dean made a mental note not to order the sausage in Stratford. He gestured to the darkness behind the house. "I saw a light down there when we first pulled in."

"Boys must be working late tonight. That's fine. Gives us the house to ourselves. Watch your step on the porch. I've been after Elijah to fix it up, but he's always so busy."

Dean carefully followed her into the house. Ruth pulled a

chain to illuminate a dim bulb swinging gently in the entry hall.

"Let's go into the kitchen," she said. "I can show you my knives."

"I don't understand," Chuck said. "How could I be valuable to you?"

Amos Farrell tapped ash from the end of his cigar and took an extra-long hit of oxygen. "This farm has been in my family for generations. I hope it will be for generations to come, although the prospect of that happening..." He glared at Elijah, who appeared to shrink under his father's gaze. "Well, anyway. We grow cotton, sorghum, peanuts, but our most important cash crop is corn. You know why that is?"

Chuck nodded toward the still. "You need it to make the corn likker."

"That is correct. This county and the neighboring ones is all dry. You could walk fifty miles in any direction and not be able to buy a legal drop of alcohol. Since Prohibition times, Farrell Farms has been supplying the social clubs and certain private buyers in this vicinity. This is a local family-run operation, and that's how it's always been. However." Farrell put his hand over his mouth and coughed for nearly ten seconds before taking another pull on his oxygen. "You being from down Austin way, I expect you're familiar with the Sixth Street Mafia. Now that I think about it, maybe you're even affiliated."

"No sir. I am from San Marcos, thirty miles south of Austin. I have no criminal affiliations up there. All I know about Sixth Street is it's a good place to get drunk."

"That's my understanding. It's also my understanding that most of the bars on that strip are controlled by one Roscoe Gamble and his Sixth Street Mafia. And I've learned that Mr. Gamble has gotten greedy. He's attempting to extend his reach up this way. A few of my regular clients have told Elijah they're getting a better deal from him. Real bootleg liquor with the label on. They say their customers prefer it. Well, I'm a purist. None of that swill has the purity of Farrell Farms moonshine. And I don't take kindly to outsiders muscling in on my territory."

"Again, Mr. Farrell, all I want is a tire and I'll be on my way."

"Understood. But you're going to do me a favor first. Elijah, what did you learn when you were down in Austin?"

"There's a delivery truck due up here tomorrow morning. I confirmed that with Dale at the Elks Lodge in Stratford. I had to break his nose to do it. He said there's usually two guys with the truck: the driver and another guy riding shotgun. I mean, for real shotgun." He tapped the one he was holding for emphasis.

"So you see, it's very simple," said Farrell. "You and my boys are gonna take that truck. You're gonna make the driver and his sidekick disappear."

"Mr. Farrell, it seems to me your boys can handle this on their own."

"Well, you don't know them as well as I do. I can think of ten ways for them to fuck it up just off the top of my head."

Elijah looked hurt. Noah's expression hadn't changed since the moment Chuck laid eyes on him.

"I don't know what makes you think I'd be any help in this matter," said Chuck. "If I might make a suggestion—and I don't mean to be rude here—I get the impression you have some pretty serious health issues. I wonder if it's such a good idea for you to pick this particular fight. Might be time to hang it up and enjoy your golden years. Cotton, sorghum, peanuts…seems to me those are crops your boys here can handle once you've retired."

Farrell's eyes tightened. "Your suggestion has been duly noted," he said. "I will also note that the more reluctant you are to do me this simple favor, the more I might be inclined to wonder if you might be affiliated with Mr. Roscoe Gamble after all."

"Never heard of the man. Not till you spoke his name. Now if you don't mind, I'd like to stand up and be on my way. It will be morning in a few hours, and if you don't want to loan me a tire, I can get a ride into town then."

Farrell seemed to ponder this a while. Then he pointed the remaining stub of his cigar at the still. "Do you know how that works?"

Chuck shrugged. "My daddy had a small one when I was a kid. He never let me near it, though."

"Well, this ain't a small one. That's a two hundred gallon still. It all starts with the mash. Corn meal, yeast, sugar…we got our own secret recipe, you don't need to know it. We ferment the mash for a few days, then we put it in the cooker there. Noah, show him how we heat the cooker."

Noah walked over and kneeled down in front of the still. He removed a panel at the bottom to reveal a furnace packed with glowing ash and burning logs.

"Wood-fired," said Farrell. "That's how we've always done it. Noah, why don't we show our guest how hot them logs get."

Noah took a set of tongs that had been resting next to the still and used them to remove a log from the furnace. One end of the wood glowed red-hot.

"Why don't you give him a little kiss on the cheek with it?"

Chuck bolted to his feet and charged for the door. He wasn't quite fast enough. Elijah stepped into his path, the shotgun butt hit him square in the forehead, and this time Chuck was out cold.

NINETEEN

Ruth set a leather bundle on the kitchen table and unrolled it, revealing a half-dozen knives with blades of different lengths and shapes sheathed in narrow pockets.

"They say there's more than one way to skin a pig," she said. "Well, here they all are."

"It's a cat there's more than one way to skin," said Dean. "According to the saying, anyway."

"Why would I want to skin a cat?"

"I hope you wouldn't. Listen, Ruth, much as I'd love to inspect your knife collection, I need to find my cousin Chuck. I figure the light he saw was the one in the building down the end of the driveway, the barn or whatever it is."

"Oh, that's the mash house. If your cousin's here, I'm sure my daddy's showing him Ugly Ethel."

"Who's Ugly Ethel?"

"That's what Daddy calls his still. It's kind of a joke, you know, ethyl being a type of alcohol."

"Y'all make moonshine out there?"

"Sure do. Would you like a taste?"

"Uh, well, I guess I wouldn't mind a little sample."

She opened a cabinet and pulled out a glass jug full of clear liquid. She took two glasses down from a shelf and poured a generous shot into each. She handed one to Dean and raised her own.

"This won't make me go blind, will it?" he asked.

"I sure hope not. I've got something I want you to see. Cheers."

They clinked glasses and drank. Dean's throat burned and his eyes watered, but he got it down.

"Goddamn," he managed. "I think my brain's on fire."

"Want another?"

"No, I believe I'm all set. What was it you wanted me to see?"

Ruth grinned and undid the knot holding her shirt together, letting it slip to the floor. As Dean had deduced earlier, she wasn't wearing a bra. "What do you think?" she said.

"No complaints."

"Perky, ain't they? You wanna touch 'em?"

"Well, normally, you know, all things being equal—"

"Come on. We'll find your cousin. But let's have a little fun first. You can touch 'em, and you can kiss 'em, too."

Dean figured wherever Chuck was, he'd understand.

The next time Chuck opened his eyes, he was no longer on the floor. Now he was bound to a rusty metal chair with a couple of bungee cords.

"He's awake, Daddy."

Chuck shook off the cobwebs. He was still in the mash house. Amos Farrell sat in front of him, flanked by his two sons. Elijah still held the shotgun.

"I was hoping you wasn't gonna give us any trouble," said Farrell.

"Oh yeah? I was hoping you wasn't gonna give me a concussion, but I've learned to live with disappointment."

"You ain't begun to hurt yet. I let Noah go to work on you, you gonna feel some pain like you never imagined."

"And who worked him over? His face looks like shit on a shingle."

Noah cracked his knuckles. Farrell grinned, revealing a mouthful of rotten teeth.

"Looks like you might have hurt his feelings. Noah, why don't you hurt our guest's feelings right back?"

Noah stepped forward and leaned down in front of Chuck. He drew back his fist and drove it into Chuck's gut. Chuck retched and dry-heaved, but there was nothing left inside him to come up. Noah hit him again and Chuck's head swam.

"That's just a taste," said Farrell. "We got some old irrigation pipes up in the hayloft. Noah can do some real damage with one of those. But there's no need for that. I'm simply asking you to do me a favor in exchange for the favor you've asked of me. You help my boys take care of this little problem and you'll be on your way. You refuse...well, I've got about three hundred acres out back. I figure won't be no trouble finding a place to plant you."

The shriveled old man in front of him looked like the Angel of Death. Chuck could only think of one card left to play.

"Elijah, why haven't you told your daddy about my cousin?"

"You said you ain't got no—"

"And you knew full well I was lying," Chuck said. "You said so yourself."

"Elijah," said Farrell. "What is this about his cousin?"

Elijah squirmed. "On the news. It wasn't just him wanted for killing that cop and his wife."

"That's right," said Chuck. "My cousin Dean. Dean the Killing Machine. That's what they call him back home. He was waiting with the truck while I came here to get the tire. But I told him if I wasn't back in an hour, come and get me. Locked and loaded. And I do believe your hour is up, so if you were smart, you'd cut me loose. I'll try to convince him to go easy on you."

Farrell coughed and took a long drag from his oxygen tank. "Elijah, you best go up to the house and see what Ruthie's up to. Just in case she happened upon this cousin of his."

*

Dean had been with a lot of women, but none of them had taken control quite like Ruth Farrell. She'd practically dragged him up the stairs to her bedroom, where she promptly tore off his shirt and had his jeans down around his ankles before he had a chance to unzip them.

"I could just eat you up," she said.

"Please, no teeth."

Her lips and tongue were enough to get his attention in a matter of seconds. Once he was at full mast, she pushed him down onto her bed, shucked off her shorts, and mounted him. He didn't have much to do but hang on and let her ride. He yelped when she raked her fingernails across his chest.

"Handle me with care," he groaned.

"Just give me what I need."

It didn't take long. Once he was spent, she rolled off him and stuck her legs up in the air.

"What are you doing?" he asked.

"Giving your seed the best chance to do its job."

"My…? Do you mean to say you don't use any kind of… pills or nothing?"

"Hell, no. That would defeat the point."

"And what is the point?"

"The propagation of the line. That is the purpose of fornication, ain't it?"

"Myself, I just do it for fun. I certainly ain't in the market for any offspring."

Ruth laughed and gyrated her hips up and down. "Don't worry, you won't be involved at all. See, if it was left up to my brothers, the Farrell line would be at an end. When them aliens took Elijah, they did experiments on him and now his stuff don't work. At least that's his story. And Noah…well, that poor boy he just never had a chance. When my daddy goes, and it won't be long, it's all gonna be up to me to keep the family business alive for the next generation."

"So, you just…used me? For my seed?"

Ruth turned and kissed him on the cheek. "I sure do think you're cute, Dean. And don't get me wrong, I did enjoy the process. But it was a means to an end."

Dean sat up and reached for his pants. "Well, I don't really know how to feel about that."

She kissed his back. "My goodness, you are a sensitive boy. What's the matter?"

He stood and pulled on his jeans. "I just need to find my cousin, that's all."

Before he could put on his shirt, he heard a door bang open downstairs, followed by a guttural voice hollering, "Ruthie Ann!"

"Who's that?" Dean whispered.

Ruth stood and started to dress. "That's Elijah. Bet he'll know just where your cousin is."

Sweat dripped down from Chuck's forehead into his eyes. Unable to wipe it away, he could only wince while his eyeballs burned.

"Hot as Satan's hoof out here tonight, ain't it?" said Farrell, offering another malignant grin. "But here I sit, cool as Christmas."

Chuck spat. "I reckon it ain't hard to stay cool when all your blood's turned to dust. I mean, look at you. You must be more cancer than man at this point."

Farrell's expression darkened. "Don't matter. I'm too goddamn mean to die."

"I guess we'll find out when Dean gets here. Hell, he's probably already up there in the house. You just sent Elijah to meet his end."

Farrell's knuckles went white as he gripped the arms of his

wheelchair. "Bullshit. I know a con man when I hear one. You think you can talk your way out of this?"

"I think I could kill you without ever getting up from this chair. Just talk you right into a heart attack. And I don't believe Noah will know which way to turn without you around to tell him. What did you do to him anyway?"

"I didn't do shit but let him keep a stray pit bull that wandered in from God knows where. Probably jumped off the back of a pickup, or more likely got thrown offa one for bad behavior. I could tell that dog was no good, but Noah said he'd take care of him, feed him, train him, the whole nine."

"Noah said all that?"

"He was a lot more verbal back then. Back before that pit bull got ahold of his head and wouldn't let go. Skippy, he named him. I mean, you could take one look at that hound and know Skippy weren't no name for him."

Chuck looked at Noah, who gave no indication he had any awareness of what his father was talking about.

"And what happened to Skippy?"

"Never you mind that. No more stalling for time. You want out of that chair, you can be in a second if you simply agree to do what I ask. Which makes me awful curious why you won't."

"Sure, I could just agree, but I doubt you'd trust me enough to let me out of this chair anyway. Aside from that, I've given it a lot of thought, and I figure there's only two outcomes if I do go along. The most likely one, me and your boys are no match for the Sixth Street Mafia and we all end up dead. Or if somehow we are successful in this mission, Elijah kills me anyway. How many other people ended up in a hole out in your three hundred acres?"

"Over time, there have been a few. That's just the price of business. But I'm a man of my word and won't plant you there if I say I won't."

"I'd like to believe that, I really would, but somehow I don't feel the word of a moonshiner who can't be more than days shy of being planted out there himself is worth a whole hell of a lot. When's the last time you looked in the mirror and saw a face, not just a skull?"

Farrell launched into a coughing fit that made his whole body shake. When it died down, he took a deep drag from the oxygen tank. "Keep it up, boy."

"Seriously, have you even seen a doctor? I would think the least you could do is have that thing removed from your neck. Probably too late for that, huh? Pull that off and your shriveled soul might just fly up out of the hole that's left."

Another coughing fit.

"There you go," said Chuck. "Just let it all out. Don't let us keep you here. You got places to go and people to see. Tell me, what are you gonna miss most about being alive?"

When the coughing finally stopped, Farrell took three deep drags of oxygen. He reached into his breast pocket for a crisp white handkerchief and put it to his mouth. Chuck heard a sound that reminded him of the garbage disposal in the Huntsville Unit kitchen he used to clean for twelve cents an hour. When Farrell pulled the hankie away from his mouth, it was stained red.

"Won't be long now," said Chuck.

"You first," said Farrell. He turned to his son. "Noah, I need you to go up to the hayloft and grab one of those ten-foot galvanized pipes. It seems our guest has outstayed his welcome."

When he and Ruth stepped into the kitchen, Dean was greeted with a twelve-gauge shotgun aimed directly at his nose.

"Elijah!" said Ruth. "Put that thing down. This is my guest."

"Your guest? Do you have any idea who this is?"

"Of course. This is Dean."

"Yeah, Dean the Killing Machine. He and his cousin killed a cop and his wife. They're fugitives from justice."

Ruth folded her arms. "Is that true, Dean?"

"Course not! I mean, yes, it's true that we're fugitives, but I didn't kill anybody. Is my cousin here?"

"We got him down in the mash house," said Elijah. "You and him are gonna do a little favor for us."

"I feel like I've done enough favors tonight. Put that thing down, will you?"

"I will not. Stay away from him, Ruthie. This is a dangerous man."

"You can come down off the cross, Elijah. I already fucked him."

Elijah reddened. He turned the shotgun on Ruth. "You did what?"

"What's the matter, big brother? Jealous?"

Elijah tightened his grip on the trigger. "You best watch your mouth, Ruthie Ann. That ain't funny. Specially in front of company."

Dean glanced at the kitchen table. Just about within reach, maybe a little beyond, Ruth's hog butchering knives were still laid out in their case.

"Me and Dean have been intimate," said Ruth. "And I already told him about you and the aliens. You want me to tell him how I know your equipment don't work?"

Dean had no interest in hearing that story. He was already writing a new one in his head. One where Elijah unloaded his shotgun at Ruth and, while he was occupied with that, Dean used the distraction to grab the biggest knife and jam it into Elijah's neck. Some part of him thought he could do it. A larger part of him couldn't let it happen.

"Hey! Elijah!"

Elijah swung his shotgun back toward Dean. "You fornicate with my sister?"

"I sure did. And from what I gather, you tried to do the same. That's pretty sick, Elijah."

"I didn't do nothin'."

"Yeah. Because the aliens broke you, right? That what you tell yourself?"

"You're coming with me. My daddy will decide what to do with you."

"Aw, and here I thought you were a grown man making his own decisions. You gotta ask your daddy's permission to pull your trigger?"

"I'm about five seconds from sending you into the next world."

"If you'll pardon the expression, I don't think you've got the balls."

Elijah racked the shotgun. He opened his mouth to say one more thing, but it never came out. Instead, blood gushed from his neck, all around the knife that was suddenly lodged there. Elijah gurgled a moment before falling face-forward, the shotgun clattering on the floor.

Dean looked at the sheath on the table. One of the knives was missing. He looked at Ruth. She winked at him.

"Holy shit," he said. "You just killed your brother."

"No. Dean the Killing Machine did that."

"What? No way. You ain't pinning this on me."

"It's not like that. You're the hero, Dean. I'm the damsel in distress. You got a flat, you stopped here to get a tire. You caught my brother assaulting me. You didn't know he was my brother, of course. All you saw was a man attacking a poor innocent girl. You saw my knives on the table, and you did what any red-blooded American would do under the circumstances."

"That's how you're gonna play it?"

"That's right. I can cry pretty good when I have to. I can pretend to be sorry. But now that I have a rightful heir, Elijah's just in the way."

"Ruth, you do understand there's no guarantee you're pregnant, right?"

"Oh, but I am. I can already feel it. Now why don't you pick up that shotgun and go find your cousin. Whatever happens to my daddy, that don't really matter. He's already a goner. But my brother Noah, I'm gonna need his help running things around here. I need him alive. So here's what you're gonna do."

Noah found a pipe to his liking and climbed down from the loft. Chuck strained against the bungee cords, attempting to work some slack into them, but they were bound too tight. The Angel of Death loomed before him.

"I'll do it," Chuck said. "I'll do what you ask."

"Too late for that," said Farrell. "No way I can let you live after the things you said to me."

"I got a big mouth. It's always gotten me in trouble."

"Then you should have learned from your mistakes by now."

"You're absolutely right. I have no excuse. I was disrespectful. Really, it all goes back to my upbringing. My daddy, he was a no-good sonofabitch. Never had a kind word for anyone, never showed any respect—"

"You're doing it again."

"Excuse me?"

"You're stalling for time, but that's something you're all out of. Noah, why don't you start by knocking out a few of his teeth?"

Noah started toward Chuck, who squeezed his eyes shut and braced himself. He heard a door bang open, followed by a familiar voice.

"Tell your boy to freeze or I blow your fuckin' brains out."

Chuck opened his eyes. He saw Dean standing behind Farrell's wheelchair, Elijah's shotgun in his hands, the barrel pressed against the back of Farrell's skull.

"Hold up, Noah," said Farrell.

Noah stood with the pipe raised in his hand. He didn't move.

"Thought you'd never get here, cuz," said Chuck. "Smart thing to do would be to shoot Noah first. That old man ain't gonna be no trouble."

Dean shook his head. He leaned down and whispered something in the old man's ear.

"Noah," Farrell said through clenched teeth. "Go on up and help your sister. She's got two hogs in the flatbed ready to be butchered."

Noah set the pipe down gently. Dean pushed the wheelchair forward to allow Noah room to get past them and out the door.

"Now," said Dean, "I'm gonna cut my cousin loose and we're gonna help ourselves to your used tire collection. Ruth is gonna give us a ride back to our truck. And we'll be on our way."

"Where is Elijah?" said Farrell.

"He made a mistake. He messed with Dean the Killing Machine, and he paid the price. But there's no need for any more killing tonight."

"Hang on," said Chuck. "Dean, you don't know what I been through out here. You don't know what he was fixin' to make that monster do to me."

Dean popped the shotgun open and shook out the shells. He picked them up and flipped them into the loft, then tossed the shotgun aside.

"What the hell are you doing? Least keep the gun until we're out of here. There's still Noah to deal with."

"Ruthie'll deal with him. She gave me her word."

"Jesus Christ."

"I'm gonna untie you, Chuck. But you gotta agree to let this go. That's just the way it has to be."

Chuck glared at his cousin. Finally, when it became clear Dean wasn't moving without some sort of response, Chuck gave him the smallest, most grudging nod possible.

Dean went behind Chuck's chair, kneeled down, and unlatched the bungee cords. Chuck stood on shaky legs and rubbed his arms where they'd been bound. When he looked at Farrell, he saw the old man's eyes were wet and his lip was trembling.

"Aw, look. There's some moisture left in this dried-up husk after all."

"It's time to go, Chuck."

"After you, killer."

Dean shook his head and made his way out of the mash house. Chuck followed. As he passed Farrell, he reached over and yanked the tube out of the old man's oxygen tank, threw it up in the loft with the shotgun shells.

"Rot in hell," he whispered.

TWENTY

At quarter after four in the morning, Giddings came upon a motel just off Interstate 25 with a dozen motorcycles parked in the front lot.

"Are the Demon Riders staying here?" he asked the sleepy night clerk.

"That sounds right. Are they dangerous?"

"I'm sure they're harmless. How long are you on duty here?"

"Until ten A.M."

"Do me a favor. If you see any of them up and about before then, give me a call in my room."

"Sure." The clerk handed him the key to number twelve. Giddings went to his room, stripped, washed his shirt and underpants in the sink, hung them up to dry, and climbed under the covers to get as much shuteye as he was able.

Antoine and Julian drove into the night, listening to AM talk radio.

"More whitey bullshit," said Antoine. "You notice these UFOs are only ever seen out in the boonies, and they only pick up hillbilly crackers. All these callers on this show, ain't one brother among 'em. Because no UFO ever set down in a black neighborhood."

"Things are different here, though. New Mexico, we've got history."

"What, you believe in this shit? Little green men?"

"I don't know about that, but we have our share of unidentified flying objects. I'm not saying they're extraterrestrial necessarily."

"Definitely not. Military, more likely. Something we'll never know about unless some whistleblower like Ellsberg comes along, or the Soviets shoot one down."

"Probably so. Still, imagine if the military got their hands on alien technology."

"You can imagine anything you want, but I keep both my feet planted in the real world."

"So you don't believe there's life anywhere else in the universe?"

"I didn't say that. Mathematically, the odds are slim this is the only planet that supports life. But if you're gonna trust the math, you gotta trust it all the way. And the math says every other place in the universe is too goddamn far away for any life form to find its way here. The speed of light ain't like the speed limits on this highway. You can't go five miles over and hope you don't get a ticket."

"That's true as far as we know. Doesn't the unknown interest you at all?"

"If I find out I don't know something, I learn about it. That's just how I am."

"But I mean the real unknowns. Like ghosts. You believe in ghosts?"

Antoine gave him the side-eye. "You know, you seemed like a very intelligent young man when I picked you up."

"I like to think I am, but I know I don't know everything. And there's no shortage of mysteries out here in this desert. I mean, we're just down the road from Los Alamos. Man had never mastered the atom, most never even dreamed it was possible, until it happened."

"Yeah, what a triumph of the human imagination. Now we can blow up our whole planet ten times over."

"'I am become death, destroyer of worlds.' But now the same facility that housed the Manhattan Project is a laboratory where cutting-edge medical research is done. They're working on the cure for cancer. The same place that created all that death might one day save millions of lives."

They passed a road sign reading SANTA FE 5 MILES.

"You're going to want to jump on 84 north," Julian said. "We'll be on that road for quite a while. We're going to pass through some sanctified territory. The Jicarilla Apache Nation Reservation, then the Southern Ute Reservation. Rugged, beautiful country. This is why they call it the Land of Enchantment."

"Do you work for the tourism board or something?"

"No, I've just always loved New Mexico. I feel a connection to it. I think I have some Navajo blood on my mother's side, but I could never get a straight answer from my folks. Why, don't you have any Texan pride?"

Antoine sneered. "Hell, no. Why would I? It never made sense to me that people could take pride in something they had nothing to do with, but I see it every day in Texas. No, I'm definitely not proud of an accident of birth, especially since my ancestors were brought to Texas in chains. June 19, 1865, Galveston, Texas. That's the day they got around to telling my great-grandfather he'd been a free man for two and a half years. Yeah, that's Texas for you. Kept slavery around as long as they could get away with it. And they still resent the shit they can't get away with no more. That sheriff I told you about, he can't get over the fact that I can eat at the same lunch counter as him. He'd probably shit himself if he knew my father was a sheriff's deputy."

"You're kidding."

"I wish I was. He was with the Travis County Sheriff's Department up until the first day of August in 1966. That's the day he was a guest speaker for a class on juvenile justice at the University of Texas. The last day of his life."

"What happened?"

"You ever heard of Charles Whitman?"

"Sounds familiar, but..."

"On the first day of August in 1966, in the early morning hours, Charles Whitman stabbed his mother to death. Then he stabbed his wife to death. Later that morning he went up to the observation deck of the University of Texas tower and starting shooting with a high-powered rifle."

"Oh, shit. That's right."

"Yeah. Deadliest mass shooting by a lone gunman in the history of this country, as far as we know. Well, my pop was there on the West Mall when it all started. He was in his uniform, he had his gun, and according to witnesses, he started shooting back up at the top of the tower. Whitman took him out with one bullet, straight through the heart."

"Oh my God. I'm so sorry."

"Don't be. We hadn't spoken in two years, not since I was sixteen and he caught me and a neighbor boy messing around. He would have thrown me out of the house if my mother had let him. But by then, I was already a big disappointment to him. He raised me to respect authority, and I never did. I read too much for his liking. I never understood how he could be an enforcer for the white man's way, but he thought he was one of the good guys. He died trying to be a hero, but Whitman stayed up there shooting for damn near an hour after killing my father, until another cop got to the roof deck and put one between his eyes."

"That's...I don't even know what to say."

"Anyway, you asked me if I believed in ghosts. I don't. But I know the dead stay with us, because I still see my pop in dreams. And when I do, nothing seems weird about it. Like, it doesn't occur to me that he's dead and I shouldn't be seeing him.

Sometimes it's just like it was, and he doesn't say shit to me, but other times we talk. One time he told me he was proud of me. That's when I knew I was dreaming."

While Chuck and Dean picked out three tires that looked like they had a chance of fitting the taco truck, Ruth made Noah drag the hogs out of the flatbed. They hopped up into it, and Ruth drove them back to where they'd broken down. For one heart-freezing moment, Chuck thought the truck was gone, but it was just a trick of the shadows. Ruth pulled over and they climbed out.

"You got a jack and a tire iron?" she asked.

"I doubt it," said Dean.

"Well, you can use mine. They're under the passenger seat."

Dean let Chuck handle the task of picking out the right tire and getting the truck mobile again. He had a few things he wanted to say to Ruth.

"Listen, I really appreciate you helping us out. Things could have gone a whole other way tonight."

"You helped me out too."

"Well, about that. You might have gathered Chuck and I are on the run. We've got a plan, but if it all goes the way we hope, we'll never be back this way."

"I told you, Dean. I don't expect any involvement from you."

"I know, but…I really hate to think I'll never know. That I might have a kid here I'll never meet."

"Dean, how many women have you had?"

Dean whistled. "I lost count at thirty-six, and that was a couple years back."

"Are you in the habit of wearing rubbers?"

"I mean, I've tried, but I find it kinda kills the mood, you know?"

"What I'm trying to tell you, Dean. You probably already got two or three kids you'll never meet. So what's one more?"

"Well, when you put it that way…"

Chuck climbed to his feet, wiping his hands on his shirt. "All set, cuz. That'll get us to Oklahoma anyway."

"All right," said Dean. "I guess this is goodbye."

He leaned in and gave Ruth a long, deep kiss. Too long for Chuck's liking.

"Come on, let's hit it. And hey, Ruth. Good luck with the Sixth Street Mafia."

"The what?"

"Your daddy told me they're moving in on your territory up here. Said there's a delivery coming in the morning, tried to get me to agree to take it down."

Ruth laughed. "I'm sure that's what Elijah told him. My poor brother, he was always trying to make himself seem more useful than he was. He told my daddy all kinds of stories, stuff he was doing to keep the competition away. He had what you'd call an active imagination."

"The UFOs?" said Dean.

"Well, no. That was real." She climbed into the cab of the pickup. "Happy trails, boys. Hope it all works out for you."

TWENTY-ONE

The phone in Giddings' room rang at 7:30 A.M.

"It's Brian at the front desk. One of those Demon Riders was just in here getting a cup of coffee and some ice. He bought a newspaper from the machine out front and now he's sitting at the picnic table."

"Thanks. I'll be right out."

Giddings' clothes were still a little damp, but he had no other options. He put on his uniform and stepped outside. It was a mild morning, and the birds were chirping away. He approached the biker and took a seat across from him at the picnic table.

"Help you?" said Uptown Mike, looking up from his paper. He had ice wrapped in a t-shirt, which he would occasionally press against his forehead.

"I'm Sheriff Giddings. I was hoping I could ask you a few questions."

"Ivor County. I saw your car this morning. Ivor County, Texas. I've lived in Texas all my life, and I've never heard of Ivor County."

"Lot of counties in Texas."

"That's true. But here's the thing, Sheriff. We're not in Texas anymore. We're just outside Pueblo, Colorado. You know those commercials on TV? Write to us and we'll send you all these free government pamphlets about how to lose weight or save money on your electric bill? Well, that's Pueblo, Colorado, and that ain't in Texas, and you ain't got no jurisdiction here. So no, I don't believe I'll answer your questions today."

Uptown Mike pressed the ice against his forehead and went back to reading his paper. Giddings didn't move. He noticed a small Band-Aid on the biker's neck.

"Cut yourself shaving?"

"That sounded like a question."

"Well, here's a statement. I know you didn't cut yourself shaving. I know that's not just a hangover ailing your head. I know it happened at the Silver Dollar roadhouse in Amarillo. And I know who was responsible. Not only that, but I know where they're going."

Uptown Mike laughed. "Big deal. I already know that, because we're going to the same place."

"Oh. Of course. Evel Knievel. I guess everyone who's anyone will be there."

"The fellas who did this to me, they ain't gonna be there long once I catch up to 'em."

"Hmm. Sounds like we've got a problem. See, I can't let you get between me and the Melville boys. You know they're wanted fugitives? One of 'em killed my deputy. My best man."

"Cry me a river."

For a brief moment, Giddings remembered Gwen lying in the morgue and thought he actually might cry. He could feel his eyes getting moist, but he shook it off.

"I'm gonna tell you something, since it's just the two of us chatting here and I'm tired of telling the same fucking lie over and over. See, I don't care that my deputy's dead. Hell, I wanted him dead myself. You don't know how many hairy situations I sent him into without any backup, just hoping for an outcome unfavorable to him. But the man was simply too good at his job. What he didn't know—what I don't think he *ever* knew while alive on this earth—is that I was in love with his wife. And she was in love with me. Now, we were both married to other people, but one way or another, we were gonna figure it out. We were gonna be together. But this same man who killed my deputy, he also killed my deputy's wife. And he's going to pay for that."

"Why are you telling me all this?"

Giddings stood up. "Because you, or anyone else who tries to get in my way, you're gonna meet with your own unfavorable outcome. This is your one and only warning."

"You have a nice day, Sheriff."

Giddings started to walk away, stopped, and turned back. Uptown Mike looked up from his paper.

"What is it now?"

Giddings pointed to the newspaper. "You planning to do the crossword?"

Uptown Mike smiled and handed Giddings the funnies.

The sun was rising when Antoine pulled into an Esso station just outside Durango to gas up.

"You want some coffee?" said Julian.

"Nah. I was hoping you could take the wheel for a couple hours while I crash out."

Julian lowered his eyes. "Antoine, I have to tell you something. I don't actually know how to drive a stick-shift."

Antoine banged his fist on the steering wheel. "Dammit, Julian. You lied to me?"

"I thought you'd leave me behind if I said no."

"And what did you think would happen when I asked you to take the wheel?"

"Well…I thought maybe you could teach me."

"Motherfucker, this ain't traffic school. I don't have time for this nonsense."

"Look, the overnight parking area is practically deserted. One lesson. Maybe I'll surprise you."

Antoine stared at him for a long moment before cracking half a smile. “All right. One lesson.”

He drove to the overnight lot and shut the car down before he and Julian switched places.

“Seatbelts, please,” said Antoine, strapping his on. Julian did the same. “All right. Your right foot is for the gas and the brake, same as you were taught. I hope. You do know how to drive an automatic, don’t you?”

“Of course. Do you want to see my license?”

“Never mind that. Your left foot is for the clutch. You’re gonna have your foot all the way down on the clutch when you start the car, got it? Go ahead.”

Julian started the car. “Now what?”

“You’re gonna shift into first gear. Put your right foot on the brake, grab the gear shifter, and push it up and to the left. Once it’s in gear, release the brake and ease off the clutch.”

Julian shoved the shifter forward, producing a grinding noise.

“That ain’t it,” said Antoine. “You gotta get a feel for it.”

Julian tried again and the shifter slid into place. He released the brake and popped his foot off the clutch. The El Camino lurched forward and stalled.

“Shit,” said Julian.

“Okay, first of all, you put it in third gear, not first. Second, I told you to ease off the clutch. You pulled your foot off it like it stung you. Third, I ain’t got the patience for this shit. Lesson over. Let’s find a place I can grab some shuteye.”

Dean and Chuck crossed the Oklahoma border just after eight A.M. They found a rundown motel called the Texahoma just across the state line and got a room. They collapsed onto the beds inside and slept until nearly two P.M.

"I'm not getting out of this bed," said Dean as Chuck began puttering around the room.

"That's fine. I'm too antsy. I'm gonna go get the tires checked and then hook up that CB radio. Maybe ask the desk clerk if there's a place delivers pizza around here."

"I can't believe you're hungry. I thought you'd never eat again."

"You would not believe the dump I took this morning. It was something out of a creature feature."

"Take your word for it. You might want to find the news on the radio, make sure we're not on it."

"You figure Ruth's story will hold up with the cops?"

"My guess is local law enforcement has been on the Farrell family payroll for quite some time. I don't know that she'll even call them, though. If she can field dress a hog, I reckon she can make Elijah disappear without much trouble."

"You fucked her, didn't you?"

"I wouldn't put it so crudely as that."

"Aw, you fall in love again, cuz? I wouldn't worry about it. You'll get over it soon as the next pussy crosses your path."

"I thought you were leaving, Chuck."

"Yeah. Someone's gotta take care of business."

Chuck headed out. Dean turned on the TV and watched *General Hospital*, followed by reruns of *Gilligan's Island* and *Batman*. The *Batman* episode ended on a cliffhanger, with Robin in the midst of being swallowed by a giant clam.

"Goddammit," Dean muttered. "I'll never see how it turns out."

Around five o'clock Chuck returned with a bucket of Kentucky Fried Chicken and a twelve-pack of Miller High Life. "Got us some chow and brewskies. Some rolling papers too." He set the food and beer down on the table, then pulled a baggie of weed out of his pocket. "I figure we might as well sample our wares."

"I've sampled 'em plenty, but good call, nonetheless."

They watched the local news and wolfed fried chicken and biscuits, washing them down with cold beer. There was no mention of the previous night's activity at Farrell Farms. When they were full, Dean opened the baggie and rolled a couple of joints. They sparked up and watched Walter Cronkite.

"I remember the first time I smoked this shit," said Chuck. "It was in my first apartment over by Aquarena Springs. I had just bought that Beatles album. Not *Sgt. Pepper*, the one before it."

"*Revolver*."

"Yeah. John Lennon singing he knows what it's like to be dead, that just about blew my mind."

"I think it was Peter Fonda said that to Lennon at some Hollywood party. I read that somewhere."

"That makes sense, I guess. *Easy Rider*. Hey, kinda reminds you of us, right? I'm Captain America and you're the other one."

"Wait, how are *you* Captain America?"

"Well, Peter Fonda's better-looking than the other guy."

"Shit, Chucky, there ain't one person in a hundred would say you're better-looking than me."

"Now that's just unkind."

"I'm not saying you're ugly or nothing. It's just a comparative thing. If I wasn't around, I'm sure you'd attract women like flies."

"Yeah. Like that one at Sonny's Icehouse. She was a beauty."

"I hate to tell you, Chuck, but I'm not so sure that was genuine attraction on her part. From what you've told me, she sounds like she was a schemer."

"I'm starting to think you're trying to hurt my feelings on purpose."

"Not at all."

"You weren't there. She really liked me, I could tell."

"Okay, then. If you say so. But..."

"But what?"

"But you did kill her. So I don't think there's much of a future there."

Chuck threw his beer across the room. It shattered against the door. "Goddammit, cousin, you're really starting to work my last nerve. I thought we were going to have a nice, relaxing evening here."

"Forget I said anything. Change the subject, for Chrissakes."

Chuck folded his arms. "What else is on?"

Dean changed the channel and found a movie he'd seen before.

"What the hell is this?" said Chuck.

"You never saw it? It's one of the *Planet of the Apes* movies. Not sure which, but I saw it in the theater."

"Well, I was locked up for five years, so I didn't get to the movies much."

"I keep forgetting that."

"I know."

"Anyway, these apes escaped in Charlton Heston's rocket after he blew up the Earth in the last one."

"Charlton Heston blew up the Earth? Why?"

"There were these mutants who worshipped the atom bomb. And then there were all those gorillas trying to kill him. So he just said fuck it and pushed the button."

"That's badass. I think I'd do the same."

"Anyways, these three chimps get away at the last minute and go back in time. They're back here now, before it all happens.

Before the human race destroys itself and the apes take over. So there's a chance to change history."

"I wish."

"Why, what would you do? Go back and kill Hitler when he was a baby?"

"Fuck that. I'd change my own life. Someone else can take care of Hitler. That shit ain't my problem."

"So where would you go? Or I guess I mean *when* would you go? What's the moment you would change?"

Chuck took another hit. "I would go back to the Silver Dollar, pull that fucking knife and fork out of my hands and tell myself to stick to beer."

"That's it? You could go back to any time. You could go back five years and not try to rob that fuckin' Sac 'n Pac with Gary Foulke. You would have never gone to prison."

"Let me tell you something, cousin. I'd do another five years in Huntsville before I ever put another 72 ounces of steak in my gut. For a minute there, I actually considered going vegetarian."

"Well, it's over now. You survived. Got away from those Farrells too. Maybe someone's looking out for you."

"Who? An angel? Jesus Christ on his throne? Don't give me that shit."

"All I know is, it's my side of the family that always seems to meet an early demise. My Dad in Korea. His brother Rick, trampled by a bull. And then my mother, trying to beat the train across the tracks so she could make it to my high school graduation on time. I mean, you want to know what I would change, that's it."

"Come on, Dean. She'd forgot all about your graduation. This was hours later. She was just trying to make it to the liquor store before they closed."

"Oh, so I shouldn't go back in time and save her? I should just let her die?"

"The point is you can't go back and save anyone. All that's left is what's ahead."

"And all I'm saying, if Mr. Death comes calling and has to pick between us, he's coming for me. Going early, that's my family legacy. I've always known that. Here for a good time, not for a long time."

They sat in silence and watched the movie.

TWENTY-TWO

After breakfast in Pueblo, Giddings called the office back in Ivor County.

"Sheriff? Oh my gosh," said Deputy Winslow. "Where have you been? Everybody's going crazy down here."

"What do you mean, going crazy?"

"Well, your wife, for one. You may want to give her a call. She's out of her mind with worry. And the county commissioners. They have some serious questions about Freddy McElroy and the accident scene."

"What kind of questions?"

"Well, I know this is just a bunch of baloney, but there's a young woman who claims she saw Freddy at the Twilight Ranch on Sunday night. And she's made up this crazy story about how he died in the middle of their...you know, fooling around. And she says she saw you come into the Ranch, and later she saw you putting something in Freddy's car that...well, looked like a body all wrapped up in a blanket."

"You're right, Winslow. That is a bunch of baloney if I've ever heard it. I can't figure why this young woman would be telling stories like that, but that's a problem you're going to have to handle."

"I wish it was that simple, but those DPS boys investigating Beau's shooting are still hanging around here and they're poking into everything."

"Whatever happened to Freddy—and it was definitely an accident—it had nothing to do with our colleague Beau Harlan being gunned down in cold blood. Now, you just need to freeze them DPS sonsabitches out. Let 'em know I'm still the law in Ivor County."

"Yeah, but that's the problem. You ain't here and they've been looking for you."

"Goddammit, I am in hot pursuit of them that killed our man. Any law enforcement officer worth a shit would understand that."

"But, Sheriff, isn't that the U.S. Marshals' job? I really think you should come back here and—"

"Who the fuck do you think you are?" Giddings thundered. "I'm about five seconds from firing your ass, Winslow."

"But Sheriff! I'm the only one left here in this department. I'm pulling eighteen-hour shifts, I'm—"

"Oh, fuck you, Winslow. You're not doing a goddamn thing down there that's half as important as what I'm doing. When I slap the cuffs on the shitbirds who killed Beau, that's when I'll be back. Until then, hold it the fuck together."

He slammed down the phone. He thought about calling his wife but didn't see how that would improve his situation in any way, so he called the Twilight Ranch instead.

"Hello?"

"Miss Mona. It's Bud Giddings."

"Bud? Where the hell have you—"

"Never you mind. What's this I hear about one of your girls telling stories about Freddy McElroy and how he met his end?"

"Marie was confused, but I set her straight."

"I sure hope you did. Because if somehow this all blows back on me, you'll be coming along for the ride."

"It won't."

"See to it."

*

"What day is this?" said Dean, spraying Right Guard under his arms.

"Thursday. No more setbacks, we'll be rolling up to Snake River Canyon tomorrow around lunchtime. They'll be setting up for the weekend, we'll find this Bob Dillon, make the deal, and count our money."

Dean pulled on a clean t-shirt with a giant Rolling Stones tongue on it. "And head for the border."

"Hey, I'm still planning to stick around for the jump."

"In that case, I wish you luck finding a ride up to Canada. As soon as I get my money, I'm gone."

"You'll regret it the rest of your life."

"I'll watch it on TV and tell people I was there. I just won't mention I left before the big event."

"We'll see. Come on, let's find some breakfast and get back on the road."

They found a pancake house in town and loaded up. When they finished eating, Chuck opened the atlas on the table.

"We'll be in Colorado within the hour. I say we bypass Denver, head straight up to Wyoming, then turn left. We can be in Laramie by five o'clock. No point busting our asses. Get a room there, and it's pretty much a straight shot to Twin Falls, Idaho tomorrow."

"How are we on cash? Bearing in mind that I have none at all."

"We'll make it. There's a little grocery next door. I'll pick up some road snacks and beverages and whatnot."

"I foresee an uneventful day."

"Sure. Sign me up for that."

Chuck went into the grocery and grabbed some beef jerky, a bag of chips, a pack of smokes, a six-pack of Dr Pepper, and a few comic books from a spinner rack near the counter. He met Dean back at the taco truck and they got on the road. Inspired by Dean's t-shirt, Chuck stuck *Exile on Main Street* into the eight-track player.

Chuck was dashboard-drumming along with Charlie Watts on "Loving Cup" when they crossed into Colorado.

"Now we're really gonna see something," said Chuck. "I mean, I've never even seen mountains in real life. Except a camping trip to Big Bend one time, but those are molehills compared to the Rockies."

"Hey, why don't you turn on that CB radio, see if we can hear anything."

Chuck turned the volume down on the Stones and clicked on the CB. "Let's try channel nineteen. According to the little booklet came with it, that's where most of the truckers do their talking."

He turned the dial to channel nineteen. After a few minutes of crackling static, they heard a voice.

"Breaker one-nine, breaker one-nine, this here's the Cleveland Steamer. Looking for a smokey report on Highway 385 north of Springfield, come on."

A reply followed seconds later.

"Cleveland Steamer, you got the Jawbreaker here. I'm on 385 coming up to Lamar, and there's a Kojak with a Kodak about five miles back. Other than that, I got nothing ahead of me but a pregnant roller skate and a thirteen-letter shit-spreader, over."

"That's a big ten-four, good buddy. Catch you on the flip-flop."

Chuck clicked off the CB and turned up the tunes.

"Well, that was helpful," said Dean. "What in the fuck is a pregnant roller skate?"

"No idea. But a Kojak with a Kodak, that's got to be a cop with a radar gun. So keep it under double nickels."

"See, I got that one. Fifty-five."

"That's a big ten-four, good buddy."

For the next few hours, they climbed twisting roads leading ever upward as the Rocky Mountains rose around them. Chuck got an eyeful of all the scenic vistas he'd hoped for: sweeping views of granite peaks and plunging gorges, cascading waterfalls and shimmering reflective lakes, majestic elks grazing on aspen sprouts, blue spruces clustered like a Christmas tree farm.

Ahead of a steep downward grade, Chuck noticed the paint had chipped away from the S on a caution sign that had once read SLOW DOWN.

"Check it out, cuz," he said. "We're on the Lowdown Road."

"Shit, Chuck. I've known that all along."

•

On Thursday morning, Antoine's memories of Wednesday night were hazy. Around one-thirty Wednesday afternoon, they had crossed into Utah. Antoine was having a hard time keeping his eyes open.

"Well, here we are," said Antoine. "The whitest state you could possibly imagine."

"Are you okay to drive? You look really tired."

Antoine massaged his forehead with his thumb and forefinger. "We're ahead of schedule. Let's find somewhere to hole up until tomorrow."

Outside of Moab, they pulled into a campground with cabins for rent. Antoine parked in front of the office.

"If anyone asks, you're my little brother. I'm driving you to college."

"Which college?"

"I dunno, BYU."

"BYU? You think they're gonna buy us as Mormons?"

"So you pick one."

"University of Washington. Seattle."

"Fine."

Antoine got a funny look from the clerk in the office, but no trouble beyond that. He paid cash and got the key to a cabin with a spectacular view of the La Sal Range. Antoine had no time to admire it, however; he was out as soon as his head hit the pillow.

He wouldn't remember his dream. His father wasn't in this one, but his Uncle Warren was. Once his pop had turned against him, Uncle Warren became the father figure in his life. Uncle Warren was the black sheep of the family. He made his living running guns down to Mexico and trafficking marijuana back the other way. He started taking young Antoine on his trips south of the border, which is what they were doing in his dream.

Antoine loved those trips to Mexico. He'd cut school if he had to. He was too far ahead of his classmates to worry about it. He was ahead of most of his teachers too. His mother used to tell him he could go to Harvard, but he just laughed at that. He already knew what he was going to do for a living. Why waste four years getting a degree when he could start making money hand over fist as a teenager? His Uncle Warren taught him everything, and if he gave a shit that Antoine was gay, he never let on.

Uncle Warren was alive in his dream, which he was not in real life. The federales caught up to him, and they were getting paid by a different drug lord than the one he worked for, so he ended up in a shallow grave in Piedras Negras. He wasn't there long, which is how Antoine knew he was dead. Dogs dug him up and he was identified by his dental records. But in the dream, he was alive, driving Antoine down through Coahuila.

They usually stayed in Saltillo overnight, and Antoine was left to his own devices. He met some Mexican boys he'd never forgotten.

Things didn't work out for him in the dream, however. Flashing blue lights appeared in Uncle Warren's rearview mirror and he tried to get away. Antoine heard gunshots and saw Uncle Warren slump against the steering wheel. The car went out of control, turning end over end, trapping Antoine inside. He heard footsteps approaching as he tried to climb out.

Sherriff Giddings peered inside. "Eenie-meenie-miney-mo," he said.

Antoine jolted awake just after six that evening, his stomach growling. Julian wasn't in the cabin, but Antoine found a note on the table: CAMPSITE 16. He sighed and shook the cobwebs out of his head. "What the hell, Julian?"

He headed out of the cabin in search of campsite sixteen. It wasn't hard to find. There was a psychedelic VW microbus parked in front of it, and he could hear the sound of acoustic guitars and off-key singing as he approached. He recognized the song as "Friend of the Devil." On the bright side, he could also smell meat on the grill.

Julian was sitting on a blanket, bobbing his head as two hippies with guitars wound their way to the end of the song. Another was grilling burgers and hot dogs, while a fourth sat on the picnic table taking sips from a bottle of Jack Daniels. When the song came to an end, Julian applauded before noticing Antoine standing a few feet away.

"Oh, you're awake! Hey, everyone, this is my brother Antoine."

One of the guitarists, a tall, lanky shirtless man with a mushroom cloud of bushy hair and a droopy mustache stood and shook Antoine's hand. He had a big, goofy grin plastered on his face.

"Good to meet you, man. I'm Creech. The lovely lady with the guitar is Shireen, that's Doob at the grill, and Ziggy on the picnic table."

The other hippies offered their own goofy grins, except for Ziggy. He had a hard stare that suggested a strong familiarity with the American penal system.

"Creech invited us to dinner," said Julian.

"We've got burgers, dogs, potato salad, pasta salad, and some cold ones in the cooler if you want one."

"Wouldn't mind," said Antoine.

Creech dug in the cooler for a can of Coors and handed it to Antoine, who pulled off the pop top and took a drink. "I noticed Vermont plates on your van here."

"Yeah, we've been on the road a few weeks now. Well, me and Shireen have. We're river guides in the summer and ski instructors in the winter. In between we just keep on keepin' on. We picked up Doob in Pennsylvania and Ziggy a couple days ago in Phoenix."

"Headed anywhere in particular?"

"Yeah, eventually. We've been seeing the country—Canada, too—but the goal is to end up in San Francisco for the Dead shows next month."

"The Grateful Dead?"

"Yeah, man. They're doing five shows at Winterland."

"It's a bittersweet occasion," said Shireen, strumming her guitar absently. "Jerry's sick of touring, so these are gonna be their farewell shows."

"Such a bummer," said Doob. "I've been to more than fifty Dead shows. I can't even fathom the idea of life without them."

"They have records, don't they?" said Antoine.

"Sure, man, but records are no substitute for the experience. Don't get me wrong, *American Beauty* is a classic album, but when you go to a Dead show, it's like a new community being born every night. The band and the crowd become one. It's pure love."

Antoine stole a glance at Ziggy, who was staring into the campfire. He didn't look like someone who had ever experienced pure love.

"Come and get it!" said Doob, spearing hot dogs into buns. Antoine didn't need to be asked twice. He loaded up a Styrofoam plate with picnic salads and a hot dog drowning in mustard and relish and took a seat at the picnic table. As the others joined him, Ziggy sulked away with his bottle of Jack.

"He all right?" said Antoine between bites.

"Who, Ziggy?" said Creech. "Yeah, he's cool. Not the most social guy, that's all."

"He filled our gas tank and bought the food," said Shireen. "So we're kind of stuck with him."

"Aw, don't say that. It's all love."

Antoine thought Creech was being more than a little naïve but didn't see the point in pursuing the matter. He happily accepted seconds when offered, but once the meal was finished and Creech was strumming the opening chords of "Uncle John's Band," he decided it was time to say goodnight.

"Damn," said Creech. "We were hoping you'd stay for dessert."

Antoine patted his stomach. "I'm full, man. Y'all saw to that."

"Me too," said Julian. "But I always like to look at the dessert menu."

"No room for these?" Creech held up a plastic baggie.

"Is that mushrooms?"

"Mellow but magical. Here, take some to go." Creech shook out a handful and held them in his palm. Julian accepted before Antoine could say a word.

"Thanks so much," Julian said, clutching the mushrooms in his fist. "It was great to meet you all."

"You too. Stop by for breakfast tomorrow if you'd like. Let us know how it went."

Antoine nodded curtly, and he and Julian headed back toward their cabin.

"Do me a favor," said Antoine once they were out of earshot. "You want to make new friends, wait 'til you're back on campus. I'm sure there's plenty of hippies there."

"What's wrong with hippies?"

"Ask Sharon Tate and her friends."

"Oh, come on. They were so nice!"

"Three of 'em were nice, I'll give you that. Ziggy, though, he's trouble. I'm not saying he's Charles Manson, but I got a real negative vibe off him."

"How can you make such a snap judgment about someone you barely met?"

"In my line of work, I have no choice. Anyway, the thing about those hippies, they're just a remnant of something that never amounted to much in the first place. That whole counterculture turned out to be a circus. It packed up and skipped town, and now there's a few clowns left wandering around that don't even know they missed the train."

"I swear, Antoine, sometimes you sound like Archie Bunker."

"I'm just being real with you. But I will admit one thing. I could unload a hell of a lot of product at five Grateful Dead shows. I'd just have to wear earplugs the whole time."

They reached the cabin and stepped inside. Julian spilled the handful of mushrooms out on the table. "What do you think?"

Antoine shook his head. "Have a good time, man."

"Seriously? You're gonna make me do these by myself?"

"I'm not making you do anything. I've got rules. And I don't get high on my own supply."

"But that's weed. This is different."

"I like to be in control. Of my mind, my plans, my environment. I'm on a mission, not a holiday."

"We've got nowhere to be. By tomorrow morning, you'll be one hundred percent."

He held one out to Antoine at the tips of his fingers.

Antoine took it, examined it. "What do you do? Just eat 'em?"

"You can. I like to make a tea with them. Goes down smoother. Makes for a mellower trip. Mellow but magical, just like Creech said."

Antoine sighed and set down the mushroom. "Fine. Make us some tea, Julian."

Julian found a kettle in the cabin's pantry and heated the water on the grill outside. He split the mushrooms between two coffee mugs and used a spoon to grind them up as best he could. When the water reached a boil, he filled each mug and handed one to Antoine.

"Bottoms up."

Thirty minutes after drinking the tea, Antoine felt sick to his stomach.

Thirty minutes after that, he watched the mountains turn to fire. A heartbeat later, darkness descended like a curtain falling. Blobs of light bobbed and weaved before his eyes. UFOs?

"Fireflies," said a voice.

A face appeared, free-floating in an incandescent bubble. "I found a flashlight in the cabin. We should go for a spooky walk."

Antoine got it. He had slipped out of the current of his real life, into a parallel stream that would link up with the original somewhere down the line. He didn't need to panic, just navigate gently until that happened.

Julian pointed the flashlight beam toward a trail winding around the campground. Antoine headed toward the light.

"How are you feeling?" said Julian.

"A little abstract. Nothing I can't handle."

"I told you it would be mellow."

Another light beam appeared ahead, accompanied by whispers.

"Someone coming the other way," said Julian.

"Yeah, I figured that out on my own."

Antoine made up a story about the couple coming toward them. The man was recently retired. He bought a Winnebago and talked his wife into traveling the country. She had a lover back in Ohio, and she planned to return alone.

"Well, hello! You boys are a long way from home."

Antoine snarled. "What's that supposed to mean?"

"Just…just that we saw you stop at the office on the way in. Your Texas plates."

"Forgive my brother," said Julian. "He's a little overprotective. He's driving me to college."

"Nice! What college?"

"University of Washington. Seattle."

"Oh my, you've still got quite a drive ahead of you. But… where's all your stuff?"

"I'm sorry?"

"I mean, the flatbed of your El Camino is empty. I know you can't fit much inside a car like that."

"I've got a furnished dorm room waiting for me. I didn't bring much. I'll buy some new clothes once I see what the style is up there."

"I see. Well, enjoy your walk. I think we saw an owl."

The couple went on their way. Antoine and Julian continued down the path.

"Do you think they bought it?"

"What does it matter?" said Antoine. "None of this is really happening."

TWENTY-THREE

Giddings pulled into a rest area outside of Provo, Utah. Once he'd finished his business and flushed it away, he opened the stall door to find a Utah Highway Patrol officer leaning against the sink.

"Evening," said the officer. "That your cruiser parked out front?"

"That's a good guess. You mind stepping aside so I can wash my hands?"

The officer did so, gesturing to the sink as he moved. "Help yourself. Take your time. But when you're finished, I'm going to have to ask you to come with me."

Giddings turned on the taps. "Now, why would I do that?"

"The Texas Department of Public Safety is awful anxious to talk to you, Sheriff Giddings. I'd wager every law enforcement agency within a thousand miles of Texas got the same alert we did."

Giddings washed his hands. He figured he had at least fifty pounds on the Utah trooper, but for now, the best thing to do was keep playing possum. "I'm sure this is all some misunderstanding," he said. "But I'd be happy to drive myself back if they're so all fired-up to talk to me. No need for you to trouble yourself."

"Oh, won't be much trouble for me. All I gotta do is drive you to downtown Provo and turn you over to the U.S. Marshals. They'll be happy to drive you back."

"But what about my vehicle?"

"That'll be safe with us until we figure out how to get it back where it belongs. No need to concern yourself on that front."

Giddings chuckled. “The Feds, huh? I tell ya, it just sounds like someone back home is playing a big ol’ prank on me. Really, they’re just making it harder and harder for good cops like us to do our jobs.”

“I wouldn’t know about that. I really don’t even know what you’re doing way up here.”

Giddings turned off the water and shook his hands. “Ain’t you curious?”

“Not really. Just doing my job, like you said.”

Giddings pumped the lever on the paper towel dispenser to no avail. “Shit, looks like this thing is empty. Either that, or the doohickey is broken. Lemme see if I can pop this open in case there’s a roll in here.”

Giddings grabbed the dispenser on both sides and yanked with all his might. It came free of the wall, and in one swift motion, Giddings turned and slammed it into the patrolman’s head. As the patrolman staggered back, Giddings swung the dispenser back upward into his jaw. The patrolman fell into the open stall, his head hitting the toilet with a solid crack.

Without bothering to check whether he was alive or dead, Giddings wiped his hands on the patrolman’s shirt and took his badge, gun, keys, and wallet. He was running low on spending cash, and the wallet had three twenties and a ten in it.

Giddings had no time for a tearful farewell to his vehicle as he climbed into the Highway Patrol car, flipped on the flashers, and put the pedal to the medal. He was already up to eighty by the time he hit the onramp.

“How about a movie tonight?” said Dean.

They had made it to Laramie, Wyoming without incident and found a cheap motel. Dean was on his bed, propped up on pillows, newspaper open to the movie listings.

"There's a drive-in double feature at the Laramie Twin. *Gator Bait* and *Truck Stop Women*, both starring Claudia Jennings."

"Who the hell is Claudia Jennings?" Chuck flipped idly through an issue of *The Brave and the Bold*.

Dean looked over in disgust. "Are you serious? Playboy Playmate of the Year, 1970?"

"It shouldn't surprise me that you've forgotten this again, but I was locked up in '70. We didn't always get the latest porn at Huntsville."

"I guess you never saw *The Unholy Rollers* either. Greatest roller derby movie of all time."

"Wow, that's quite an achievement. How many Oscars did it win?"

"Anyway, I've been wanting to see both these flicks, and here they are. Show starts at dusk."

"You go if you want. I'm gonna stay in, read my comics, and turn in early. I'm still a little skittish about going out after dark, if you can believe that."

Dean sat up and pulled on his boots. "Can you advance me ten bucks? I might want to get some popcorn."

Chuck took his wallet from the dresser and pulled out a twenty. "That's for gas in the morning, too."

"Got it," said Dean, taking the bill and stuffing it in his jeans pocket.

"Don't get in any trouble. Just go, watch your movies, and come back."

"Yes, mother."

"I'm serious. Our whole future is in that truck, and we're so close now. You fuck it up at the last minute, I'll hunt you down in hell."

"I don't doubt it."

*

The morning after their spooky walk, Julian was naked in Antoine's bed and the cabin window was wide open. Antoine swore under his breath, got up and closed it, pulling the shades down tight.

"Wake up," he said, swatting Julian's bare ass with his t-shirt.

Julian rolled over and yawned. "I'm up. What's happening?"

"You're getting dressed and we're getting the fuck out of here. Did you open the window last night?"

"You did. It was stuffy when we got back here."

"Goddammit. Did we make a lot of noise last night?"

"That's how I remember it."

"Shit. It's not funny, Julian. Anyone could have heard us last night. Anyone could have looked in that window this morning."

"You didn't care anything about that last night."

"Well, I do now. For all I know they can legally burn you alive for sodomy in Utah."

"Sure. You can have as many wives as you want, but you have sex with one man..."

"This is not a debate. You have two choices, Julian. The first, and I'm leaning hard toward this one, I take you as far as Salt Lake City and put you on a bus back to Albuquerque."

"I don't like the sound of that. What's the second choice?"

"My way or the highway. No more driving lessons, no more psychedelic interludes, no more fucking around. This is supposed to be a business trip for me. If you're staying with me, it's all business until I've accomplished my goal. You do what I say when I say it. Otherwise, we part ways."

Julian pulled on his underwear. "I'm with you, Antoine. I'm sorry. I've been treating this like a vacation because that's what it is for me. But you're right, this is your trip. I just want to be with you."

Antoine stroked his cheek. "Look, it's partly my fault. I allowed myself to be persuaded by you against my better judgment, because…well, let's just say most of my bar pickups, there's a whole lot less stimulating conversation. Less stimulation all around."

Julian patted the bed beside him. "One for the road?"

"Nope. Finish getting dressed. I'll be outside."

An unpleasant surprise awaited Antoine when he stepped out of the cabin. Ziggy was leaning against the El Camino, arms folded.

"Afraid we won't be joining y'all for breakfast," said Antoine. "We gotta hit the road."

"There's no breakfast. I need a ride."

Antoine glanced over at the camping area. The psychedelic microbus was gone. "They left your ass, huh?"

"Peeled out of here at three o'clock in the morning."

"I guess it's not all love after all."

"Don't really want to talk about it."

"Well, as you might have noticed, this is an El Camino. There's no back seat, so you'll have to find a lift elsewhere."

"I can ride in the flatbed."

"No, I don't think so. Could you please step away from the car?"

Ziggy cracked his knuckles. "How about I just kick your faggot ass and take the car from you?"

Antoine smirked. "Now, see, I had a feeling you were going to say something like that."

"I heard you and your 'brother' last night. I sure hope he ain't really your brother, or we got a whole other level of sick shit going on here."

"You know, Creech defended you last night. Said you were just quiet. You ain't so quiet this morning. Anything else you want to call me? Better get it out of your system now."

"I ain't a racist if that's what you're getting at. I've fucked plenty of black chicks."

"I doubt that, but it wouldn't matter even if it's true," Antoine said. "Now move your filthy hippie ass away from my mother-fucking ride."

Ziggy made a clumsy attempt at a sucker punch, but to Antoine, he looked like he was moving underwater. One quick side-snap kick to the midsection doubled Ziggy over. A knee in the nose put him on his ass.

"Don't get up until we're gone," said Antoine. He glanced over his shoulder to see a wide-eyed Julian standing right behind him. "Come on, my brother. Let's roll."

Giddings pulled over three cars trying to find a driver roughly his size. The fourth time was the charm. It was easy for Giddings to tell, even though it was dark. The rider was on a Harley.

"In a hurry to see Evel Knievel, are you?"

"Was I speeding, officer?"

"A little bit. I don't think we need to make a big deal of it. But I do need to show you something. Leave the bike and come with me."

The biker looked a little concerned, but he did as he was told. Giddings walked him back toward the patrol car.

"Traveling alone? You're not with one of those motorcycle gangs?"

"Nope. Just me. I've only had the bike six months or so."

"I haven't ridden one in years. I wonder if it's like...well, like riding a bike. It just comes back to you."

"I wouldn't know."

Giddings glanced up and down the road. He waited for a stray car to pass. "I'm fixin' to find out."

He fired two shots into the biker's head. The biker fell behind the car, hidden from the road. Giddings stripped off his uniform and helped himself to the biker's clothes and leathers. By now every cop in the state would be looking for the Texas sheriff who stole a Utah Highway Patrol vehicle. They wouldn't be looking for a lone biker on his way to Idaho.

TWENTY-FOUR

The sun was beginning to set as Dean pulled up to the gate of the Laramie Twin Drive-In. He rolled down his window and held out a five-dollar bill. He'd already broken the twenty he got from Chuck buying a six-pack of Coors at a gas station.

"You hidin' anyone in the back?" said the curly-haired young woman in the booth.

"You want to check it?" Dean winked and blew a bubble until it popped.

"I'll take your word for it. You seem like an honest fella." She took the fiver from him.

"You seen these flicks yet?"

"Three or four times. *Truck Stop Women* is okay, but *Gator Bait* is the real deal. Claudia Jennings is one tough chick. She's not just on the screen to look good and scream and get rescued by the hero. She kicks ass. I mean, her Cajun accent isn't much, but who cares?"

"She get naked in that one?"

"I don't want to ruin it for you."

"Well, you decide you want to see it again, just come find me."

"That reminds me, you need to park near the back, behind the smaller vehicles."

"No problem...what did you say your name was?"

A horn sounded behind Dean.

"I didn't," she said, raising the gate. "But it's Ginny."

"I'm Dean. Check you later, Ginny."

*

It was just after midnight when Giddings pulled into Twin Falls, Idaho. He had trouble remembering what day it was. He'd slept less than four hours out of the past forty-eight and it was all catching up to him now. He needed to find a bed.

"My friend, you are shit out of luck," said the night clerk at the Moonlight Inn. "There's not a room in town available. They've all been booked for weeks."

Giddings felt naked without his badge. As far as this clerk was concerned, he was just another biker. His usual means of intimidation were lost to him.

"Is it possible you had a cancellation tonight? I mean, I'll take anything. A cot in the boiler room if you've got one." Giddings took a twenty out of the Utah patrolman's wallet and slid it across the desk.

The clerk checked his registry and the keys hanging behind him. "Well, I'll let you in on a little secret. Mr. Knievel's people paid us in advance to keep a room open for him just in case. He's got a trailer out at the jump site, but he does enjoy having a drink or two at the local taverns, perhaps meeting a young lady or two as well..."

"I understand. Is that room currently unoccupied?"

The clerk tapped the twenty on the desk. Giddings added another.

"It is. However, if Mr. Knievel were to show up tonight, no matter the time, you would have to be out of that room in a flash."

"Got it. Here's hoping he decided to retire to his trailer early tonight and have a nice glass of warm milk before bedtime."

"We can always hope." The clerk handed him a key. "Room 236. If the phone rings, don't even bother to answer it. Just make the bed and leave. And in any case, you'll have to be out by eight A.M. That's when I'm off-duty."

"Understood. Appreciate your help."

"Enjoy your stay at the Moonlight Inn."

Truck Stop Women was nowhere near as exciting as the ad in the paper had made it look, but there was enough nudity to hold Dean's attention. He'd worked his way through half his six-pack and was about to head to the concession stand when he heard a familiar voice calling, "Popcorn here! Hot popcorn!"

He leaned out the window and saw Ginny walking between the cars with a tray of popcorn supported by a neck strap. He whistled and she walked over.

"Popcorn?"

"Perfect timing." He handed her a dollar and took a bucket off the tray.

"How did you enjoy the movie?"

"Well, it was kind of feminist, wasn't it? But still had plenty of bare breasts. A good combination, but there wasn't much action."

"You'll have more fun with *Gator Bait*."

"Sure you can't stay and watch it with me?"

"Gotta work. This is my last night. Just a summer gig, but if I want to get paid, I've got to see it through. But hey, my band is playing tomorrow night if you want to come see us."

"Aw, shoot. Wish I could, but we're leaving town in the morning."

"Who's we?"

"Me and my cousin. We're headed to Idaho for that Evel Knievel deal."

"You're kidding. I'm gonna be there too."

"Really? You're an Evel fan?"

"No, but he was here in town a couple weeks ago, doing his

little publicity tour for the jump. His manager saw us play at this bar we're gonna be at tomorrow night, and he liked our stuff. So we're gonna be playing Saturday night in Twin Falls. Part of the whole weekend celebration, I guess."

"Tell me where and when, and I won't miss it."

"Right out at the jump site. Nine o'clock on the main stage."

"Cool. What do you play?"

"I sing and play a little rhythm guitar. We're called Ginny and the Juicers. We do a few originals, but mostly covers. Rock, country, and a little bit of soul."

Again, their conversation was cut short by a beeping horn. A guy in a Chevy van was hollering for popcorn.

"Can't wait. See you in Twin Falls."

Dean cracked open another beer, shoveled a handful of popcorn into his mouth, and settled in for the late show.

Just outside Salt Lake City, traffic slowed to a crawl.

"Is this the morning rush hour?" said Julian.

Antoine craned his neck out the window. "Can't tell from here. Might be an accident up ahead and we're caught behind rubberneckers."

They inched along the highway.

"So you know karate?" Julian said.

"I've been taking classes down in San Antonio. I was supposed to go for my blue belt this week, but...I guess that will have to wait. But yeah, I got into it. A man should know how to defend himself."

"You weren't at all inspired by how cool it looks."

"I admit I do love a good kung-fu movie. Not the TV show with the white dude, that's bullshit. But Bruce Lee, *Fist of Fury*, *Way of the Dragon*. Shaw Brothers, *Five Fingers of Death*, that's my favorite."

"I like foreign films too, but I'm more into Godard, Bunuel, Antonioni."

"Shit, brother, I never said I was *only* into flicks where dudes get kicked in the face. I'm down with Godard. He's one of the only cats who really gets it. Or did, anyway. His newer stuff doesn't do much for me."

"You didn't like *Tout Va Bien*?"

"Didn't see it."

"You should."

"Maybe," Antoine said. "Though I gotta say, much as I love movies, they can't compete with books. For one thing, you can actually find books written by black folks. Movies, even something like *Across 110th Street*, it's a good flick, but it was directed by a white dude."

"Pretty sure a white dude wrote the novel it's based on, too."

"Shit," said Antoine, but it wasn't the news about *Across 110th Street* that troubled him. "It's some kind of police roadblock ahead."

"Roadblock? What are we going to do?"

"Nothing we can do. No way off this highway before we get to it. Just play it cool. Nobody up here is looking for us, and we ain't doing anything wrong."

Antoine wasn't quite sure he believed his own words. He knew Giddings had put out an APB on him in Texas. If a Utah cop called in his driver's license, would that information be available to him? Antoine didn't know how that kind of interstate cooperation worked, but there was nothing he could do about it now.

They approached the roadblock. He saw several officers looking into cars and waving them through. When it was his turn, Antoine pasted on a smile.

"Good morning, officer."

"Morning." The officer leaned down and looked into the El Camino. "From Texas, are you?"

"That's right. Just driving my little brother to college."

"Well, we're looking for a man from Texas, but it's pretty clear neither one of you is him."

"I see. What did this man do?"

"It's been all over the news. He killed a highway patrolman and stole his car. Later we found the car abandoned with another dead man beside it. You wouldn't believe it, but this killer is a sheriff from Texas. Anyways, he's a white man. You two can move along."

The officer slapped the roof of the car. Antoine drove on through the roadblock.

"A sheriff from Texas?" said Julian.

"Gotta be Giddings. The one I told you about. The man is a stone-cold psychopath, apparently. And he's going where we're going."

Giddings woke up at seven on Friday morning. He showered, shaved, and went downstairs. The night clerk was still at the desk.

"Slept like a baby. Much appreciated."

"We're just lucky Mr. Knievel never showed up last night. If you're staying for the jump, you're going to have to find somewhere else to sleep."

"I will. Just one more favor I need to ask you." He dug the Polaroid out of his pocket and showed it to the clerk. "You see either or both of these boys, I want you to let me know. I'll be popping in periodically to check."

"Who are they?"

"Just some friends I'm supposed to meet up with here. I've got no way to get in touch with them, and they aren't going to be able to find a room either."

“Sure thing. I’ll keep an eye out for them.”

Giddings headed out. He spotted Lucky’s Diner across the street and went in to have some breakfast.

“Lotta strangers in town?” he asked the waitress.

“Like never before. It’s gonna get real busy here shortly and it’s gonna stay that way. I saw this fella I recognized from *Wide World of Sports* in here last night. They say Elvis is coming. And Steve McQueen.”

“No kidding? Well, I’m supposed to meet up with some friends here. Haven’t seen them, have you?” He showed her the Polaroid.

“Don’t think so, but like you said, lotta strangers here this week.”

“Well, if you do see them, I’d appreciate if you’d let me know next time I drop in. But don’t say I’m looking for ’em. I want to surprise them.”

“You got it. More coffee?”

“Please.”

After breakfast, he found a pay phone outside the diner and placed a call.

“Sheriff’s office.”

“It’s Giddings. What’s the latest, Winslow?”

“The latest? The latest is I’m cleaning out my desk.”

“Why are you doing that?”

“Because I don’t work here anymore.”

“Winslow, when I said I was five seconds from firing you, that was just me blowing off some steam.”

“You don’t understand, Sheriff. You don’t work here anymore either.”

Giddings felt his face reddening. “You can start making some sense anytime now, Winslow.”

“The county commissioners held an emergency meeting yesterday afternoon. They voted to dissolve the Sheriff's Department and contract county law enforcement out to DPS for a two-year trial period. That came right after their vote of no confidence in you."

"I don't give a fuck whether they have confidence in me or not. I am an elected official. They can't do this."

"Technically, I guess, you're still the elected sheriff. It's just that you don't have a department or any authority. You could fight it in court, I suppose. But you'd have to come back down here. Which you really should do, anyway."

"Winslow. Is DPS there now? Tracing this call?"

"Well, the thing is, Sheriff—"

Giddings hung up the phone. He stormed back into the diner and found the restroom, where he splashed some cold water on his face. He looked into the mirror, and for the first time saw himself in his biker garb. All at once, the tension slipped out of his body.

He was free. His career in law enforcement, which he'd never wanted in the first place, was over. He'd left all that behind when he'd abandoned his cruiser at the rest stop. Of course he could never go back. By now the word was spreading far and wide about the state trooper he'd killed. Whether that word had reached Texas yet or not, the county commissioners had done him a favor by dissolving the department. He was the sheriff of nowhere.

The man looking back at him from the mirror, that was who he always should've been. And he knew what he had to do now.

TWENTY-FIVE

"I met a girl last night."

"Oh, Jesus," said Chuck. "Did you have sex in this truck again?"

"No, as a matter of fact. She was somehow able to withstand my charms."

"I'm sure that was humbling."

Dean signaled and took the exit for Route 30 west. He figured they were five hours from Twin Falls. They'd be in town by mid-afternoon.

"Only a temporary setback," he said. "We have a date tomorrow night."

"How the hell do you have a date tomorrow night? You're going back to Laramie?"

"Nope. She's gonna be in Twin Falls with her band."

"I see. So now you're planning to stick around this weekend. Just to get laid."

"It ain't like that."

"Oh, so you're in love again. I told you it wouldn't take long."

"This one's different. Worth putting in the effort."

"Yeah? You two have some deep conversations, did you?"

"Not really. We hardly got a chance to talk at all. But I have a sense about these things."

"You mean you have no sense about these things."

"We'll see how it goes. By tomorrow night, I'll be a rich man. Maybe I can talk her into coming to Canada with me."

"What about her band?"

"They have musicians in Canada, don't they? Neil Young,

Joni Mitchell…all the guys in the Band except one were from Canada."

"They all left Canada and came here. I don't think it works the other way around."

"No point in getting ahead of myself, I guess. But Neil Young sounds like a good idea."

Dean stuck *On the Beach* in the eight-track player and cranked "Revolution Blues" as loud as it would go.

The bars in Twin Falls were all opening at eight A.M. for the week, and all were crowded by mid-morning. Giddings showed the Polaroid to all the bartenders, none of whom remembered seeing Chuck and Dean, most of whom said they wouldn't remember if they did. He rode the Harley block by block around downtown, looking for a black-painted taco truck. He figured he'd beaten the Melville boys to town, which is what he'd planned, but he had one more place he wanted to check first. He spotted an ABC news van near the Moonlight Inn. A couple of grips were unloading camera equipment.

"Excuse me," said Giddings. "You guys know the way to the jump site?"

"Can't miss it. Just head east on this street for two miles until you hit Hankins Road, then hang a left. It's the only road in. They've got a little guardhouse with a gate rigged up. Not sure if they're letting the general public in yet."

"Oh, I'm working security for the event."

"In that case, I'm sure you'll find someone who can help you up there."

Giddings thanked him and headed out. On Hankins Road, the houses and other buildings grew fewer and farther between until he reached an intersection with a DEAD-END sign straight ahead. To his left, a billboard read SNAKE RIVER CANYON JUMP

SITE with a blue arrow beneath it marked WELCOME. The arrow pointed toward the dead end, so Giddings continued straight. Soon he was riding through a rugged landscape of dirt and dust. As he'd been told, the road came to an end at a guardhouse.

"Help you?" said the burly, bearded man in charge of the gate.

"I've got it," said Giddings. "I've got the picture."

"What the hell are you talking about?"

"Didn't you hear? These two idiots tried to sneak into Evel's trailer last night. Here." Giddings handed him the Polaroid. "You seen 'em today?"

The guard eyed the photo carefully. "Nope, I don't believe so."

"Well, you keep that photo there in the guardhouse. You or anyone else working here sees these two, Evel wants you to call and leave me a message at the Moonlight Inn."

"Leave you a message? Who are you?"

"I'm Buddy G. Evel put me on this one personally, so if you see 'em, don't try to handle it yourself. Just call the hotel and leave a message for Buddy G."

Shortly after 1:30 P.M., Antoine parked in front of a saddle store in downtown Twin Falls. It was the only parking spot available as far as he could see.

"I've got a feeling we won't be able to get a room in town tonight," he said, taking a couple of twenties out of his wallet and handing them to Julian. "Why don't you see if you can find us a couple of sleeping bags at that sporting-goods store we passed? We can sleep in the flatbed tonight, outside of town. I've got a phone call to make."

Antoine waited while a reporter called in a story from the phone booth outside the Moonlight Inn. When the reporter was done, Antoine called the salvage yard office back in San Marcos.

"T.J., it's Antoine."

"Holy shit. Boss, what the hell is going on? The cops have been here looking for you. They said you assaulted a sheriff's deputy in Lubbock."

"That was self-defense. Anyway, it's a long story."

"Well, when are you coming back here?"

"I don't know. Sounds like there's gonna be quite a welcoming committee if I do."

"But Antoine, we've got some pissed-off partners expecting to re-up—"

"No business on the office phone. Go to the phone booth outside the Biscuit and call me back." Antoine gave him the number and hung up. Five minutes later, the phone rang.

"You were saying. Pissed-off partners?"

"Our dealers need product. If they can't get it from us, they'll go elsewhere."

"Elsewhere meaning San Antonio?"

"Manny has been looking to expand his territory for a while now. This is his chance. By the time you get back—"

"All the more reason for me not to come back."

"Where will you go?"

"I dunno. New Mexico holds some appeal. But first I gotta get back what's mine."

"Any luck with that?"

"Not yet. But I'm in the right place. It's just a matter of time."

Dean and Chuck were the last to arrive in Twin Falls, on Friday, September 6 at 3:23 P.M.

"Looks like the circus is in town," said Chuck.

"It is, isn't it? Evel Knievel's Flying Circus."

"I guess we better try to get a room for the night."

"Might as well give it a shot, but I think we're sleeping in the truck tonight."

They paid two dollars to park in a lot and headed for the

Moonlight Inn. The NO VACANCY light was on. They decided to talk to the desk clerk anyway.

"Nope," he said. "Not even a cot in the boiler room. And people have asked." He squinted at them. "Oh, hey. Your friend has been looking for you."

"Our friend?" said Chuck. "We don't have any friends here."

"Well, he showed me a picture of you. Said to let him know if I saw you."

"Who was this guy?"

"Didn't get his name. Big biker type. Stayed here last night and he's stopped in a couple times since."

"Biker type, huh?" Chuck leaned over and whispered to Dean. "Uptown Mike. Guy from the roadhouse in Amarillo."

"How'd he get a picture of us?"

"No idea." Chuck turned back to the desk clerk. "Hey, if he comes back, do us a favor and tell him you haven't seen us. We kinda want to surprise him."

"He was a good tipper."

Chuck grimaced and pulled out his wallet. He set a twenty on the desk. The clerk pocketed it.

"Don't suppose I'm obligated to tell him anything."

"Appreciate that."

They headed out. Dean noticed a sign for Lulu's Lounge down the block. "Wouldn't mind wetting my whistle."

"Yeah, but I've got twenty bucks left. After that, we're flat broke until we make this deal. Let's head out to the jump site and see if we can catch this Bob Dillon today and get it over with."

Giddings was growing impatient. He'd been in Twin Falls for nearly thirty-six hours, and there was still no sign of the cousins Melville. He was drinking whiskey in Suicide Kings when he saw a familiar face. The biker he'd chatted with at the motel outside Pueblo was shooting pool with another member of the Demon Riders.

Giddings didn't figure he'd be recognized out of uniform, but when the biker came to the bar to order another round, he gave Giddings the once-over.

"I know you, don't I?"

"I guess we've met."

"Oh, right. You're the sheriff from Texas. You like the crossword."

"And you read the newspaper. Read any the past day or two?"

"Can't say I have. I miss something?"

"Never you mind. Don't think I caught your name."

"I'm Uptown Mike. And before you ask, there was a Downtown Mike, but he's dead now. But I still like being called Uptown Mike."

"Fine by me. And you can call me Buddy G."

"Well, Buddy G, you caught up with them boys caused all that ruckus in Amarillo yet?"

"Was just about to ask you the same."

"Ain't seen 'em. But my eyes are open, as you just learned."

"You remember me telling you not to get in my way?"

"I have a selective memory about things like that. I do remember thinking how much fun I'm gonna have tearing those motherfuckers limb from limb. That I recall."

"Just know that you're looking at a man with nothing left to lose."

Uptown Mike got the bartender's attention. "Another round of Schlitz. And whatever my friend here is having."

The bartender set a fresh whiskey in front of Giddings. He raised the glass to Uptown Mike.

"May you be in hell an hour before I know you're dead."

*

Dean leaned out the window to talk to the guard at the jump site gate.

"How you doing?" he said. "Concessions?"

"Drive on in and turn to the right. You'll see where they're setting up."

"You happen to know if Bob Dillon is around?"

"Bob Dylan? He supposed to be here, too? I heard Elvis was coming. And Frank Sinatra."

"D-I-L-L-O-N. He's in charge of concessions."

"No idea. You can ask when you get up there."

The guard raised the gate and Dean drove through. As the truck passed, the guard glanced down at the Polaroid he'd been given. He made a note to leave a message for Buddy G. at the Moonlight Inn.

TWENTY-SIX

The concession stands were lined up along the western end of the lot. A dozen or so workers were in the process of unloading delivery trucks parked nearby.

"The guy with the clipboard is probably him," said Chuck. "The boss always carries a clipboard so he doesn't have to carry anything else."

The man nodded as they approached. "Help you?"

"I hope so," said Chuck. "Are you Bob Dillon?"

"Nope. I'm Benny. Bob's gone."

"Do you know when he'll be back?"

"He won't be back. Evel fired his ass."

Chuck felt his guts churn, as if the 72-ounce steak had somehow rematerialized inside him. "You're kidding."

"Nope. Fired him this morning."

"Why?"

"Evel says he was stealing from the petty cash, making up fake invoices to be paid, taking kickbacks from the vendors…I mean, who knows how much of it's true, but when Evel gets a bug up his ass, there's no stopping him."

Dean popped a fresh stick of gum in his mouth and started walking toward the canyon. Near the rim was a fenced-off area in which a red, white and blue launching pad that looked to be about a hundred feet long was angled on top of a mound of dirt. Several large tents were set up nearby, with trucks and trailers parked around them. Most of the canyon was wide-open, though, and Dean wondered if he wouldn't be better off walking straight off the edge.

"Do you guys have a delivery?" Benny asked Chuck.

Chuck considered his answer carefully. Maybe the deal could still be made, but this wasn't the time to present it. "No, I really just need to talk to Bob."

"My guess is he's drowning his sorrows at Lulu's Lounge."

"All right. Well, maybe we'll be back tomorrow. I'm Chuck, by the way."

"Okay, Chuck. I gotta get back to work."

Chuck jogged after Dean and caught up to him. "What are you doing?"

"Just staring out at this canyon. Contemplating the infinite and whatnot."

"Don't panic. We came here to do a deal, and we're gonna get it done. Let's go back to town and have a word with Bob Dillon."

"Sure. We can ask him how many roads must a man walk down."

There weren't many restaurants in Twin Falls, but they were all packed, with lines snaking out the doors. An enterprising townie had set up a half-dozen grills in a vacant lot and was selling hamburgers and hot dogs as fast as he could cook them. Antoine waited in line for fifteen minutes before buying two burgers.

"Quite a scene," said Antoine, handing over a fiver.

"Most excitement we've had in this town since the fire of '57!"

Antoine didn't care to hear anything about the fire of '57. He took the burgers and went back to the El Camino, where Julian was sitting in the flatbed. Antoine climbed in and handed him a burger.

"The sooner we can get out of this town, the better," he said.

"What's the plan? I mean, I know you're here to get back

what belongs to you. But how are you going to accomplish that, exactly?"

"That's nothing for you to worry about. What I do, I'll do alone. And when I have what's mine...well, I don't think I can go back to Texas. That psycho sheriff, who's probably somewhere around here by now, he fucked things up for me back home."

"Are you telling me I might need to find a ride back to Albuquerque?"

"No. I'm telling you I might be staying in Albuquerque when I take you back there. Not with you. I'll get a place of my own, but...what would you think about that?"

Julian wiped burger grease from his lips and grinned. "I'd love to show you around."

"That campus of yours...a lot of heads around?"

"Heads?"

"You know, potheads."

"Oh. Well, yeah, like any college campus, I guess."

"Well, hopefully it won't come to that. Whatever deal the Melville boys had set up here, that's gonna be my deal now."

A different clerk was on duty in the crowded lobby of the Moonlight Inn when Giddings dropped by on Thursday evening. She looked harried and ready to do almost anything else for a living.

"No rooms," she said before he could say a word.

"I know. I'm camping just outside of town, but since I don't have a phone, I've been asking people to leave me messages here."

"Name?"

"Buddy G."

"That's it? Just Buddy G?"

"That's the name the messages would be under."

The clerk flipped through a pad of hotel stationery. "How about that. Message for Buddy G. from Jack O. at the jump site. Says to tell you the two guys in the picture showed up at the gate in a black truck around quarter to six tonight. They left twenty minutes later."

"Shit."

"Excuse me?"

"Sorry. I mean, thanks. I'll check in again later."

She didn't care and had already moved on to a real guest. Giddings stormed out of the lobby and stomped around the block. He jumped on the stolen Harley and started to make the rounds, looking for that black taco truck.

"Why the hell did we have to park so far away?" said Chuck.

"You see any parking anywhere near downtown? There's gotta be a couple thousand Harleys alone taking up space, and it's only gonna get worse."

"I just don't like the idea of leaving the truck unattended."

"Well, I wish I could put it in my pocket, but I just don't have room for it."

"You know, there was a guy up at Huntsville used to make smartass remarks like that. I figure someone must have told him he was funny once, not knowing the damage they would be responsible for down the road. I put up with it once or twice because I'm a good sport, but the third time I put him in the infirmary for a week."

"Oh, and you don't make smartass remarks? You must not listen to yourself—which, come to think of it, is not a bad idea."

Like everywhere else in town, Lulu's Lounge was packed. Business spilled out onto the street, and if there was a public drinking ordinance in Twin Falls, no one was enforcing it. Chuck and Dean waited for an opening and squeezed inside.

Chuck managed to elbow his way up to the bar. Eventually, he got the bartender's attention.

"I'm looking for Bob Dillon. And no, I don't mean Mr. Tambourine Man."

"Oh, I know Bob. He's in the last booth toward the back. He's been here all day."

"Thanks."

Chuck pushed back into the mob. Lulu's looked like it had been given a quick makeover in anticipation of the crowds drawn by the big event, but the mood lighting and glittery wall hangings made a poor disguise for a place that catered mostly to unemployed and retired alcoholics. At least the jukebox was up to date. Barry White crooned "Can't Get Enough of Your Love, Babe" as Chuck and Dean made their way to the back.

Two men were seated in the last booth. One was completely bald and wore a Nehru jacket. He reminded Dean of Blofeld from the James Bond movies. All he needed was a white Persian cat. The other sported Elton John glasses and a black leather jumpsuit with yellow lightning bolts embroidered on the chest. For a second, Dean thought this might be Evel himself, but the man in black leather was at least ten years too young.

"Excuse me," said Chuck as they reached the booth.

"You want an autograph?" said the man in black. "I'll be signing tomorrow at the jump site. This is my relaxation time."

"No, I need to talk to Bob. Is that you?" Chuck said, pointing to the bald man, who flashed a crooked smile.

"You've found him! Welcome to Lulu's Lounge, where dreams go to die. Join us, won't you?"

The two men in the booth made room for Chuck and Dean.

"You'll have to excuse him," said the man in black. "He's in a shit mood today."

"Correction! I was in a shit mood. Now I'm just drunk. Ooh,

I love this song," said Bob as ABBA's "Waterloo" struck up on the juke.

"I'm Chuck Melville and this is my cousin Dean."

"In town to see the wise and powerful Evel Knievel kiss his ass goodbye?"

"No, we're here to see you. We have a mutual friend who set up a deal between us."

"Let me tell you something about Evel Knievel," said the man in black, as if in the middle of an entirely different conversation. "You better enjoy him while you can, because this is his last hurrah. After this weekend, Dynamite Dave Dixon takes his proper place as America's favorite daredevil."

Chuck ignored him. "Our friend from Huntsville," he said to Bob. "You knew him as Double H, although now he goes by Triple H. But that's neither here nor there. We have a deal, you and I."

Bob bugged his eyes. "Oh, you mean Hank! I always just called him Hank. Yeah, now I know who you are. Oh, man. Shit, that was gonna be one sweet deal. Cost me my job, but I was gonna lose that anyway, right? Just as soon as Evel drops in that river and drowns or crashes into the side of that canyon and splatters into a million pieces. So I figured there was no harm in using his money to make this deal with you. I mean, I couldn't tell him about it. He never would have gone along with it. Make no mistake about it, Mr. Robert Knievel is the cheapest man on God's green earth. And he comes off all sanctimonious and anti-drugs, but the man is drinking double shots of Wild Turkey for breakfast. Yeah, but this would have been a damn good deal for all of us. I'm so sorry to have wasted your time. Let me at least buy you a drink."

Getting no reaction from Chuck, the man in black turned to Dean. "That's me. Dynamite Dave Dixon. You want an autograph?"

"Uh, well, I don't want to interrupt your relaxation time," said Dean. "I'll just get one tomorrow. But, um, someone said something about buying drinks?"

"Go get us a round and tell Terry to put it on Bob Dillon's tab. I'm having whiskey sours and Dynamite Dave, what are you drinking again?"

"Brandy Alexander. Make sure they don't forget the nutmeg."

"Chuck?"

"Double Wild Turkey sounds good to me."

"See, I'm one of the opening acts for the big suicide on Sunday," said Dynamite Dave, still oblivious to any topic of conversation besides himself. "We got the Flying Wallendas and some other stunt guys, but really, I'm the main attraction. I'm gonna jump—"

"Excuse me, Diamond Dave," said Chuck.

"*Dynamite* Dave."

"Yeah, let me just have a word with Bob here. Now, Bob, I'm real sorry to hear about your misfortunes, losing your job and all that. But you and I have a deal. I brought the product up here from Texas at great personal hazard. You don't even want to know what I went through to get here, believe me. But I am here, and I want my money."

"There is no money. Well, I mean there's *some* money, petty cash I got my hands on, but nothing like what we talked about. Plus, now I don't have the sales outlet. See, this was gonna be a black-market concessions thing. I had it all worked out, you know. Pay twenty bucks for a popsicle and get a couple joints on the side. Now, even if I had the money, I'd have nowhere to sell the product."

"But you just said you have *some* money. So let's start there. Maybe you can't buy all of it, but surely an enterprising gentleman such as yourself could figure out a way to sell some of it. All these people in town, bikers, freaks, redneck tweakers.

You've got a consumer marketplace right here in Twin Falls."

"Well, you see? You just solved your own problem."

Dean returned with the drinks.

"I'm Dynamite Dave," said Dynamite Dave.

"Yep, we established that. Here's your Brandy Alexander."

"With nutmeg?"

"I made sure he sprinkled on the nutmeg." Dean passed out the drinks and took a seat. "What did I miss?"

"Bob here is about to solve all our problems. That right, Bob?"

"Not exactly. Think about what you just said to me. All these people in town, crazy characters, the perfect target demographic for your product. And it is *your* product. You follow? You don't need me at all. You can cut out the middleman and sell your product directly to the people."

"How? Set up a lemonade stand on the corner?"

"Well, you'll have to be a little more discreet than that."

"You mind letting me out?" Dynamite Dave said to Dean. "I think it's about time for Dynamite Dave to get his dick sucked."

"Oh, by all means." Dean stood and allowed Dynamite Dave to stumble out of the booth.

"Who wants to suck Dynamite Dave's dick?" he hollered as he disappeared into the crowd.

"He's really a sweetheart," said Bob. "Had a few too many tonight."

"Look, man," said Chuck. "You owe us for our time and trouble. You don't want any product, fine. But that doesn't let you off the hook. We want a kill fee."

Bob finished his drink and chewed the ice. "What kind of kill fee?"

"Say…a hundred grand."

Bob spit ice back into his glass. "Tell you what. Let me pay for your travel expenses. How's two hundred bucks sound?"

"Sold," said Dean.

"Whoa, whoa, whoa," said Chuck. "Two hundred bucks? Are you serious?"

"Cousin, we are out of money. We take the two hundred, we go home, we bring Antoine his product, and we beg for forgiveness."

"That's the shittiest plan I ever heard. Listen, Bob. You think I'd be able to work something out with the guy they got running concessions now? Benny?"

"Well, Benny wasn't in on my plan. But Stevie, the guy running the beer stands. You might be able to set something up with him."

"Can you introduce us to Stevie?"

"It will have to be first thing tomorrow morning. I've got a flight to New York out of Boise at noon. Already got a new gig. Friend of mine hooked me up with the Lynyrd Skynyrd tour. They're playing in Syracuse tomorrow night, and I might just make it."

"I bet they'd buy some pot."

"I'm not taking it on the plane, that's for sure. Cocaine, maybe I'd take a risk. You got any cocaine?"

"No."

"That's too bad. All right, boys. I pay your travel expenses, I make the introduction tomorrow, and we're square. Right?"

"Yeah. We're cool," said Chuck.

Bob counted out two hundred dollars in cash. Dean grabbed it and pocketed it. Piercing screams from the front of the bar caught their attention. They turned to see a burly man in biker gear wearing a ski mask and holding a gun on the bartender.

"All the cash!" he hollered.

The bartender opened the register and dumped the drawer into the shopping bag the burly man had handed him. The man snatched the bag and ran out the door. The bartender grabbed a shotgun from under the bar, jumped over it, and headed out after him. Gunshots followed.

Bob raised his glass. “Never a dull moment in Twin Falls, eh?”

TWENTY-SEVEN

Giddings was out of gas and out of money. He had just enough left to buy a ski mask at the sporting goods store. He knew one way to get money in a hurry. There was a ton of cash flowing into Twin Falls, and much of it flowed into the bars. He had no chance of finding a quiet one—they were all equally crowded. The bartender at Lulu's Lounge had been rude to him earlier in the day, so he picked that one.

Happy revelers were milling on the sidewalk as he approached. He took the ski mask out of his shopping bag and pulled it on. He pushed through the crowd and into the bar, raising up his sidearm.

"Freeze, this is a robbery!"

Shrieks went up from the crowd immediately surrounding him. Some raised their hands, some dropped to the floor, a few ran out the door. He aimed his .38 at the bartender and handed him the shopping bag. "Empty the register into that bag in one smooth motion. All the cash!"

The bartender complied, as if this happened every day. Once the bag was full, Giddings snatched it back and bolted out the door.

As he ran down the block, he heard what sounded like a shotgun blast behind him. He whirled to see the bartender taking aim at him. Giddings fired twice, and the bartender twitched and tumbled, screaming all the way. Giddings took off around the corner. He was already out of breath. It had been a while since he last chased a suspect on foot. He reached the Harley, hoping it had enough juice to get him away from the immediate area. He started it up and rode half a mile west. The bike was sputtering when he pulled into the nearest gas station.

"Fill it," he said to the attendant. "Hell, give me the good stuff."

At midnight, Antoine and Julian were in the flatbed of the El Camino, about five miles from town at the end of a dirt road to nowhere.

"It gets chilly up here at night," said Julian, snuggling up next to Antoine under the sleeping bag.

"Don't get any ideas."

"I know. No sex until the mission is accomplished."

"My rules."

"I'm just trying to stay warm. You want to tell me a story?"

Antoine snorted. "Tell you a story? Like a bedtime story?"

"A story about you. Your childhood or some special memory. A get-to-know-you kind of thing."

"There's nothing I want to remember about my childhood. Until about eighth grade, I was small for my age. I got the shit beat out of me on a regular basis."

"When did it change?"

"I guess between eighth grade and high school I had a growth spurt. And I worked hard that summer. This salvage yard that belonged to my uncle. Now it belongs to me. Fourteen years old, I could strip a car down to its frame. First day of high school, I was bigger and stronger than all of them that used to beat on me."

"So you kicked their asses."

"Well, no. They still had a numbers advantage on me, and I still didn't know how to fight. But I came up with this plan, and I got my uncle to go along with it. Uncle Warren, he was bigger than me. He had a mean look to him, though he was never that way with me. Anyway, me and my uncle practiced fighting, but fake fighting. It was like a dance routine, you know. Choreographed. We got it so it looked really good, convincing. My uncle even rigged up this little bag of fake blood. I'd hold it in my fist and squeeze it as I swung at him so it would look like I broke his nose.

"One day Uncle Warren posed as my father picking me up after school. He looked enough like him, not that it mattered, since none of my schoolmates knew my Pop anyway. We staged this whole scene where I refused to get in the car with him. We got to yelling, swearing, and a crowd gathered. Uncle Warren slapped me upside the head, and the dance began. After I 'broke his nose,' he ran to the car and drove away, leaving me in the parking lot yelling after him, 'Don't ever fuck with me again!' It wasn't hard to pull off the acting job, I just pretended I was yelling at my real Pop. Anyway, I got suspended for three days. And by the time I got back, the legend had spread through the whole school. No one ever fucked with me again. And a couple of those kids that used to beat on me? They work for me now."

"Wild."

"Yeah. Okay, your turn. Storytime."

"Oh, I don't have any cool stories like that."

"You gotta have something. I need to get to know you better, too."

"I had a pretty happy childhood, actually. Loving, supportive parents. We weren't rich, but we weren't living in poverty either. I got picked on a little, but nothing too bad. I guess I could tell you about Donna, my first and only girlfriend."

"Oh, yes. I gotta hear this."

"This was in high school. I was fifteen years old. Donna sat next to me in biology class, of all things. We dissected a frog together. She did most of the work, truth be told. I barely held it together. But she liked me a lot, I could tell. And I liked her.

She was cool, she was pretty, she was funny...but there was something missing. Of course, I know now what that was, but at the time, I was just..."

"Confused."

"Exactly. Anyway, we started going steady. All that meant was we'd have lunch together, and I'd walk her home from school, go to a movie once in a while. There was some kissing, but nothing too salacious. I knew Donna wanted to go further, and my friends were egging me on. Well, one Friday night Donna was babysitting her little sister. She told me to come over, and she told me to bring rubbers. I actually had to ask my friend Lenny what that meant. He had a box of 'em in his locker, so he gave me a couple. And he told me, 'When it happens, think about baseball.' "

Antoine laughed. "Oh, shit."

"I mean, I get it now. It's a way to keep from ejaculating prematurely, right? But at the time, I didn't know anything about baseball. There was nothing for me to think about. But I knew basketball, because we'd been playing it in gym class. Shirts versus Skins. So anyway, Donna's little sister goes to bed, and Donna brings me into her bedroom, and we get naked. And we're fooling around and stuff, but nothing is happening...with my equipment, right? And she's taking notice. She asks me what's wrong. I don't answer her, but I start thinking about basketball. Specifically, I'm thinking about Marlo Danielson playing for the Skins team, his pecs all glistening with sweat."

"Boner time."

"That's what happened. I didn't even get the condom on. I just...made a mess all over her sheets."

Antoine was laughing uncontrollably now. "You're killing me here."

"Anyway, that was my one and only sexual experience with a

woman. Donna was done with me after that. And my confusion was…cleared up." He kissed Antoine on the cheek. "Sorry. I know the rules."

"Well…I was thinking maybe we could bend the rules."

"Really?"

"Yeah, well, I was just laying here thinking about baseball, and…" He rolled over on top of Julian. "Boner time."

Chuck and Dean arrived in the lobby of the Moonlight Inn for their morning meeting just in time to see Bob Dillon step off the elevator. He was wearing a lime-green turtleneck and carrying a suitcase. He gestured to a man with long, stringy hair and a beard sitting in the lobby thumbing through a magazine.

"Gentlemen, let me introduce you," said Bob. "Stevie!"

The stringy-haired man stood as they approached.

"Stevie, these are the boys I made the arrangement with. Uh…remind me?"

"Chuck. And my cousin Dean."

"Right. Chuck and Dean, this is Stevie. Maybe you can work something out. I gotta check out and head to Boise."

"Wait," said Dean. "Do you have a room here? One you won't be using?"

"That's right."

"Can we have it?"

"Hell, I'm not paying for it. It's covered through Monday morning courtesy of our friend Mr. Knievel. All yours." Bob handed Dean the room key. "I'm off to New York. Good luck, fellas."

As Bob departed, Dean and Chuck sat with Stevie in the corner of the lobby.

"How much do you know about our deal with Bob?" said Chuck.

"Not that much, but I'm aware of the product."

"We've got two hundred and fifty pounds. Our deal with Bob was for eight hundred and fifty grand, but we understand the situation has changed, so we're willing to make you a sweetheart deal. Let's say half a million."

"Let me slow you down here," said Stevie. "Bob might have thought he could get his hands on that kind of money, but there's no way I can. Especially now. Evel and his promoters have clamped down on the expenditures."

"So let's negotiate."

"Our options are limited. I mean, I could set you up with a spot on the concession line, but you can't exactly be selling that shit out in the open. You wouldn't last five minutes, and we'd all end up in jail. But I'm thinking there's another way we could go."

"All ears."

"Half these motorcycle clubs up here are criminal gangs. Dealing drugs is what they do. Now, we've got these boys call themselves the Northern Warriors working security for us. And from what I've observed, they are about as outlaw as it gets. Now, I don't know about two hundred and fifty pounds, but fifty? Maybe a hundred? They might be able to do that."

"What's your end of this?" said Dean.

"All I'm looking to do is bring you up to the site and introduce you to their club president, Driller. If you're able to work out a deal with him, all I ask is you slice off a couple pounds for me and my boys. Personal use."

"Driller. Nice guy, is he?"

"Not that I've noticed. Were you expecting to do a major drug deal with a nice guy?"

"Fair point. All right, let's meet Driller."

TWENTY-EIGHT

Giddings found a motel room in Appleton, twenty miles northwest of Twin Falls. When he got to his room, he counted his haul from the Lulu's robbery. He had nearly six hundred dollars in all denominations. He turned out the light and got the first good night of sleep he could remember since his last night at home.

He made the morning news out of Boise twice. First came a report on an unidentified masked man who'd robbed Lulu's Lounge in Twin Falls, shooting and wounding bartender Terry King, who was now in intensive care. That was followed by an update on rogue ex-sheriff Edwin "Bud" Giddings, the subject of a nationwide manhunt following the slaying of a Utah state trooper and a lone biker.

Giddings sat up with a start when he saw his wife Megan being ambushed by a reporter outside their home. Her eyes were red, and her voice trembled when she spoke.

"I don't know where my husband is, but I can tell you everything they're saying about him on the news is nothing but lies! My Bud has served his country and Ivor County faithfully, and he is not capable of such things as they're saying. Now, please! I have to go to the store."

He hated to see Megan like that. He knew she'd never understand, but he owed her a phone call at least.

"Hello?"

"Megan, it's me."

"Oh, Bud! Oh my God, Bud, what—"

"Just listen to me, Megan. I know DPS has tapped this phone

and they're trying to trace this call, so I need to make this quick. I can't ever come back home. I think you know that. We won't be seeing each other again."

"Bud, no!"

"Just listen. When you think of me, I want you to remember the good times. I know there haven't been many lately, but I'd like you to think about when we were young and first courting. Long before I pinned that stupid badge on my chest. Remember when I picked you up in my '57 Chevy and we went out to the lake?"

"Of course, Bud. That's the night we fell in love."

"That's right. I remember it was a full moon. I pulled your dress up over your head and you undid my belt and pulled down my khakis and we went skinnydipping. Remember? And I said we better be careful because there's water moccasins out here, and then I slipped my fingers inside you for the first time and you moaned like a wildcat—"

"Bud! What on earth are you talking about? That never happened and you know it."

That's when Giddings realized he hadn't been talking to his wife at all, but rather the real love of his life, Gwen Harlan. "I know. Just trying to entertain them DPS shitbirds listening in, since they ain't never gonna catch me. Goodbye, Megan."

He hung up the phone and stared at the floor. When he thought about Gwen, he couldn't bring her face into focus. He could remember her perfume, though. He wondered if she'd truly loved him, or if he was just a means to an end.

It didn't matter. Now he only had one thing left to do in this life. He was a creature of pure vengeance, and he would avenge her, true love or not. He picked up his saddlebag and headed out for the ride back to Twin Falls.

*

Chuck and Dean rode with Stevie the beer guy up to the jump site. The night before, they'd slept in the taco truck, parked behind an abandoned lightbulb filament factory on the outskirts of town. Dean was already daydreaming about their room at the Moonlight Inn.

"I think ol' Bob got swept up in the hype," Stevie was saying. "At one point, Evel was saying he expected two hundred thousand people to show up here, then he scaled it down to fifty thousand. Personally, I'll be surprised if we hit twenty thousand. Tickets are twenty-five bucks for the weekend pass that gets you onto the thirty-four acres Evel leased for the event. But the farmer who owns the hundred-some acres next door, he's charging forty bucks a night for campsites. You ask me, he's the one getting rich on this. Honestly, I think Evel's gonna take a bath on this thing."

"What about the closed-circuit TV deal?"

"Sure, ten bucks a pop to watch the jump live in a theater. But those ticket sales have been slow compared to the heavyweight fights they've shown on closed-circuit. I'll let you in on the worst-kept secret in town. You see all these ABC-TV trucks around here? That's because they're airing the jump a week later on *Wide World of Sports*. If people knew they could watch it for free from their couch just by waiting a few days, ticket sales would really go in the shitter."

"You think he's gonna make it, though, don't you?" said Chuck. "Seems like everyone we talk to thinks this is a suicide jump."

"I'll let you in on the second worst-kept secret in town. They did a test of the X2 last week—an exact duplicate of the Skycycle Evel is being shot off in. The test was a complete failure. The X2 nose-dived into the Snake River. If Evel had been aboard, he would have drowned, no question."

"They've had time to fix it, though, right?"

"I guess. Evel puts up a good front, but I know he's scared shitless. See, this is why I think this thing is gonna be a financial bloodbath. Who are Evel's fans, for the most part? Kids. They're the ones that drive the toy sales. Well, this is not an event for kids. No one is gonna bring their little ones here to watch someone die. This thing, it's more like a biker rally than anything else. Speaking of which…"

Stevie reached the gate and waved to the guard, who let him through. Activity had picked up considerably since the day before. Rows of portable toilets were being set up, along with drinking fountains. Several more tents had been erected, one of which was swarming with press. Fans who showed up early were about to learn that there wasn't much to do at the jump site other than drink beer, eat hot dogs, and watch Evel's engineers tinker with the Skycycle. To Dean, it looked like a recipe for trouble.

Stevie parked near the concession stands. "Let's find Driller."

"Hey, Chuck, you mind handling the business? It's your deal, really. I just want to wander around a bit."

"Do whatever you want," said Chuck. "Just as long as you're satisfied with a sixty-forty split."

"How quickly you forget who saved your life at Farrell fucking Farms."

"We doing this?" said Stevie.

Chuck went off with Stevie, while Dean ambled over to the concession area. He bought a bag of peanuts and a beer. Hell, it was after nine A.M. He smiled as he spotted someone he recognized sitting at a folding table with a stack of eight-by-ten photos and a black marker.

"Dynamite Dave," he said, stepping up to the table.

"You want an autograph?"

"Actually, we met last night. At Lulu's Lounge?"

"Did we? I gotta confess, I might have had one Brandy

Alexander too many last night. My head is pounding like Keith Moon."

"Yeah, you were a little tipsy. But here you are, bright and early."

"Yeah. Too early. My fans aren't out in numbers yet, but neither are Evel's. They got a couple of stands over there selling posters, buttons, and all that, but nobody's buying."

"I never asked: What exactly are you doing here this weekend?"

Dynamite Dave grinned. "See that big tent over there? It's hiding a Styrofoam replica of Mount Rushmore. Twenty-five feet at its highest, it'll take me a hundred and fifty feet to clear it and land safely on the other side."

"That sounds pretty cool."

"It's just a warmup for me. Here's what's gonna happen. Evel is gonna crash into that canyon or drown in the river. Now, they won't want to show that on *Wide World of Sports*, but they've already got the time booked. So what are they gonna do? They show Dynamite Dave Dixon jumping Mount Rushmore instead. America's gonna have a new favorite daredevil. And that's when I announce the big event."

"Which is?"

Dynamite Dave beckoned Dean to lean in close, then whispered. "The World Trade Center. I'm gonna jump from one of the twin towers to the other."

Dean whistled. "Sounds like a hell of a show. Will they give you a permit for that?"

"If they won't, I'll do it anyway. Like the French guy who walked the tightrope between them."

"I'll definitely be watching that."

"So you want an autograph? You can say you knew me when."

"Sure, give me one."

Dynamite Dave signed one of the glossies. "It's a buck."

Dean smirked, digging a dollar out of his jeans. "Well worth it. See ya around, Dynamite Dave."

Dean made his way to the edge of the canyon and stared across it. The other side looked like the surface of Mars, or so he imagined. It was rocky and desolate, and looking at it made him feel lonelier than he ever had in his life.

Stevie led Chuck to a ten-by-twenty-foot party tent with SECURITY stenciled on the side. Inside, two Northern Warriors sat at a picnic table playing checkers. Another was busy dumping beers into an enormous cooler full of ice. A fourth stood at the back of the tent in front of a cabinet stocked with shotguns, in the process of loading one. He was shirtless, revealing enormous black wings tattooed on his back. Chuck thought he might have been the tallest man he'd ever seen.

"Driller," Stevie called.

The tall man turned around. His head was shaved, and his bushy beard dyed blood-red. He wore dog tags around his neck, and eye black streaked with sweat ran down his face, reminding Chuck of the band Kiss. Tattooed across his chest were the words DEATH FROM ABOVE. When he licked his lips, Chuck could see a bolt piercing his tongue.

"Driller, this is Chuck, the guy I was telling you about. I'll let you two talk business."

Stevie headed out. Driller motioned for Chuck to join him.

"How's it going?" said Chuck, doing his best not to appear intimidated. Driller grabbed his hand and squeezed like he was trying to turn coal into diamonds. Chuck managed to hold his poker face.

"Couldn't be better."

"You sure about that? Because I think you could be."

"That your sales pitch?"

"Don't need one. The product sells itself."

"If that was true, you wouldn't be here."

"Figure of speech."

"I know. I'd actually prefer if it did sell itself. I don't like dealing with people I don't know."

"I'm Chuck from Texas. I have a truck full of weed."

"Did you serve, Chuck?"

"I served five years in the Huntsville Unit as a guest of the Texas Department of Criminal Justice. That kept me out of Viet Nam, but I'm guessing you were there."

"Good guess."

"Death from above, that's airborne, right?"

"Seventh Bomb Wing. Spent two years giving the Cong hell all along the Ho Chi Minh Trail. Ever heard of Operation Niagara? Khe Sanh?"

"I don't believe so."

"They called it Operation Niagara because we rained bombs from our B-52s like a waterfall."

"Is that where you got the name Driller?"

"Nah, I got that playing high school football."

"You were a defensive tackle?"

"Nope. I was QB one. The cheerleaders gave me the name Driller."

He winked and Chuck realized Driller didn't really care to know who he was doing business with. He just wanted to talk about himself. What Chuck would never know was that his new business partner had been given the nickname Driller after he flunked out of dental school. He'd played chess in high school, not football, and no cheerleader had ever looked twice at him. The war had given him the opportunity to rewrite his past, and he'd sunk his teeth into it.

"How was the weed over there? I heard about that Thai stick."

"It was good and it was cheap. You could buy a bottle of gin at the PX for a buck and trade it for twenty sticks. They were the size of cigars and potent as firecrackers."

"And since you got back?"

"It's crap. Nothing but skunk weed."

Chuck took his box of Winstons out of his sleeve and produced a tightly rolled joint from within. "First ride is free."

Driller plucked the joint from Chuck's fingers and stuck it in his mouth. He took a Bic lighter out of his jeans and sparked it up. He inhaled deeply and held it. He slowly exhaled and coughed.

"Oh yeah," he said. "That'll work."

"I don't know what Stevie told you, but I've got two hundred and fifty pounds of that shit. I had a buyer who was gonna pay a cool million, but he flaked out on me. I'd be willing to cut you a deal."

"A million, that ain't gonna happen. Not even close. A hundred grand, I could maybe scrape together."

"That gets you fifty pounds."

"Make it a hundred and you got a deal."

"A thousand bucks a pound. That's damn cheap."

"It's a buyer's market, no?"

"You think you could find buyers for the rest? Affiliated clubs or whatever?"

"I bet I could."

"All right. In that case, you've got a deal."

"Cool. I'll need a few hours to pull the cash together and spread the word."

"I'm staying at the Moonlight Inn. Room 318."

"You'll be hearing from me."

*

"There you are. Thinking deep thoughts again?"

Dean turned to find Chuck approaching. "I dunno how deep it is, but I was just looking over there at the other side of this canyon. And I was thinking that, best case scenario—I mean if every single thing goes right—that's where Knievel ends up. No Vegas neon, no showgirls, no cheering fans. Just that desolate stretch of rock and dirt. Meanwhile, there's a thousand things could go wrong. He could get maimed, he could drown, he could get burned alive. Every single thing has to go right." Dean pointed across the canyon. "And that's what he gets."

"Well, that's life, ain't it? Every single day there's a thousand things could go wrong. And the best you can hope for is what? Live to be a hundred, house as big as Graceland, die on a bed stuffed with thousand-dollar bills. You're still dead forever, just like every other poor sonofabitch in the world. Look at it that way, you're stupid *not* to try to jump this canyon."

"That didn't make me feel any better. What's the good word?"

"We have a deal. Driller's crew is gonna buy a hundred pounds for a hundred grand. I know it's not the kind of money we hoped for, but he's gonna talk to his contacts from other territories who are up here. Another couple sales and we'll unload the whole stash."

"Shrewd negotiating. Well worth sixty percent of the cut."

"What's up your ass? You're still gonna get out of here with six figures to start a new life."

"Here's the difference between you and me, cousin. I liked the life I had. It wasn't perfect, but I had a lot of fun."

"Good for you. Listen, Driller needs a few hours to pull the cash together. Let's grab the shuttle back into town and check into our room. I could use a shower."

"You said it, not me."

"What's that you got there?"

"Autographed photo of Dynamite Dave Dixon. It's gonna be a collector's item someday."

Antoine parked the El Camino in the pay lot in town. The man with all the grills who had taken over a vacant lot was now serving up bacon and eggs, so he and Julian each bought a plate and scarfed them down.

"All business today," said Antoine.

"What does that mean?"

"It means I need some time to myself. Can you keep busy for a couple hours?"

"No problem. There's a used bookstore a couple blocks over."

"Good. Let's plan to meet up in the Moonlight Inn lobby, say three o'clock. If I'm not there, ask the desk clerk if there's a message for you."

"Okay. Be careful, Antoine."

"Don't you worry about a thing."

Julian appeared to be going in for a hug, but Antoine gave his hand a quick shake and walked away. His plan was to walk each block, checking all the restaurants, shops, and bars. He'd already called the few hotels in town and determined that the Melville cousins had not checked in anywhere, at least not under their own names. It was possible they'd been able to get into town, do their business, and leave without him seeing them, but he didn't want to think about that. Such thoughts wouldn't lead him anywhere good.

The roar of motorcycles was a more or less constant background noise as he did his search. Downtown Twin Falls resembled the set of some Roger Corman biker flick, and when he passed people who looked like they could be actual residents, their expressions ranged from wary to deeply alarmed.

Antoine made a loop through the big parking lot in the center of town on the off chance a black taco truck might be parked there. He didn't see that, but he did spot a familiar vehicle: a psychedelic VW microbus. Creech leaned against it, smoking a cigarette.

"Fancy meeting you here," said Antoine.

"Oh, hey! Yeah, Julian told us you were heading this way, so we thought we'd check it out. I don't know that we're staying, though. The vibe is a little…dark."

"Yeah. Kinda like the vibe coming off Ziggy the other night. Heard you left him in the lurch."

Creech blushed. "I don't like to think the worst of people. But Ziggy—he had some ideas about free love that weren't cool at all. Like, he thought he was entitled to have his way with Shireen. Not cool."

"Well, don't worry about it. I kicked his ass before we left."

"Oh, dude. Violence? That's never the answer."

"Is that right? You ever read James Baldwin?"

"I don't think so. I know who he is. Seen him on Cavett."

"Yeah, well, you should read *Notes of a Native Son* and *The Fire Next Time*. One thing Baldwin said, and I'm paraphrasing here, but people like me and him grew up rooting for Gary Cooper. Like every other kid. Until that one shocking day we woke up and realized we were the Indians. Now Gary Cooper in *High Noon*, he had to wrestle with his conscience. Whether violence was the answer. But the Indians were never given the choice. See what I mean?"

Creech nodded. "Right on, man."

Antoine gave him a fist bump and moved it on down the line.

A bus rolled past. On the side, in star-spangled lettering, it said EVEL KNIEVEL SNAKE RIVER CANYON SHUTTLE.

Antoine considered jumping on it at the next stop and riding out to the jump site. Dean and his cousin could be doing their business up there without ever setting foot in town.

The bus stopped in front of the Moonlight Inn. Antoine started jogging toward it as passengers got off. That's when he saw something that froze him in his tracks.

Getting off the bus and heading into the hotel were Dean Melville and the man who had to be his cousin Chuck.

Antoine smiled. "Gotcha, motherfuckers."

TWENTY-NINE

"There's only one bed in here," said Dean.

"It's mine," said Chuck, flopping onto it.

Dean opened a closet and found a rollaway bed inside. "Fine. You're the boss, right? Except it was my quick thinking that got us this room in the first place."

"You can have the first shower."

Dean performed an elaborate salute. "How very generous, your majesty."

He did his best to use up all the hot water. His only change of clothes was back in the truck, so he tossed his tighty-whiteys in the trash and went commando. Drying his hair, he walked back into the main room, where Chuck was watching the noon news. The content didn't vary much from the broadcast Giddings had watched that morning.

"Hey, this is last night," said Dean. "The robbery at Lulu's."

"Yep. Bartender's in intensive care, poor bastard."

"They catch the guy?"

"Nope. If he tries it again, every bartender in town will be ready for him, I guarantee."

The report on the rogue sheriff out of Texas followed. It was the first either Melville had heard of it.

"Ivor County?" said Dean. "Isn't that…?"

"Sure is. That's where the shit went down with the deputy and his wife."

"And my car."

"That's not important right now. The question is, what is this sheriff doing way the fuck up in Utah?"

"Killing people, sounds like."

"I know that. You don't find it awful coincidental that he's in the same part of the country as us?"

"You think he followed us up here?"

"No, but maybe he knew where we were going."

"How the hell would he know that?"

"Did you tell anyone?"

"No. Did you?"

Chuck went silent.

"Chuck? Did you tell anyone where we were going?"

"No. But Triple H knew. And my daddy knew I met up with Triple H the day before we left, so—"

"Jesus Christ. So you stole Red's mad money, he got pissed off and called Triple H to find out where you were going? But why would Triple H give you up?"

"I'm sure he didn't know that's what he was doing, but he never was the brightest star in the Milky Way."

"So Red sold you out to this loco sheriff. He could be here now looking for you. You killed his deputy."

"But I had your car, so he's probably looking for both of us."

"Jesus H. Christ. This is just perfect. Your master plan is clicking on all cylinders."

"There's a nationwide manhunt for this sheriff. He's not gonna show his face around here. You seen those state cops patrolling around?"

"You know what, I think I'm gonna head over to Lulu's and get a drink."

"I'm staying here. I told Driller to ring this room when he has news."

"Fine. Enjoy your bed."

Their room was on the third floor, but Dean didn't bother with the elevator. He had a lot of steam to blow off, so he took the stairs two at a time. The lobby was crowded as usual. He headed out to the street and went to the corner to cross. Before he could do so, he felt something press up against the small of his back.

"Keep walking," said a voice he knew. "Over to the parking lot."

"Antoine—"

"Walk if you don't want a bullet in your back."

Dean let two bikers pass and started across the street, Antoine right on his heels.

"Antoine, you gotta believe me, this was all my cousin's idea."

"Oh, I don't doubt that for a moment. If you think that gets you off the hook, you're dreaming. See the El Camino in the second row? That's where we're going."

"We can work this out."

They reached the car. Antoine held the gun at Dean's head while he unlocked the driver's side with his free hand. "Get in."

Dean complied and Antoine slammed the door on him. He walked around the front of the car, keeping the gun trained on Dean through the windshield until he climbed into the passenger seat. He handed Dean the keys.

"You're driving."

"Where are we going?"

"Do you still have my product?"

"Yes. All of it. Well, we smoked a little, but—"

"Take me to it. Now. Don't try anything stupid. I know that's gonna be hard for you, but I will not hesitate to pull this trigger if you give me any reason at all."

When Giddings pulled up to the jump site's front gate, he recognized the guard on duty.

"Do you remember me? I gave you that Polaroid?"

"I remember. They were up here yesterday. I left you a message."

"I got it. Have you seen them since?"

"Matter of fact, they were here earlier with Stevie the beer guy."

"Are they still here?"

"Not sure about that."

"Where can I find Stevie the beer guy?"

"I'd try over by the beer."

Giddings nodded and rode over to the concessions area. A server at one of the beer stands directed him to Stevie, who was looking over some paperwork at a nearby picnic table.

"Stevie the beer guy?"

Stevie looked up. "Who's asking?"

"I'm Buddy G. I'm looking for Chuck and Dean Melville."

"Oh, Driller must have got in touch with you. You're repping one of the other clubs looking to make a deal with Chuck?"

Giddings said, "That's right."

"Well, I'm not sure if he's still up here, but you can always check in with Driller. Otherwise, you can just hang out. I'm sure they'll be around today. Although I wouldn't bother with Dean if I were you. He seems pretty checked out on the whole deal. Chuck is the guy to talk to."

"Yeah. I'm quite eager to talk to him."

"I'm really disappointed in you, Dean. You were my number one guy. We were making a lot of money together. Hell, I even gave you a generous advance when you needed it. And this is how you repay me? You disrupted the whole supply chain. My dealers are going to my competitors for product, and what do you think that's going to do for my bottom line?"

Dean drove toward the abandoned factory where the taco

truck was parked. Antoine held the gun on him, level and steady.

"I swear, Antoine, you were always gonna get your cut when we made this deal. I insisted on that before I agreed to go along with it. We were gonna get rich together."

"Mm-hmm. And what exactly was this master plan? Because it's sounding like a past-tense thing to me."

"Chuck had a connection with the guy running all the concessions for the jump. Eight hundred and fifty grand for the whole stash. Half that would have been yours."

"But."

"But that guy got fired, so the whole thing fell apart. Now Chuck has a deal to sell a hundred pounds to this biker gang doing security for the jump, and maybe the rest to other gangs."

"Uh-huh. Well, that deal isn't Chuck's anymore. It's mine. Where the fuck is this truck?"

Dean turned the corner. The factory was ahead on the left. "It's behind that building. It's all yours. You can just drive away in it, and I'll—"

"Fool, we are not negotiating. I'm taking what's mine, and what happens to you is not something you have any say about."

Dean thought back to his kin and their early deaths. He knew the Grim Reaper had to be close. He turned into the factory parking lot and drove around to the back, hoping for a miracle. Instead, he got a reprieve.

"It's not here," he said.

"What the fuck, Dean? You playing games with me?"

"No! It was here. It was parked right here. But it's gone."

THIRTY

The hotel room phone rang just after three o'clock, and Chuck answered.

"It's Driller. I've set up a meet for you."

"Just tell me where and when."

"Six o'clock, back up here at the site."

"No problem, I'll take the shuttle back up."

"No. You need to bring the truck. These guys want to inspect the product first. And come to think of it, so would I."

Chuck felt the back of his neck get hot. "Now wait a minute. How do I know I'm not driving into an ambush? Just me against a whole pack of bikers?"

"This does not sound like the spirit of trust and cooperation that fuels good working relationships. I've been doing the legwork here, finding buyers for the rest of your product, but there's no deal if we don't see the merchandise."

"Put yourself in my shoes. You're a smart guy, you've been in the shit. I'm sure my concerns are not all that mysterious to you."

"Sure, I get it. But it's not like you're walking into a dark alley. There's thousands of people up here, more arriving every minute. What exactly do you think we're going to do in front of all them witnesses? Just pull the truck up by the concessions and my boys and I will take a peek in back. If we like what we see, you get your money, and we go our separate ways."

Chuck still didn't like it, but his other options looked even worse. "All right. I'll be there. I'll be armed. My cousin will be up there too, and you won't see him."

"You're being paranoid, but that's your choice. Six o'clock by the concessions."

Chuck hung up the phone. He took a quick shower, got dressed, and headed out to find his cousin at Lulu's.

Dean wasn't lying. The space where he and Chuck had left the taco truck that morning was empty. Elsewhere in the parking lot, a man in an orange vest was waving cars into spots and taking cash from the drivers.

"You'd best not be fucking with me, Dean."

"I swear. We slept in it last night. This place looked like it had been abandoned for years. There was no one else around."

"Well, there is now. Let's go talk to the dude in the orange vest."

They got out of the car and started walking. The man met them halfway.

"You wanna park here, it's five bucks. The shuttle will be stopping here on the half-hour."

"I left my truck here this morning," said Dean. "I didn't know about any of this. The place looked completely deserted."

"Oh yeah, the factory has been shut down for years. But someone bought the property last year, and they're planning to tear it down. Don't know what they're putting up in its place, but for the next couple days, this is a shuttle stop for the Snake River thing."

"But what about my truck?"

"I had to have it towed. I looked around for the owner first, but I couldn't find you so…"

"You had it towed? Why did you have to do that? I would have gladly paid you five bucks if you'd been here. Or given it to you now."

"I had no way of knowing that. And the people who pay me

were very clear. No free parking. I'm sorry, but I had to do it."

"Where is it now?" said Antoine.

"The impound lot."

"And where is that?"

"Oh, it's out on 93 past Hollister. It serves the whole county, you know."

"How far from here?"

"Probably a twenty-minute drive or so. You'll see it off on your left. You hit Amsterdam, you've gone too far. Now if you'll excuse me, I've got paying customers."

"Thank you for your time," said Antoine. He gestured with his hand in his pocket toward Dean. "Let's go."

The previous night's robbery hadn't put a dent in the popularity of Lulu's Lounge. If anything, it was even more crowded as Chuck squeezed his way inside, where it smelled about as pleasant as you'd expect from a place jammed with several hundred sweaty bikers. If there was a fire inspector in town, his palm had long since been greased.

Chuck pushed his way to the back, craning his neck all the way, hoping for a glimpse of Dean. It wasn't that he expected his cousin to be of any help when it came to dealing with Driller and the other buyers. He needed to find Dean because Dean had the keys to the truck. After that, fuck him. Chuck was the one putting it all on the line. Chuck was going to be across the border with all the money while Dean was still hoping to get laid.

Except Dean wasn't in Lulu's Lounge. Chuck had made two complete loops and he was certain his cousin was elsewhere. Maybe up at the site, looking for the chick he'd met in Laramie. Chuck swore under his breath, cursing himself for not getting the keys from Dean before he left the hotel room. Surely Dean had taken the shuttle bus up to the site. He wouldn't drive the truck up there.

Would he?

Chuck burst out of Lulu's and started jogging in the direction of the factory where they'd parked the night before. Halfway there he was out of breath and had to walk the rest of the way. It was farther than Chuck remembered. When he got there, his first thought was that he must have come to the wrong place. What had been an abandoned parking lot was now full of cars, none of which were the taco truck he'd left sitting there that morning.

"Excuse me," he said to the orange-vested man who appeared to be in charge. "What's going on here?"

"This is one of the stops for the shuttle going out to the Snake River jump site. Did you need to park your car? We only have a few spots available at the moment."

"No. I was already parked here. A panel truck painted completely black, Texas plates."

"You had one of those too?"

"What? What is that supposed to mean?"

"A couple guys were here not half an hour ago. They said it was their truck. I directed them to the impound lot."

"The truck was towed?"

"That's right."

"Well, who were these guys? Describe them to me."

"Young guys, mid-to-late twenties. White guy with long hair and a mustache, black guy with one of them little Malcolm X beards."

Chuck could feel his heartbeat throbbing in his throat. Could Dean have sold him out to Antoine? Called him and told him where he could find his stash? Worked out a deal for his safe return to Texas?

"These two…they seem to be getting along okay?"

"Far as I could tell."

"How far is this impound lot? Can I walk there?"

"No, it's fifteen or twenty miles from here."

Chuck's mind raced with possibilities. There hadn't been enough time since the deal with Bob Dillon collapsed for Antoine to get a call from Dean and drive all the way up from San Marcos. If Dean had sold him out, it had happened before that. Or maybe Antoine had somehow figured it out on his own or heard it from someone. Whatever the case, Chuck needed help. And the only help available to him was up at the jump site.

"When is the next shuttle due?"

"Any minute now. You got a ticket?"

"What ticket?"

"Admission ticket for the event. You need it to get on the bus. I can sell you one for twenty-five bucks."

Chuck got out his wallet.

"How did you know we were coming here? Did you hear it from Chuck's father?"

"Chuck's father?" said Antoine. "Who the fuck is Chuck's father?"

"You must know Red, or at least see him around. He's usually holding down one end of the bar at Rusty's Tavern."

"I don't frequent Rusty's Tavern. No, I figured it out myself. And I'm not the only one. There's this batshit crazy sheriff who's probably up here too unless they caught him by now."

"The one from Ivor County? I saw that on the news."

"Yeah. You and your cousin sure know how to win friends and influence people. Really, you're lucky I found you first. He's got a real hard-on for your cousin."

"Antoine. I don't want to die."

"I haven't decided what I'm going to do with you yet. Let's get my product back first. We been on the road, what, fifteen minutes? This place should be coming up."

"That town up ahead must be Hollister. He said it was just past there."

"Right. Just be smart and get us there in one piece."

"Where did this El Camino come from anyway? What happened to your Trans Am?"

"That sheriff I told you about. He made trouble for me back in Texas and I had to ditch that Firebird. I don't know if I can go back. That's another thing I hold you responsible for."

"I'm sorry, Antoine. It was Chuck who—"

"Man, you just can't stop throwing your cousin to the wolves, can you? I mean, you did it right from the second you felt that gun in your back. Whatever happened to blood being thicker than water?"

"He'd give me up just as fast, believe me. He dragged me into this mess in the first place by stealing my car and using it for his crime spree. The truth of the matter is, I didn't give him up fast enough. I knew he had my car. I should have reported it stolen, but...Chuck saved my life once. At least he's always said he did. He's held it over my head ever since. Well, without going into all the gory details, a few days ago I saved *his* life. Now I wonder why I bothered."

"Maybe blood *is* thicker than water. But the fear you're feeling? That's thicker than blood. Look, up there on the left. That's it. Let's get this over with."

The shuttle bus pulled up and the crowd piled in. Chuck was at the back of the line, and by the time he got on board, there were few seats left. He showed his ticket to the bus driver and sat down next to a young black man with his nose buried in a book.

"Whatcha reading?" he asked once the bus got underway. His seatmate showed him the cover: *Bury My Heart at Wounded Knee* by Dee Brown.

"Oh yeah. They had that in the pris—uh, the college library. All about how we fucked over the Indians, right?"

"That's…one way of putting it. I've been meaning to read this for a while. I found a copy at the used bookstore in town."

"I've got some Cherokee blood on my mother's side. At least that's what my father always said. He used to call her 'half-breed' when he was pissed off, which was most of the time. You know, like that Cher song."

"Right. I have some Navajo ancestry myself. Or so I'm told."

"Who really knows, right? I mean, I don't think my mother was any half-breed. Maybe an eighth breed. Anyway, Little Bighorn was somewhere up around here, right?"

"In Montana. Northeast of here, I think."

"Yeah, I remember learning about Custer in school. You know why he's so famous? He's one of the few white guys in history to come out on the losing side."

"That's an astute observation."

"Thanks. Hey listen, I hope you don't mind me saying, but… I'm pretty sure you're the only black guy I've seen around here."

His seatmate laughed. "Pretty close. It is very white up here."

"You an Evel Knievel fan?"

"Not at all. No, I'm more interested in this event from a sociological standpoint. I'm a student, and I think I might be able to get a paper out of this."

"So you came up here all alone?"

"No, I'm travelling with…a friend. We were supposed to meet back up at the hotel in town, but he didn't show up or leave me a message, so I thought I'd take a ride out to the site. Do some…preliminary research, I guess you'd say."

"Right. So, you and your friend, that makes two black people in town for this, huh?"

"So far, yeah."

"Well, hey, my name is Charles." Chuck offered his hand. His seatmate shook it.

"I'm Julian."

"Really good to meet you, Julian. And I'm looking forward to meeting your friend, too."

THIRTY-ONE

Giddings decided to check out the campground set up on the land adjacent to the jump site. It cost him forty bucks to get in, but he was flush at the moment. He'd had no luck finding the Melvilles in town, but he hadn't considered the possibility that they might be camping out.

It quickly became evident that this was not a family-friendly campground. As far as Giddings could see, he'd stumbled into a completely lawless gathering of criminal biker gangs with a few hippies and redneck weirdos sprinkled on top. The ground was blanketed with empty beer cans, pill bottles, and cigarette butts. Open drug use was rampant, nudity—much of it unsightly—was prevalent, and every few minutes he witnessed a fight breaking out. An improbably hairy biker in the midst of receiving oral favors from a naked woman covered in red, white, and blue body paint winked and gave a thumbs-up as Giddings passed.

His lawman instincts had him itching to call in the National Guard to perform an airstrike on the entire campground, but he was no lawman anymore. These were his people now. This was the land of pure freedom he'd been yearning for, and his only job was to learn to enjoy it. But he had no time for that. Not yet.

"Hey. Hey, I know you!"

Giddings turned to see a man in a rainbow wig and a Tarzan loincloth pointing at him.

"You know me?" said Giddings.

"Yeah, your face is all over the news. You're that killer sheriff from Texas, right?"

"No, I'm not. I used to be, but not anymore. Can you understand that?"

"Yeah, man. Far out. Hey, I used to be someone else too."

"That's what I thought. What do you suppose our former selves are up to tonight?"

"Oh, wow." The rainbow man rubbed his chin. "That's a good question."

"Tell you what. Why don't you give it some thought. You come up with any answers, come find me and let me know."

Giddings left the rainbow man behind and faded into the crowd.

The bus arrived at the front gate and the guard waved it through. The driver discharged his passengers right in front of a souvenir stand as instructed, all the better to encourage those impulse buys.

"Look at all this crap," said Chuck. "Beach towels. Lunch boxes. Electric toothbrushes."

"It's the American dream, isn't it?" said Julian, taking notes on a small pad. "People sitting down to breakfast and drinking their coffee out of a mug with your face on it."

"If he makes it, they'll put him on the Wheaties box. That's the American dream."

"And if he dies, what is the value of all this stuff? To some, it immediately becomes worthless. To others, they'll be collector's items worth hoarding. How would you like that? Knowing some fine folks out there are hoping you'll die tragically so that their souvenir plates with your face on them might double in value."

Chuck thought he'd picked up on something in Julian's body language and manner of speech before, but somehow his delivery of that last remark made it clear. Or maybe it was the thing about the souvenir plates. Did they all talk about them? That couldn't be. But Bill Browder at the barbershop sure as hell had, on and on about the vultures feeding off poor dead Judy Garland, when all Chuck had wanted was a simple trim, not all the gossip from sunny Hollywood. But now Chuck was glad he'd sat through it.

"Happened when Judy died," Chuck said. "Poor thing. The vultures came out."

"Judy, huh?" Julian looked like he was reappraising him. "You a fan of hers?"

"You're not? Oh, I shouldn't assume, I know. But I'm up here with a 'friend,' too. I thought you'd understand, but maybe I—"

"I do understand. I'm just…surprised. I didn't get that vibe from you at all."

"You grow up where I grew up, you get good at hiding it. My best friends would have dragged me behind a truck and buried me in the swamp if they'd ever guessed. Don't want to think what my enemies would've done."

"Oh my God."

"Perils of a redneck upbringing. You…don't have to hide it?"

"It depends. My parents know. They're very understanding. Some friends at school."

"Like the one you're up here with?"

"Oh, I don't know him from school. We met at a bar, actually. He was just passing through, but we hit it off."

"Just passing through from where?" As soon as he said it, Chuck had a feeling he'd pushed too hard.

"Listen, I'd love to chat more, but I should probably see if I can find my friend."

"Me too. Why don't we look together, maybe we'll be lucky enough to run into both of our friends."

*

The impound lot was surrounded by ten-foot-high corrugated metal fencing, making it impossible to see from the outside whether the taco truck was on the premises. Inside the office, a man in gray coveralls sat behind a glass partition watching *Wide World of Sports* on a small black-and-white television. Dean approached the window, Antoine hovering over his shoulder.

"Excuse me. I'm here to pick up my truck."

The man glanced up and slid a card under the glass. "Make, model, and license plate, please."

Dean picked up the pen on the counter, froze, and set it back down. He motioned for Antoine to step away from the window with him.

"What now?" said Antoine.

"The license plate. We switched it back at the salvage yard. I don't know what it is now."

"Just tell him you can't remember the license number. You think that's never happened before?"

Dean went back and knocked on the glass. The man looked up, annoyed. Dean saw a name stitched on his coveralls: FINLEY.

"I'm sorry, Mr. Finley, but I can't remember the license plate. It's a jet-black Ford panel truck with a food service window built into the side. You can't have more than one of those in here."

"License plate number should be on your insurance card, which you need to get your vehicle back anyway."

Now Dean had another problem. He did have an insurance card in his wallet, but it was in Gonzo's name and had a license plate number that wouldn't match the one on the truck.

"I don't have the card on me."

"Then you can't prove the vehicle is yours. And I can't give it back to you."

"I have the keys. Isn't that proof enough?"

"Nope."

"Look, how much is it to get the truck out of impound?"

"Towing fee is twenty-five, plus twenty a night for storage. So it's forty-five at the moment."

"But it hasn't been here overnight."

"As soon as it gets here, that's twenty. Each additional night is another twenty."

"Fine. How about I give you a hundred and you let me drive it out of here?"

"Oh, you mean like a bribe."

"A tip, Mr. Finley. Not a bribe."

"Not gonna work. My books have to show that I noted the name and insurance information for each vehicle I release."

"Just make it up. Who's gonna know?"

"If there's nothing else, I'm watching the stock car races."

Antoine had heard enough. He walked up to the window and banged on the glass with the butt of the Lubbock deputy's service revolver. When Finley looked up again, Antoine pointed the gun in his face.

"We're taking the truck."

"That's bulletproof glass."

"You really want to test that?"

"I have tested it. Now I'm calling the police."

"Antoine," said Dean. "Let's get the fuck out of here."

Antoine almost pulled the trigger anyway. He got himself under control, shoved the gun back in his jacket, and followed Dean out the door.

"What now, motherfucker? You best have a plan for coming up with my money."

"Same plan," said Dean. "We get the truck. Let's drive around to the back of this place. I get up in the flatbed, I can hoist myself over that fence."

"And how are you gonna drive out of there?"

"I won't know that until I'm in the lot. Worst that happens, I get trapped in there, you get away. Let's do it now in case he's really calling the cops."

Chuck figured his luck was finally changing. Unless he was badly mistaken, Antoine the revered and feared marijuana kingpin of Central Texas was secretly a homosexual. And his boyfriend was Chuck's new best pal. If Antoine had indeed reclaimed his stash, Chuck had the leverage to get it back.

The crowds at the jump site had built steadily throughout the afternoon. The initial excitement of seeing the famous canyon along with the launch ramp and X2 Skycycle quickly dissipated. It soon became clear that the promoters had provided precious little in the way of entertainment for the weekend leading up to the jump. At the moment, the only officially sanctioned activity was taking place on a small bandstand laughably designated the Main Stage. That's where a man in a cream-colored suit, suspenders, and a straw boater was playing the likes of "Puff the Magic Dragon" on a banjo.

As the performance went on, the musician's expression devolved from cheery to concerned to terrified. With nothing else to do but drink beer, the audience started to make its own fun, which mainly consisted of hurling beer cans at the performer, not all of them empty.

"This is perfect," said Julian, taking notes. "Exactly what I was looking for."

"How do you mean?" said Chuck.

"The decay of the great American experiment. It ties in with Watergate, the president resigning, the tawdriness of the popular culture. This event is symbolic of where we are today. Westward expansion, the genocide of the natives, and it all leads to this. Evolution in reverse. I mean, the ideas need some refining, but the raw materials are all here."

"Julian, I need to use the men's room. Will you be right here?"

"There's nowhere else to go."

Chuck made his way to a row of portable toilets. Each had a line of people waiting, so he picked the shortest. The banjo player introduced an original called "The Legend of Evel" to general indifference and scattered boos. "He never acted out of anger or malice," he sang. "He jumped the fountain at Caesar's Palace."

After waiting ten minutes, Chuck finally got into a Porta-Potty and relieved himself. The smell inside reminded him of the mash house at Farrell Farms. That night already seemed like a lifetime ago, yet he didn't think he'd ever shake it off. He shuddered and stepped outside. He felt an iron arm wrap around his neck.

"Long time, no see," said Uptown Mike. "Let me introduce you to my friends."

THIRTY-TWO

For once, Dean knew something Antoine didn't know. He knew the M16 Chuck had taken off T.J. back at the salvage yard was still in Chuck's duffel, stashed on top of a couple of marijuana bales under the sink in the taco truck. He saw no reason to share this information as he hopped up onto the flatbed of the El Camino and grabbed the top of the fence surrounding the impound lot.

"If you do pull this off, you'd best not try anything stupid," said Antoine, as if reading his mind. "I'll be waiting right outside with my gun."

"Understood. I'm just hoping to survive the next five minutes." He hoisted himself up and scrambled over the top, dropping down inside the lot. There were fewer than twenty impounded vehicles, so it wasn't hard for him to find the taco truck. He sprinted toward it as the rear entrance to the office popped open and Finley came running out with a baseball bat in his hand. He had twice the distance to cover as Dean, who reached the back door of the truck and fumbled the keys out of his pocket.

"Get the fuck away from that truck!" Finley hollered as he continued to close the gap.

Dean stuck the key into the lock and turned it. He yanked the back door open. He could hear Finley getting closer, but he didn't look back. He hopped up into the truck and launched himself toward the sink. He flipped open the cabinet and pulled out the M16 just as Finley reached the back door.

"Back the fuck up!" said Dean, raising the machine gun.

Finley dropped the bat and took a step back. "Are you out of your mind?"

"Open the gate and let me out of here."

"I called the police! They're on their way."

Dean aimed at the windshield of a Buick LeSabre and opened fire. Finley ducked and covered his head as the windshield shattered.

"Jesus Christ! All right, I'll open it!"

Outside the lot, Antoine heard the burst of automatic gunfire. His first thought was that Dean was now lying dead on the ground and it was time to give up on getting his stash back. The next sound he heard was a gate being rolled open around the corner of the lot. He hit the gas and rounded the corner just in time to see the taco truck tearing out of the lot toward the road.

"Goddammit, Dean. Just when I was thinking I might let you live."

As he followed the truck onto the road back toward Twin Falls, he heard a siren and saw flashing blue lights approaching from the west.

"You better let go of me. I know the head of security." Chuck's voice was little more than a wheeze with Uptown Mike's arm wrapped around his throat.

Uptown Mike laughed. "You think there's any security here?"

The sentence was no sooner out of his mouth than four filthy speed freaks who had been rocking one of the portable toilets back and forth managed to tip it over. A river of human waste poured forth to a chorus of cheers. One of the speed freaks tackled another into the shit creek and they wrestled in the feculence.

"Let's go," said Uptown Mike, releasing Chuck's throat and grabbing his arm. He dragged Chuck through the crowd, dust devils swirling around them in the late afternoon sun. "We're over in the camping area. You're gonna be our guest of honor."

"Listen, I got something going on here. Big money. I can cut you in."

"Cut me in on what?"

"I've got a truck full of weed. Two hundred and fifty pounds of it. Drove it up from Texas. I'm selling a hundred pounds to this guy Driller and his gang. I'll give you and your gang the rest. That's a hundred and fifty pounds of product, no charge."

"Very generous offer. Where is this truck of yours?"

"Well, it's not here at the moment. You let me go and I can get it."

"Right. I let you go and never see you again. Except I've got such a fun evening planned."

"Listen. The guy who has it now, probably, is named Antoine. He's a homo. His boyfriend is right over by the bandstand. Julian. He's the only colored guy up here. We use Julian to get Antoine to give us the product."

"Good plan. My favorite thing about it? I don't need you to make it happen."

"No, you do! Julian, he thinks I'm his new best friend. I even convinced him I'm a homo too! He'll never suspect me—"

"Shut up. Even if I believed there's a hundred pounds of pot and a homo named Antoine and all the rest, it wouldn't stop me from doing what I'm gonna do to you with a little help from my friends."

They reached the campground. Hours of drinking and drug use now manifested in a contest to find out how many things could be set on fire. Campers cheered as their eight-person tent went up in flames, unconcerned about where they'd be sleeping later.

"My opinion," said Uptown Mike, "this jump is never gonna

happen. That whole fucking site is going up in smoke tonight. We're gonna bust down those fences and dump that rocket in the canyon, then we're gonna break into Evel's trailer and cornhole him with a broken beer bottle. And you're gonna miss the whole thing."

"I think you're overreacting, man. We had a little barroom brawl. They happen all the time."

"You threw up on me. And I told you nobody ever puked on me and lived."

"You watched me eat a 72-ounce steak, and then you bought me shots. Really, you brought it on yourself."

Uptown Mike paused their march long enough to punch Chuck in the stomach. Chuck doubled over as the campground spun around him.

"Might as well puke again," said Uptown Mike. "I can only kill you once."

Dean had the pedal to the metal. The truck hit ninety miles an hour. He doubted it could reach a hundred.

Antoine had no such problem. He was quickly gaining on Dean, with the police cruiser right behind him. The highway was one lane in each direction, and as it straightened out, Antoine gunned his engine and pulled up alongside Dean in the westbound lane. Antoine was raising up his gun when the cop switched lanes and came up behind him, siren blaring. Dean slammed on the brakes and both cars flew past him.

An oncoming car approached in the westbound lane and Antoine swerved back into the eastbound, leaving the police cruiser in the path of a head-on collision. Dean hit the gas and drove up close behind Antoine, preventing the cop from maneuvering out of harm's way. At the last second, the oncoming car went off the road, its fate unseen by either Dean or Antoine.

Dean saw Antoine's brake lights come on in time to squeal

over to the westbound lane, right behind the police cruiser. A blind curve awaited several hundred yards ahead. Antoine hit the gas again and passed the cruiser, which immediately veered into the eastbound lane behind the El Camino. That left only Dean in the westbound lane as a beer truck rounded the curve and headed straight toward him. The trucker blared his horn and Dean jerked the wheel, just managing to get over before the beer truck passed. Now the cruiser was sandwiched between the El Camino and the taco truck, all in the eastbound lane.

As they came around the bend into Hollister, Dean felt a surge of adrenaline. Different outcomes flashed through his mind, one on top of the next. The cop blowing out Antoine's tires and Dean sailing past them both to freedom. The police cruiser pancaked against an oncoming eighteen-wheeler. Dean making his last stand with the M16, going down in a blaze of glory.

All at once, the fight went out of him. He could only see one outcome now—the only rational one available to him. He turned on the CB, grabbed the microphone, and pressed the button.

"Breaker one-nine, breaker one-nine, this here's the…Gonzo Taco. Can someone out there tell me how to get the cops on this thing?"

The radio crackled. "Channel nine is for emergencies. If you got one, take it there, Taco."

Dean switched to channel nine. "Attention all law enforcement, especially the Twin Falls County cop pursuing me on eastbound 93 in Hollister. Actually, I'm right behind you at the moment, but the point is this. I'm surrendering. There's a McDonald's ahead on the right. I'll be waiting for you there."

Giddings finished a complete loop of the camping area. He saw no sign of the Melville boys, but he did spot a campsite occupied by the Demon Riders. He didn't see the biker he'd spoken to back in Pueblo, but the situation bore revisiting later. For now, he was thirsty.

"You mind if I crash this party?" he said to a group of campers gathered around a cooler and listening to *American Top 40* on the radio. "I'll give you five bucks for a beer."

The four men and two women looked more like long-haul truckers than bikers or hippies. As Casey Kasem introduced Stevie Wonder's "You Haven't Done Nothin'," a man in a Chicago Cubs cap gestured to the cooler.

"Help yourself. You can keep your five bucks. We delivered the beer, so it didn't cost nothing."

Giddings nodded and reached into the cooler, pulling an Old Milwaukee out of the ice. He opened it and took a long swig. "Oh, that hits the spot. Much appreciated."

"Alcohol is a depressant," said a woman with a large bandage on her nose. "Maybe you want to put your five bucks toward something that'll keep you sharp and alert. Might be some crazy shit going down tonight."

"I'm counting on it," said Giddings. "What do you have?"

"We call 'em West Coast Turnarounds. The truck driver's best friend. You ever driven overnight through the Dakotas, you know what I mean."

Giddings handed over his five dollars. The woman passed him five black pills. He threw them in his mouth and washed them down with beer.

"I was gonna suggest you pace yourself," she said. "But I guess that'll work."

Dean was on his knees next to the taco truck, his fingers laced behind his head, when he saw the police cruiser returning. The cop had either lost Antoine or decided to take the easy collar. The cruiser squealed into the McDonald's parking lot and came to a stop behind the truck. Dean could see the cop eyeing him through the windshield as he removed his seat belt. Before the cop could get out, the El Camino came rocketing in behind the cruiser.

Antoine didn't put on the brakes. He was still wearing his seat belt.

Dean watched the cop's head shatter the windshield as the El Camino rammed the cruiser into the back of the taco truck. Antoine stumbled out of the car, rubbing his neck with one hand, holding his gun with the other.

"Not smart, Dean. Not smart at all."

"What could I do? The cops were coming. I didn't have time to stop and explain myself to you."

Remarkably, the cop was still conscious. His forehead bloodied and his face embedded with glass, he struggled to get his door open.

"Get back in the truck, Dean," said Antoine. "You're driving us back to the jump site. We're gonna make that deal, at which point our partnership will come to a very sudden end."

Antoine shot out the police cruiser's rear tires, just in case.

Chuck wasn't paying much attention as Uptown Mike introduced him to his fellow Demon Riders. He didn't anticipate any future social occasions where he'd have to recall their names. The only one that stuck with him was Ricky Teardrops.

"I told them all about what happened at the Silver Dollar," Uptown Mike was saying. "And we started brainstorming what to do with you once we got our hands on you. We came up with some fun ideas, but Ricky Teardrops had the winner. Tell him, Ricky."

True to his name, Ricky Teardrops had tattooed tears running from his eyes down his cheeks, all the way to his neck. He spoke with a mouthful of hot dog, bits of which achieved escape velocity and came to a landing on Chuck's face.

"This goes all the way back to thirteenth century England. You've probably heard the term 'drawn and quartered.' Really nasty method of execution. You drag the prisoner to the gallows by a horse. You hang him by the neck but cut him down while he's still alive. You chop off his dick and balls while he watches, then you disembowel him. If he's somehow still breathing at that point, you chop off his head. You finish off by cutting the body into four parts. That's what they call quartering. We got anymore hot dogs?"

Another Demon Rider passed Ricky Teardrops a fresh frankfurter and he went to work on it, continuing his monologue. "Now, this process was refined over the centuries. The guy who assassinated King Henry IV in France, his name escapes me, but you know what they did to him? They tied each of his limbs to a different horse. His arms, his legs, four different horses facing different directions. On a signal, they whipped all the horses at the same time, and they all ran. They tore that motherfucker apart. They drew and quartered him."

"Now, we don't have no horses," said Uptown Mike with a snicker. "But we got plenty of horsepower."

"And chains," said Ricky Teardrops as two Demon Riders grabbed Chuck, one by each arm. He struggled to no avail.

"You're really going to do this in front of all these people?" Chuck said.

"You really think they're going to care? Look around you. We're back in the wild west. If anyone here even pays attention, they'll just think it's part of the show."

"We do need a little more room to pull this off, though," said Uptown Mike. "How about the four of us ride over to the eastern edge of the campsite? Chain Chucky here up to my bike and I'll drag him over."

"This is the 'drawn' part of the process," said Ricky, clipping a chain to the back of Uptown Mike's motorcycle. "Hold his legs steady for me."

Chuck managed to kick one of the bikers in the face before he could get a grip around his shins, but it was a short-lived victory. Ricky wrapped the chain around Chuck's squirming legs, pulling it tight and clipping it in place with a quick link. Uptown Mike started his bike and revved the throttle.

"I'll lead the way," said Ricky Teardrops, starting his own bike and weaving his way through the campsites. Two other Demon Riders followed.

"You'll be bringing up the rear," said Uptown Mike.

"Fuck you," said Chuck.

Uptown Mike accelerated and Chuck's legs went out from under him. He hit the dirt and flailed as the bike dragged him through the campground. His back scraped against the hard ground, kicking up dust and small rocks that pelted his arms and face. Finally provided with some entertainment, campers cheered as they passed.

Chuck gritted his teeth as he felt the flesh of his back ripping open, leaving a blood trail behind him. He didn't want to give the Demon Riders the satisfaction of hearing him scream. He held his arms up, his fists clenched, fingernails tearing into his palms. He tried to keep his eyes shut tight, but dust and dirt still penetrated his eyelids.

He folded his hands together above his head and prayed to no one in particular. *Just give me one more chance. Just let me live long enough to kill these motherfuckers. Send me to hell, I don't care, as long as they get there first.*

Uptown Mike squeezed his brakes and the chain went slack,

causing Chuck to jackknife into the motorcycle's back tire headfirst. The world spun around him, but he didn't lose consciousness. He felt himself being lifted from the ground, and when he was finally able to open his red, puffy eyelids wide enough to see, Uptown Mike was standing in front of him, grinning.

"Enjoy the ride? Man, your back looks like you've been tied to the whipping post. I wouldn't worry about the scars, though. You've been drawn, now it's time to get quartered."

Chuck took a swing and missed Uptown Mike by a mile. The Demon Riders laughed as Ricky Teardrops kidney-punched Chuck from behind, dropping him to the ground once again. Chuck felt his arms and legs being pulled, felt chains digging into his flesh, but the fight had gone out of him. His prayer would not be answered, in heaven or in hell.

The four Demon Riders moved their bikes into position, stretching his limbs until his body hovered above the ground.

"On three," said Uptown Mike, revving his throttle.

"One."

Chuck braced himself for the end.

"Two."

A gunshot, followed by three more.

Chuck hovered a moment longer before the chains around his legs went slack and he hit the dirt again. He felt the links around his wrists loosen before hands under his arms lifted him to his feet. He saw Uptown Mike and Ricky Teardrops crumpled under their fallen bikes, their foreheads blown open, blood and brains leaking onto the earth. The man holding him up turned him around.

"Got 'em all," he said, nodding to where the other two Demon Riders were splayed lifelessly on the ground.

"Th-thank you," Chuck managed.

"Don't thank me yet. Do you know me?"

Chuck peered through his swollen, cracked eyelids. "I don't think…wait. You were on the news."

"My name is Bud Giddings. I used to be the sheriff of Ivor County. I just saved you from an agonizing death I would have very much enjoyed watching. So just imagine what I'm going to do to you now."

THIRTY-THREE

By the time Dean and Antoine arrived back at the jump site, the sun was setting and the front gate was gone. It had been torn out of the ground, presumably by the same people who set the guardhouse on fire.

"What in the living fuck is happening here?" said Antoine as Dean drove on. Half of the portable toilets were burning and the rest had been tipped over, creating a churning brown river of human sewage. The concession stands had been abandoned by their operators and were in the process of being torn apart by the mob looting them for souvenirs, food, and beer. Burly, hairy men were passing women around, tearing off their clothes or reaching under what they had left to grope them.

"This is some end times shit right here," said Antoine. "*Lord of the Flies* with a bunch of redneck peckerwoods. Let's get this deal done before this whole thing goes nuclear."

"We need to find Chuck first. He made the deal with this Driller dude. I never even met the man."

"So let's find him. Park this thing somewhere safe."

"Somewhere safe? Are you serious? Look around you and tell me where that would be."

"See those two trucks over by the base camp? Just park between them and pretend you belong."

One of the trucks belonged to ABC Sports. The other had a mural of Evel Knievel in midair airbrushed on the side, and presumably contained equipment related to the jump. No one stopped Dean from parking between them.

"Out the back," said Antoine, gesturing with the gun. As

they made their way through the taco truck, he suddenly froze in his tracks. "Hold up."

"What is it?"

Antoine gestured to an open backpack sitting on the prep counter. The corner of a hardcover book was sticking out of it. "Is that my library book?"

"Huh? Oh. *Jaws*. Yeah, I'm still reading it. Brody and Hooper are on the boat with the crazy fisherman."

"Quint."

"Right. It's getting really good now."

"Fool, you left Texas without returning my library book?"

"Well, Antoine, it all happened kind of fast."

"It's not bad enough you stole a million dollars in product from me. You also stole from the fucking library?"

"I didn't steal it! It's not due until Tuesday. I'll mail it back."

"Someone will mail it back. I sincerely doubt it will be you. Let's go."

The next time Chuck opened his eyes, he was sitting in a camping chair by a fire.

"You passed out," said Giddings.

Chuck's vision went in and out of focus. He thought he could see five other people sitting around the fire, including Giddings. Three of them appeared to be asleep. One man in a Chicago Cubs cap was roasting marshmallows. The radio was playing *American Top 40*. Casey Kasem was nearing the end of the countdown.

"Written by reggae artist Bob Marley, and originally recorded by Marley with his band the Wailers, our next song has climbed much higher on the charts in this version by a guitarist and singer known for his work with Cream, the Yardbirds, and Blind Faith. Holding steady at number two, here's Eric Clapton with 'I Shot the Sheriff.'"

Despite all the pain, Chuck couldn't help but laugh.

"What's so funny?" said Giddings.

"Like the man says, I did not shoot the deputy. That's why you tailed me all the way up here, right? To get your revenge? Well, you wasted your time. It was the deputy's wife who killed him."

To Chuck's astonishment, Giddings' eyes grew moist, and a smile lit up his face.

"She did love me," he said.

"What?"

"For months we plotted how to get rid of her husband. She figured it out. You were the patsy. You were supposed to be found dead on the scene."

"Yeah, I know. I figured that out just in time. Wait, I don't get this. You came here to kill me because you thought I killed your deputy, right?"

"No, you fucking moron. Gwen and I were in love. Harlan was in the way. I don't give a shit that he's dead. You killed the love of my life."

"I…she didn't give me any choice. It was self-preservation. If she got away, she would have gone to you, you would have arrested me—"

"And you would have been found hanging in your cell. See, this was always leading to the same place for you. I was the death waiting for you all along."

Chuck couldn't let himself believe it. He had survived that night, and he had made it out of the mash house at Farrell Farms and he had narrowly escaped being torn apart by the Demon Riders. He hadn't gone through all that just to die now. It didn't make sense. He tried to ignore the pain and gather his inner resources to cheat death one more time.

"Marshmallow?" said the man in the Cubs cap. Chuck and Giddings both ignored him.

"Do you know why I came to Twin Falls?" Chuck said. "Do you know what's in that truck my cousin and I drove up here?"

Giddings leaned in with an exaggerated expression of interest. "Antoine Lynch. You stole something from him."

"You know Antoine?"

"We've crossed paths. I'm eager to see him again. And your cousin as well."

"First thing you should know, my cousin had nothing to do with what happened in Ivor County. I took his car without his permission. He didn't know I had it."

"Noble effort. But at this point, I'm all in. I might as well kill him too."

"What if I could deliver you Antoine? And Antoine's product?"

"Which is?"

"I figured you knew. Marijuana. Two hundred and fifty pounds of it. Yours for the taking. Sell it, do whatever you want with it. Hell, bring it back to Texas with Antoine in cuffs, maybe you can cut a deal."

"Oh, come on now. There's no going back for any of us. I think you know that."

Casey Kasem had moved on to the number one song in the country. For the third week in a row, it was Paul Anka's "(You're) Having My Baby." Chuck didn't want to die listening to that.

"It's worth a million dollars. I'm not saying you'll get that much, but you'll be rich. You can go wherever you want, start a new life."

The man in the Cubs cap looked up, gooey marshmallow running down his chin. "A million dollars, you said?"

Giddings opened his vest, flashing his gun. "Time for you to take a walk."

The man wiped the goo from his chin, glanced at his snoozing comrades, and got up from his chair. "I'm taking the radio," he said.

"Please do," said Chuck.

Once he and Paul Anka were gone, Chuck inched closer to the fire.

"Chilly evening, no?" said Giddings. "Don't worry. You're gonna be in a hot place soon. Hotter than Texas."

"If there is such a place, we'll definitely meet again."

Giddings laughed. "If there is such a place, I'll be running it within a week."

"I'm not ready to go. I've made my offer. A million in weed plus Antoine."

"You've got nothing to offer. I take what I want and leave a trail of dead behind me."

Chuck had nothing left to say. The sheriff was too far gone. But Chuck had a plan. One last shot. There was a burning log perched at the top of the fire, within reach of his foot. If he was quick and a little bit lucky, he could kick it at Giddings. That would provide the momentary distraction he needed.

He visualized it all. Giddings jumping up and batting at the sparks while Chuck exploded out of his chair and ran, disappearing into the crowd. Finding Dean, who had managed to get the truck back while getting rid of Antoine. Making the deal with Driller and splitting for the Canadian border, where they would say their goodbyes and start new lives under new names.

But none of that happened, because as soon as Chuck flinched toward the fire, Giddings pulled his gun and put a bullet between his eyes.

The sleepy truckers were suddenly wide awake. They saw Chuck slide out of the camping chair, his face a crimson waterfall. Someone nearby screamed.

"Dammit," said Giddings. "I should have let them bikers finish you off. It's never as satisfying as you think it's gonna be."

THIRTY-FOUR

The main stage was, miraculously, still standing. Mostly because the few members of Driller's security team who hadn't abandoned their posts to participate in the carnage were lined up in front of it, arms folded. A band was setting up. Dean knew the singer.

"Ginny."

"Say again?" said Antoine.

"The curly-haired chick on stage. Ginny. We had a date tonight."

"Oh, I see. You're trying to make me cry now."

"I just don't want her to get hurt. All this craziness. If you had someone you care about up here, you'd understand."

Antoine clenched his jaw. "I need to find a phone."

"Up here? I dunno, I guess you could try the press tent. I'll just wait here."

"You really think you're slick, don't you? You think your charm works on everyone, not just horny women with no other options."

"Hey, that's not cool. You think of the hottest chicks in San Marcos, I guarantee I've had 'em all."

"Congratulations. You want that on your tombstone?"

"You jealous?"

Antoine laughed. "You don't have a clue, do you? What I'm all about."

"Hey, for all I know, you could be married and have kids. Antoine the family man."

"Not even close."

"Well, it's not like we've ever gone out for drinks after work and discussed our personal lives."

"And now is not the time. Let's just find your cousin and get this over with. I'll make my call later."

Ginny and the Juicers launched into their set with a cover of Santana's "Evil Ways." Almost immediately, they were pelted with a shower of beer cans and half-eaten hot dogs. The security team lining the stage surged into the crowd and a melee broke out.

"See what I'm talking about?" said Dean. "She's gonna get hurt up there."

"Hey, everybody," said Ginny during the guitar solo. "We're all here to have a good time. If you came here to fight, there's a big empty canyon behind us. You're welcome to it."

Cheers went up through the crowd. For the moment, the security team had gotten the skirmish at the front under control.

"She's got this," said Antoine. "It's rock and roll, right? Come on, let's check the concession area."

As Giddings approached the jump site, he saw flames licking the sky. A mob of looters carrying cases of beer swarmed past him, heading to the camp sites. He clocked their faces as they passed. No one took any notice of him.

Killing Chuck had only made him angrier. He'd wanted to torture him slowly, over a period of days, but he'd thrown the chance away the moment Chuck made a move toward him. His gut reaction was chickenshit. He didn't have to pull the trigger to defuse the threat; Chuck was so weakened that a punch in the nose would have put him back down in a flash. He'd denied himself his full measure of revenge, and now he had a gaping hole to fill.

A young longhair in a coat of many colors approached, holding a sign reading "John 3.16." Giddings tore it out of his hands.

"What does this mean to you?"

The young man smiled beatifically. "For God so loved the world that he gave his one and only Son, that whoever believes in—"

"I know the Bible verse. I'm asking what it means to you. Why would you come here with this sign? Don't you see that we're in hell?"

"What better place to spread the Word?"

"You don't get it, son. When you're in hell, it's already too late." Giddings ripped the sign in half. The young man's smile didn't falter until Giddings knocked out three of his teeth.

As the young man ran screaming into the crowd, Giddings headed for the flames.

Half of the concession stands were still burning, while the other half had been completely ransacked and torn apart. As Antoine and Dean approached, four men with fire extinguishers were doing their best to get the blaze under control, but they were severely overmatched, and they knew it.

"I know that guy in the denim jacket," said Dean. "Stevie the beer guy. He helped Chuck set up the deal."

"So let's talk to him," said Antoine.

Stevie's extinguisher had just gone dry when Dean stepped up to him. "Hey, how's it going?"

"How's it look like it's going?" said Stevie, tossing the extinguisher to the ground.

"Like no one's in charge and nobody has a clue how to get things under control?"

"That's about the size of it. Turns out firing the event manager two days before the event wasn't the smartest idea Evel ever had. There was no plan for this shit. Our so-called security team is doing most of the damage at this point. All we could do was gather up as many fire extinguishers as we could find, which wasn't nearly enough. As you can see. We're just gonna have to let it all burn itself out."

"Yeah. Well, I know you're busy—"

"Fuck it. I'm not busy anymore. All the beer is gone. My work here is finished. I'm getting the fuck out of here."

"I'm just wondering if you know where I could find my cousin."

"No idea. Haven't seen him since I introduced him to Driller."

"And where is Driller?" said Antoine, stepping forward.

"I know you?" said Stevie.

Antoine flashed his pistol. "I think you know enough."

Stevie raised his hands. "Look, I got nothing to do with this. I just made the introductions. Last time I saw Driller, he was over in the base camp."

"That's behind the fence, where the rocket is?"

"That's right."

"Come on, Dean. We don't need your cousin anymore. Let's get this shit over with."

He saw them from a distance. The white one, who he knew only from a photograph, was talking to someone in front of a charred souvenir stand. The black one, who he'd encountered twice before, joined the conversation and pulled a gun. After a moment of chatter, they headed off in the direction of the canyon.

Giddings followed.

*

Having run out of things to burn and steal, the mob turned its attention to the base camp. A crowd of several hundred, at least six deep, surrounded the fence and started chanting and banging on it. A few tried to scale it, only to be knocked back when they reached the top by the few members of Driller's security crew still willing to do their job. It looked like an untenable situation, as those inside the fence were vastly outnumbered.

"How are we supposed to get anywhere near that fence?" said Dean.

"I've still got a gun, don't I?"

"You're gonna shoot your way up there? You have unlimited bullets?"

"I've got one with your name on it."

Dean folded his arms. "I don't believe you."

"Excuse me, motherfucker?" Antoine aimed the gun at his head.

"Antoine, you've had every opportunity to kill me by now if that's what you wanted to do. You don't need me anymore. I don't know this Driller at all. You can make the deal without me. But you're not a killer, Antoine. You're just a businessman whose business happens to be illegal."

"That's a very nice speech, Dean. I can tell you've been thinking on it. But like I already told you, you don't know a goddamn thing about me."

"I'll work with you on this, Antoine. You don't need to keep threatening me. You're still my boss, right? So I'll do what you say for a cut of the money if we get it."

Antoine stared at Dean as if he'd just proposed a trip to the moon together. "I'm almost impressed. I didn't think you had any balls on you at all. I know this whole thing was your cousin's idea and you just went along with it. But now, after stealing from me, after making me chase you all the way up here to the end of the world, you want to discuss your cut? While I'm pointing a gun at your face?"

"I don't want a lot. Just enough to get across the border and live on for long enough to find some kind of work up there. I doubt they have taco trucks, but I'll find something."

Whatever Antoine planned to say next, he didn't get the chance. He never saw what hit him, but Dean did. He was a big man wearing motorcycle leathers, his face painted with red streaks. He knocked Antoine out with one blow to the jaw and picked up the gun when it fell from Antoine's limp hand.

"I don't know if he was going to shoot you or not. But I have other plans for you, and him, too."

"Do…do I know you?" said Dean.

"Name's Giddings. I'm from Texas, too. Maybe you've seen me on the news."

"The sheriff."

"Once upon a time. You see my face? That's your cousin's blood. You're not gonna see Chuck again in this world."

"You…what are you saying? Chuck is dead? You killed him?"

"I thought it would satisfy me, but all it did was get my bloodlust running hotter. So I'm gonna have to take that out on you and Antoine here."

"But…Chuck is dead?"

"Yeah, that's what happens when you kill someone. They die. You want to know something? He begged for his life. He told me it was you who killed my Gwen, and he was just along for the ride. He said he'd serve you up to me if I let him live."

Dean felt frozen in place. He couldn't see anything beyond this moment. Giddings snapped him out of it with a slap across the face. "You hear what I said to you?"

"Listen," said Dean. "You don't have to do this. I've got—"

"Yeah, yeah, you've got a million dollars' worth of marijuana in your truck. I'm up to speed. Don't worry, I'm gonna take that, too. But we're not gonna do any negotiating."

Antoine twitched and stirred.

"Help him up," said Giddings. "And let's go see this truck of yours."

THIRTY-FIVE

"You with me, Antoine?"

Antoine rubbed his jaw as his vision came back into focus. "How the fuck did you get the drop on me?"

"It wasn't me," said Dean.

"Antoine Lynch," said Giddings, a gun in each hand. "We meet again, as I knew we would."

"Oh, fuck this."

Giddings held up the gun in his left hand. "You took this off that deputy in Lubbock, didn't you? If he worked for me, I would have had his badge for that."

"What do you want, Giddings?"

"I just want to make sure you don't get what *you* want."

A light appeared in the sky. As it drew closer, the rotors of a helicopter could be heard. An amplified voice followed.

"Attention. Attention. Please disperse and return to your campsites. The jump site is closed until tomorrow morning. Attention..."

The message continued, but Giddings gave no indication of compliance. "Take me to your truck," he said.

Antoine and Dean started walking, Giddings two steps behind them.

"He killed Chuck," Dean whispered. "He killed my cousin and smeared his blood all over his face. He's crazy."

"I'm well aware."

"What are we going to do?"

"We? There is no we."

"Look, however we ended up here, we're in the same boat now. We stand a better chance if we work together."

"Oh, so you have a plan?"

"Sort of. Think about what's still in that truck. If you can keep him distracted—"

"That's enough whispering," said Giddings, poking them each in the back with a gun barrel. "However you think you're gonna get out of this, it ain't gonna happen."

"Shit," said Dean. "Look."

The trucks that had been parked on either side of Gonzo's were both gone. The taco truck was still there, but it was under siege. Bikers smashed the hood and side panels with pipes and wrenches. The windshield and the door windows were already shattered. Two of the vandals danced on the roof, while another was busy trying to pry open the back door with a crowbar.

"Better hit the deck," said Giddings, cocking his pistols. Antoine and Dean didn't need to be told twice. As they dropped to the ground, Giddings opened fire. One bullet hit the crowbar-wielding biker in the neck, painting the truck's rear door with red Jackson Pollock spatters. Another took down one of the dancers on the roof.

"Y'all got a choice," Giddings bellowed. "Fuck off or die."

The remaining bikers fucked off.

"Get up," said Giddings. Antoine and Dean slowly climbed to their feet. "Open it up. I want to see the goods."

"Those guys who just left," said Antoine. "They're gonna come back with a hundred more."

"You think that worries me?"

"No, I don't. Because I think you've completely lost your mind."

"I know what you're trying to do. You want to make me angry, so I snap and shoot you. Give you a quick, easy death. Well, I made that mistake once already. Open the fucking truck."

As he got out the keys, Dean made brief eye contact with

Antoine. He hoped they had an understanding. He unlocked the back door and opened it. The M16 was sitting on the prep counter, six feet away. He looked back at Antoine, who stood in Giddings' way.

"Move it," said Giddings.

"You made a mistake. Do you know what it was?"

"Get out of my way."

"You could just shoot me, but you won't. No satisfaction in that."

"Plenty of satisfaction in this." Giddings pistol-whipped Antoine across the face, knocking him to the ground again. When Giddings looked up, he saw Dean Melville holding a machine gun.

"This is for Chuck," he said.

Giddings' body rippled and shimmied as it was peppered by a spray of bullets. Somehow, he got off one shot before dissolving into a psychedelic cascade of gore. His bullet found the taco truck's gas tank. In a movie, it would have exploded. Instead, it drizzled gasoline onto the ground.

"Holy shit," said Dean, lowering the gun.

Antoine sat up, rubbing his jaw. "Damn. One of us is a killer, that's for sure." He stood, raising his hands. "Might as well get this over with."

"Goddammit, Antoine. I don't want to kill you. The offer still stands. We're partners."

"Partners? No, that's not what you said. You said you still work for me."

"Well, now I'm holding a machine gun."

"Yeah. That says it all, don't it?"

"I want to trust you. But I'm going to need you to keep your hands up while I collect those guns."

Antoine complied. Dean knelt, picked up the Lubbock

deputy's pistol, and stuck it in his jeans. Then he picked up Giddings' .38 and tossed it to Antoine.

"What is wrong with you, man?"

"Maybe I know you better than you think I do."

Antoine stuffed the .38 into his waistband. "What now?"

"Same plan. Find Driller, do the deal, go our separate ways."

Antoine bent down over what was left of Giddings and dug through his pockets. He came up with a roll of bills and riffled through it.

"Looks like about six hundred bucks."

"It's a start."

A second helicopter had joined the first, circling over the jump site. The periodic announcements hadn't made a dent in the crowd, nor dampened its enthusiasm for trying to breach the gates to the base camp. The time for more drastic measures had arrived.

As one of the choppers swooped down low, Antoine and Dean saw two men in gas masks leaning out either side. They both tossed smoking canisters into the crowd.

"Tear gas," said Antoine. "Hold your breath and follow me."

As Dean followed Antoine away from the base camp and the fumes, the crowd began to disperse amid the sounds of coughing and choking. Two more gas canisters plummeted from the sky. Running with the M16 in his hands, through the smoke of burnt-out concession stands, past shadowy figures emerging from the clouds of gas, across a dusty, desolate landscape, Dean felt as if he'd been plunged into some surreal war zone in a far-off land. At one point he looked up to see a giant edifice looming ahead in the swirling smoke. With a start, he realized it was Mount Rushmore. The mob had torn down the tent covering it. Someone had painted a Groucho mustache and glasses on George Washington.

He heard music. He heard a voice, strong and gritty like Janis Joplin. He saw the stage up ahead. The band was still playing. Ginny was singing "Sweet Home Alabama." About two hundred people were still gathered in front of the stage, where Driller's security force had dwindled to four Northern Warriors. Some in the crowd were dancing and singing along, with the occasional skirmish or full-on fist fight interrupting the fun.

Dean caught up to Antoine at the back of the pack.

"We've got to wait for that tear gas to dissipate," said Antoine. "Hopefully by then the crowd will be gone and we can find Driller."

"Fine by me. I wanted to see Ginny's band anyway."

If he could have gotten closer to the stage, he would have seen a studious-looking young black man scribbling in a pocket-sized notebook, grinning to himself, lost in his own mind, oblivious to the encroaching chaos. He would have seen the larger man standing next to him, beer bottle in hand, staggering as he took a swallow. It wouldn't have meant anything to him, but he would have seen it. Antoine, to whom it would have meant something, was looking in another direction entirely.

As it happened, all they saw was a crowd. When the band launched into "All Along the Watchtower" and Ginny sang that there must be some kind of way out of here, Dean saw a ripple in the crowd as a disturbance broke out near the front of the stage. He saw one of the Northern Warriors leave his post to dive into the middle of whatever was happening. A chorus of screams went up. Ginny stopped singing in mid-verse and motioned for the band to stop playing.

"Hey!" she shouted into her microphone. "Everybody back the fuck away from the stage! Someone's hurt!"

A few onlookers fled the scene, but most stayed, gawking at something on the ground out of Dean's line of sight.

"What now?" he muttered.

Antoine craned his neck. "I'm going up there."

"Why?"

"For my peace of mind."

Dean watched Antoine go, considered his options, and followed.

"We need a doctor!" Ginny screamed from the stage. "Is there an ambulance here? Is there anyone in charge of this fucking thing?"

Antoine pushed through the crowd, pistol in hand. Dean followed, still wielding the M16. No one messed with them. Up in the air, one of the helicopters peeled off from the base camp, heading for the stage area.

Antoine ran into a tight scrum at the front. He pointed his gun at the sky and fired. "Out of my fucking way!"

The crowd parted. Dean followed Antoine to the front. He saw Antoine drop to his knees. He heard Antoine wail, a keening sound he never could have imagined coming from the man he'd called his boss.

A man was sprawled on the ground, gasping for breath. He had his hands pressed to his abdomen. A knife was lodged just above his fingers, sticking out of his gut. His shirt was soaked in blood.

"Julian," Antoine said. "Julian, it's me. It's Antoine."

Julian managed a half-smile. "I'm…sorry…"

"Sorry? What are you sorry for?"

The chopper touched down twenty yards away, people scattering to get away from its whirling blades. A man in a paramedic uniform came running out with a first aid kit.

"I…should have waited…for you…"

"Julian, tell me who did this to you."

"I…never saw him before…"

"Julian—"

"Step aside," said the paramedic. He leaned down, opened the first aid kit, and pulled out a roll of cloth medical tape.

"I'm going to need to pull the knife out," he said. "Julian, is it?"

Julian took one last breath, trying to gather the strength to answer. Antoine watched the light go out of his eyes.

"Julian?" said the paramedic.

"He's gone," said Antoine. "Can't you see that he's gone?"

The paramedic took Julian's pulse. Judging from his reaction, he found none.

"I'm sorry," he said. "Are you the next of kin?"

"Yeah." Antoine's eyes welled with tears. "I'm his brother."

"Okay. Can you help me carry him to the chopper? You can ride to the hospital with us."

"I'll help you carry him. But I'm not going with you. Not right now."

"That's up to you. Grab his legs for me."

Dean watched them lift Julian's corpse and carry it to the helicopter. He turned to the surrounding crowd, wielding the M16 like he meant business.

"Anyone see who did this?"

"I saw it," said a hoarse, raspy voice behind him. He turned to see Ginny, wiping one sleeve across her eyes.

"Ginny. It's me, Dean. From the drive-in the other night."

Her eyes went wide. "Dean? What are you—what the hell is going on here?"

"What did you see, Ginny?"

"The kid, Julian, he was so sweet. We talked before the show. He said he was going to write a paper about all this. He took notes. And he was right up front when we played."

"And what happened?"

"He was watching the show, and this big oaf was drunkenly

dancing around and slammed right into him. He gets mad at Julian and starts yelling at him like it's his fault. Like he was in the way and should have known better. I couldn't hear what they were saying, but I could tell what was going on. And then I did hear one word the guy said, really loud. I bet you can guess what it was."

"Jesus Christ."

"Yeah. And Julian got mad and started yelling and poked the guy in the chest. Not hard, as far as I could tell. But the big oaf, he hauled off and clocked Julian."

"And stabbed him?"

"No! He didn't stab him. That was the security guy. One of those Northern Warriors. They were grappling, Julian and the guy who'd hit him, and the security guy shoved them apart and just whipped out his knife and, and—It was in his belly before I even realized what was happening. It was like history repeating, you know? Like Altamont all over again."

"Do you know who it was? Which Northern Warrior?"

"Dean, what are you doing with that machine gun?"

"It's a long fucking story. Do you know which one it was?"

"When he ran off I heard one of the other Northern Warriors call to him. Called him something like...Digger? Dipper?"

"Driller."

"Yeah. That's it—Driller."

THIRTY-SIX

Dean found Antoine sitting alone on the ground, his head in his hands. The chopper had taken off a minute earlier, and its light twinkled on the horizon. The air was still hazy with dissipating tear gas. Dean cleared his throat.

"Antoine? You okay?"

Antoine looked up, dazed. It took him a moment to focus. "Yeah. Never better."

"I'm sorry, man. I didn't even know you had a brother. What a fucked-up situation. Me losing my cousin, you losing your brother on the same night."

"I didn't."

"What?"

"I didn't have a brother. I've only known Julian for…I don't even know. Three days? Four?"

"Oh. Well…I'm still sorry, I guess. He was, what, a hitchhiker?"

"I guess you could say that. He was…an innocent, you dig? Not part of our world."

"Yeah. Well, if it helps, I found out who stabbed him."

Antoine stood. "You're goddamn right it helps. Who was it?"

"Funny thing. Turns out Driller wasn't at base camp after all. He was heading up security at the main stage."

"He saw who did it?"

"No. It was him. It was Driller that did it."

Two of the Northern Warriors sat in camping chairs at a makeshift table comprised of stacked beer cases, playing five-finger fillet. The game involved placing one's palm flat on the table, fingers spread, and using the other hand to stab between the fingers with a switchblade as quickly as possible. It was a simple game, and a dangerous one, particularly when the participants were drunk or high on methamphetamine or, as seemed likely in this case, both.

Dean walked up and fired three shots into the table, causing beer cans to explode and one of the bikers to slice his pinkie to the bone. As he howled and rolled to the ground, Dean aimed the M16 at the other Northern Warrior.

"I need to see Driller. Now."

"Shit, all you had to do was ask," he said, standing up.

"Somehow I doubt that. Toss that knife aside."

The biker did so and motioned for Dean to follow him. He led Dean into a tent where another Northern Warrior was busy snorting cocaine off the naked buttocks of a woman passed out on a picnic table. At least, Dean hoped she was only passed out.

"Driller," said the biker who'd led Dean inside. "Man here to see you."

Driller looked up, rubbing a finger under his nose and sniffling. "Who the fuck is this?"

"I'm Dean Melville. You met my cousin earlier. Chuck."

"Oh yeah. He was supposed to meet me hours ago. What happened?"

"He's not going to be able to join us. But we're equal partners in this, so I'll be handling his end."

"Is that right? What's with the heavy artillery?"

"I don't know if you've noticed, but things have gotten a little crazy around here tonight. This is purely for my own protection."

"Can't say as I blame you. Thing is, the other buyers I had lined up, they ain't around now. Why don't you come back tomorrow after we've all had a good night's sleep?"

"That's not going to work. If you're the only buyer, it's all yours, but this gets done tonight."

"Shit, man, I ain't got that kind of money. I mean, I was able to pull some cash together, but not the kind of money like your cousin was talking about."

"Make me an offer."

Driller grinned, revealing a mouthful of crumbling teeth. "Those concession stands that got burned down? They didn't go up in flames with the cash still in 'em, I made sure of that. I don't have an exact count, but I'd say I've got close to fifty grand. Lotta small bills, but they add up."

"Fine. Fifty grand for all of it. All two hundred and fifty pounds."

Driller's repulsive grin grew larger. "Everything must go, huh?"

"Get the money and I'll take you to the stash."

"That's kinda rude, man. I don't like being talked to like that."

"I'm making you the deal of the century here and you want me to be polite about it?"

"Just fuckin' with you, man. Hey, you want some of this nose candy before we go? You can do it off my old lady's ass cheeks if you want."

"That's very generous, but no thanks. Is she all right?"

"Tell you the truth, I've had better."

"I mean, is she breathing?"

"Oh. Last I checked, yeah." Driller grabbed a shotgun from the rack. "I'm sure you don't mind if I carry some protection too."

"Why would I mind?"

With his free hand, Driller picked up a large, overstuffed hiking backpack from a corner of the tent, set it on a picnic table, and unzipped the top. A few tens and twenties fluttered out of it. He zipped it back up and flung it over his shoulder. "After you," he said, gesturing to the tent flap with his shotgun.

Antoine flicked the lighter in his hand and stared at the flame. He clicked it shut and then ignited it again. One minute there was light, the next it was gone.

He pocketed the lighter and pulled out Julian's notebook. He'd found it on the ground near where Julian had fallen, after the helicopter carrying his body vanished into the night. He flipped through the pages. Julian's handwriting was impossibly neat and stylized, like the writing in a children's book of fairy tales. On one page he'd doodled a sketch of Antoine's face. Antoine felt acid bubbling in his throat.

He saw them coming. Dean with the M16, a biker wearing a heavy backpack and wielding a shotgun. He stayed in the shadows, Giddings' corpse at his feet where he'd dragged it.

"That's it," said Dean, gesturing to the taco truck. "Hell, you can have the truck too, if you want it. Some of your guests did quite a number on it, though."

"You got the keys?"

"Drop the backpack and they're yours."

"I haven't seen the merchandise yet."

"You're welcome to inspect the truck. But the backpack stays here."

Driller sneered and shrugged off the backpack. "You'd best not try to fuck me. My people are still all around here, and you will not get out alive."

Dean tossed him the keys. "All yours."

Driller walked to the back of the truck and unlocked it. He leaned his shotgun against the bumper. Antoine stepped out of the shadows.

"Hey."

Driller spun around. "Who the fuck are you?"

"My name is Antoine Lynch. You took someone very special away from me."

He flicked the lighter and tossed it. The pool of gasoline under the truck ignited.

"Jesus fuck!" Driller's pants caught fire and he dropped to the ground, rolling to smother them. Unfortunately for him, he only managed to soak himself in gasoline. He howled as the flames engulfed him.

In a last-ditch effort at salvation, Driller pulled himself up onto the truck's rear bumper and crawled in through the back door. He rolled on the floor of the truck, across old grease stains that did nothing to slow the spread of the inferno. He knocked open a supply cabinet door and a bale of marijuana tumbled out and immediately caught fire. In seconds, the entire truck was ablaze.

Dean shouldered the backpack. "Let's go."

"I want to watch this a little longer."

"Antoine, his people could be here any minute. It's over. We need to get the fuck out of here."

Antoine stared into the flames.

THIRTY-SEVEN

The only bar in Metaline Falls, Washington was called the Bigfoot Lodge. A ten-foot statue of the mythical creature stood just outside the entrance, surrounded by lush greenery. A soft rain began to fall as Dean approached. He still wore the backpack he'd taken off Driller a week earlier. He tipped his cap to Bigfoot and stepped inside.

It was almost four-thirty on a Saturday afternoon, and the place was nearly empty. Dean was a half-hour early for his appointment, so he leaned the backpack against a barstool and took a seat.

"What'll ya have?" said the bartender.

"I don't suppose you have Lone Star."

"Lone Star beer? Naw. It's not distributed up here. You from Texas?"

"Not anymore. I guess I'll take a Schaefer draft."

The bartender poured it and slid it to him. On the television above the bar, an announcer was telling America about the thrill of victory and the agony of defeat.

"They're showing the Knievel jump today," said the bartender. "If you can even call it a jump. My buddy Hank paid ten bucks to see it live in a theater in Spokane last weekend. I'll never let him hear the end of it. Complete rip-off, but what do you expect from a con man like Knievel?"

Dean sipped his beer. On the screen, a *Wide World of Sports* correspondent in a mustard yellow ABC blazer stood at the jump site, the X2 Skycycle visible over his shoulder. "It's Evel Knievel versus the Snake River Canyon, with the canyon as the sentimental favorite. Before he even attempts this death-defying stunt, the famous daredevil has been overshadowed by two late-breaking news stories. Most notable, of course, is President Ford's controversial pardon of Richard Nixon, announced the morning of the jump and guaranteed to push Knievel off the front page no matter how things turn out for him. And then there's the bizarre story of Edwin 'Bud' Giddings, the former Texas sheriff whose multi-state reign of terror came to a bloody end not far from where I'm standing now. Giddings is believed to be responsible for the murders of at least eight people before himself being gunned down by an unknown assassin. Knievel has made no comment about the violence and destruction that has plagued the weekend leading up to his jump attempt. When one reporter dared ask about it, Knievel physically shoved him and had him removed from the site. Coming up after these messages, a look at Knievel's opening acts, followed by the main event."

The bartender set two shot glasses on the bar and filled them with whiskey. "I tell ya, I got no love for Knievel. Wouldn't have cared if he drowned. But whoever iced that crazy sheriff is a hero in my book, and I'll drink to him."

He pushed one of the shot glasses to Dean, who reluctantly picked it up and clinked it against the bartender's before shooting it down. *Wide World of Sports* returned from commercial with Jim McKay in the studio introducing a package of highlights from the previous Sunday morning at Snake River Canyon. Karl Wallenda walked a high wire above the canyon's edge. A woman hung by her hair from a helicopter as it buzzed over the canyon. Dynamite Dave Dixon attempted to jump a Styrofoam replica of Mount Rushmore, only to clip Abraham Lincoln's nose on his descent, sending him flying from his motorcycle, which rolled over him as he lay in a crumpled heap on the ground.

"Some sad news earlier this morning," said Jim McKay, back in the studio. "Dynamite Dave Dixon, who has been in a coma since his accident last Sunday, succumbed to his injuries and died at St. Luke's Medical Center in Boise, Idaho. He was just twenty-six years old."

"Pour me another shot," said Dean. When the bartender did so, Dean raised his glass. "Here's to you, Dynamite Dave." He tipped back the glass and swallowed.

The front door swung open, and a man hurried in out of the rain. He shook off his umbrella and hung it up on a rack near the door. He wore a long black raincoat over a dark blue suit and carried a briefcase. He took a seat at the bar, with a stool between him and Dean.

"What'll ya have?"

"Club soda with a lime, please."

The man set his briefcase on the bar in front of the empty stool. He glanced up at the television, where Evel Knievel was being strapped into his rocket. "Is he trying again?"

"Nah, this is just the film from last weekend." The bartender set a club soda with lime in front of him.

"My kid loves the guy. He's got the little toy and everything. I dunno. When I was a kid, we wore coonskin caps like Davy Crockett. I guess every generation has their own kind of hero."

"That's what worries me," said the bartender. He stepped out to check on a couple sitting in a booth near the jukebox.

Dean tapped the briefcase. "Something in here for me?"

"Depends if you've got something for me."

Dean reached into his jacket and pulled out a thick envelope. He slid it to the man, who opened it and riffled through the contents.

"Looks about right," he said. He popped open the briefcase and gestured to a manila envelope sitting inside it. Dean took it and slid a thumb under the flap. He dumped out the contents: a Washington driver's license and a U.S. passport. He examined the license. The photo of him had been taken two days earlier in Spokane, after he'd cut his hair and shaved his mustache. He still wasn't used to seeing his boyish face in the mirror. His new name was Daryl Manning.

"At least I won't have to change my monogrammed towels."

"What's that?"

"Just joking," said Dean, pocketing the ID and the passport. The man threw the envelope of cash into his briefcase and closed it. He picked it up and stood. "Well, pleasure doing business with you. You've got my card if you ever need it."

"Stay dry out there."

The man grabbed his umbrella from the rack and headed out into the downpour. Dean returned his attention to the TV screen, where the final 30-second countdown had begun. The bartender came back just in time to see the launch. The Skycycle shot off the ramp in a burst of thunder and smoke, and the parachute deployed almost immediately. Whether or not Evel Knievel had triggered it himself was still a matter of debate. The rocket appeared to be on course for a splashdown in the Snake River, but it kept drifting back until it came to a landing on the rocks below the jump site.

Evel didn't succeed, but he was still alive. Dean could relate.

As the daredevil was led from his rescue copter to a scrum of reporters, the bartender changed the channel to a baseball game. Dean ordered another beer. The bartender couldn't help but notice that he kept glancing at the door.

"Expecting someone?"

"I'm not sure."

"It's really coming down out there now."

"I guess I'll wait it out."

As the afternoon turned to evening, the bar started filling up. Every time the door opened Dean craned his neck to see who was coming inside. The rain lightened, eventually stopped. He was considering settling up and heading out when the door opened again and Antoine walked through it.

He took a seat next to Dean and ordered a gin and tonic. "Almost didn't recognize you, babyface," he said to Dean.

"You got my message?"

"Yeah. I called T.J. at the office, and he told me. How did you get away?"

"I hitched a ride with Ginny. They had a gig in Missoula, Montana the next night, so I rode there with 'em. I paid for the gas, so they were happy."

"You and Ginny get along?"

"We did. I thought so, anyway. I asked her to come with me. She turned me down as nice as she could. What about you? Last I saw, you were standing there by the truck, watching it burn."

"I hid out until dawn. You remember that money I took off Giddings? About six hundred bucks? I spent five hundred on a motorcycle. This guy down in the camping area had four bikes he was selling. I had no idea where he got them until I saw on the news about those four Demon Riders our friend Giddings shot dead. Anyway, the bike was in good shape. Got me this far."

"You must be running low on cash by now."

"Yeah, well, I didn't come here just to catch up on old times."

Dean unzipped the backpack. He pulled out a shoebox and set it on the bar. "I got to Spokane four or five days ago. Did some banking, traded in the smaller bills for bigger ones. It's all in there, your cut. Twenty-five grand."

Antoine sneered and shook his head. "A million dollars in

product. Up in smoke. That business is dead to me now. Even if I could go back, T.J. says all my dealers have gone to the competition. My cartel contacts have moved on. They'd probably cut my head off if they ever found me. But yeah, I'll take this new pair of shoes. It's time to walk on."

"Where will you go?"

"No idea. I was thinking New Mexico for a while, but…no reason for me to go there now."

"Julian?"

Antoine nodded and signaled for another drink.

"You two were…close?"

"I wish I'd never met him. No, that's not true. I wish I'd made him stay in Albuquerque. Instead, I dragged him into my world. He couldn't survive that."

"You can't blame yourself. It was complete chaos down there."

"I do blame myself. That's the difference between you and me—one of many. I don't go blaming my problems on other people."

"Is that what I do?"

Antoine tapped the box in front of him. "If the shoe fits. Julian got killed because he fought back, and he got that from me."

"You don't know that."

"I know. I have to live with it."

Dean stared into his drink. "You know what Giddings said to me? He said Chuck begged for his life. He said he tried to give me up to save himself."

"You said the same thing to me. After you tried to hang Chuck out to dry so I wouldn't kill you, you said he'd give you up just as fast if he got the chance."

"I said it, but I didn't believe it."

"So why do you believe it now? Because Giddings said so?

He was a sadistic motherfucker. He would have said anything to make you feel like shit before he tortured you to death."

"I guess I'll never know for sure."

"I wouldn't think another minute about it. You're a new man now, right? Where are you going?"

"We're a mile from the border. I guess I'll try to get a ride. Walk across if I have to."

"Canada, huh? I don't know if that's far enough away for me. Maybe Australia. That's as far as I can go without leaving the planet, right?"

Dean dug a business card out of his pocket and slid it to Antoine. "If you need a new name, this is the guy."

Antoine picked up the card. "How did you find him?"

"Asked around when I got to Spokane. Oh, something else I got for you." Dean dug around in his backpack until he came up with a hardcover book. He set it on the bar.

"*Jaws*," said Antoine.

"I found it in a bookstore in Spokane. Since your library copy went up in smoke, thought you might like to send them a new one."

"You finish it?"

"Last night. Shame about Quint, but Hooper had it coming. Fucking the chief's wife like that."

"Maybe you can work your way up to *Moby Dick*. Not the comic book, the real thing."

"No point. My name's not Melville anymore. Hey, when you mail that, you mind sending this too?"

Dean pulled an addressed package out of his backpack and set it on top of the book. Antoine read the recipient's name. "Who's Emilio Gonzales?"

"He's the Gonzo in Gonzo Taco. I'm sending him five grand for his truck. Figure it's the least I can do."

"What's to stop me from keeping the five grand?"

"Nothing at all. But I don't think you will."

Dean finished his beer and stood. He zipped up the backpack and shouldered it. "I guess this is goodbye. I don't imagine we'll cross paths again."

"I wish life was that predictable."

Dean extended his hand. Antoine stared at it a moment before giving it a quick shake. Dean left a twenty on the bar and headed outside. He followed the street out to Route 31 north and stuck out his thumb. He heard a distant rumble of thunder as the rain began to fall again.

THIRTY-EIGHT

Dean was in heaven.

This was his happy place. Floating in a tube on the Guadalupe River, sipping a cold beer on a hot day. It was Memorial Day weekend, and the summer was just getting started. He was making good money without working very hard. He had a cool car, a hot girl, and his cousin was fresh out of prison.

Chuck floated up beside him and raised his Lone Star. "This was a good idea, cuz."

"I do have my moments." They clinked their cans together and chugged their beers.

"It's been five years since I've done this. Hell, it's been five years since I've done anything worth doing. I threw away my prime years."

"You're just hitting your prime now. All you gotta do is stay out of trouble. Life is good, man."

"You talk to your boss about me?"

"Who, Gonzo?"

"Your other boss."

"Shit, cousin, what did I just say? Stay out of trouble. You're on parole. You need a straight job. What about the car wash?"

"Yeah, looks like that's gonna work out. But that ain't gonna pay me enough to move out of my old man's place."

"Look, I mentioned you to Antoine, but he ain't hiring any ex-cons. He says that's looking for trouble."

Chuck sneered. "Like I'd work for someone like him anyway. I really don't understand how any self-respecting white man could."

"That's Red talking." Dean drained his beer, crumpled up the can, and tossed it onto the riverbank. He plucked a fresh one from the mesh bag tied to his tube and dangling in the cold water.

"Being on the river like this," said Chuck. "It reminds me of that time we went canoeing on the Blanco. You remember that?"

"Yeah. You saved my life. Or so you tell me. Truth be told, I don't remember it. I hit my head on a rock."

"Maybe I should have just let you go. Maybe I should have let you slip under the water and go right over the falls. Maybe then I would've had your life instead of mine."

"You made your own choices, Chuck. I had nothing to do with them."

Later at the campsite, Loretta took their picture with a Polaroid camera. Chuck had never seen one before.

"It didn't work," he said, looking at the photo. "It's blank."

"Just give it a minute," said Dean.

The image appeared out of nowhere. Chuck and Dean with their arms around each other's shoulders, raising their Lone Star cans in salute.

"That was cool," said Chuck. He glanced over at Loretta's friend Missy, who was laying on a towel with her back to the sun, her bikini top undone.

"Why don't we get the burgers and hot dogs going?" said Dean.

"Sure, cuz."

Standing at the grill, Chuck leaned in and whispered. "You think she's gonna fuck me?"

"Missy? Probably not right away. She's getting over this guy Lewis. They were together since high school."

"Shit, only time I've been laid since I got out was at the Twilight Ranch. That redheaded whore down there."

"I wouldn't know, Chuck. I never pay for it."

Chuck gazed at Dean's 1970 Dodge Challenger gleaming in the sunlight. "Yeah. Your life's damn near perfect, ain't it?"

Dean flipped the burgers and tossed on slices of American cheese. "Nobody's got a perfect life, cousin."

"Well, I'll tell you one thing. I ain't never going back where I was. I'm gonna get me a car like that and a girl like that and I'm never looking back. I'm gonna forget I ever spent one minute in the Huntsville Unit."

"I hope so, cuz. I wish that for you, sincerely."

Chuck grabbed two more Lone Stars from the cooler. "Here's to us, then. May this summer never end."

After dinner, Dean and Loretta went for a hike in the woods. When they got back to the campsite, Missy was alone, and Dean's car was gone.

"Where the fuck did he go?" said Dean.

"He said he just wanted to take the Challenger for a ride and see what it could do. He tried to get me to go with him, but… I'm sorry, Dean, I just think he's creepy."

"That's one word for him. Goddammit, he was half in the bag already. He better bring it back in one piece."

On the last day of summer, 1974, a diver in Canyon Lake was surprised to discover a fully intact 1970 Dodge Challenger resting on the sandy bottom.

THE
END

ACKNOWLEDGMENTS

I was seven years old when Evel Knievel made his ill-fated attempt at jumping the Snake River Canyon. Of course I had the Evel Knievel Stunt Cycle. You couldn't be an American boy in 1974 and not have one, or at least envy those who did. At the time I thought Evel was a real-life superhero, and I'm pretty sure the first stories I ever read in the newspaper were in the days leading up to the jump and immediately after.

My reaction to the news that he hadn't succeeded was one of confusion. How could Evel have failed? At the time I didn't understand that the Stunt Cycle toy encapsulated the Knievel experience perfectly. It rarely went where I wanted it to go, and on the few occasions it did, the result was a failed jump ending in a crash.

I revisited Evel Knievel as an adult while writing my first nonfiction book, *Hick Flicks: The Rise and Fall of Redneck Cinema*, in which I wrote about the biopic starring the catastrophically miscast George Hamilton as well as Knievel's lone starring role as himself in *Viva Knievel*. In my research I came across a 1974 *Rolling Stone* article by Joe Eszterhas called "King of the Goons." Long before he penned *Showgirls*, Eszterhas went full gonzo journalist on Knievel's Snake River Canyon event, making it sound like something out of a *Mad Max* movie.

Eszterhas may have taken some liberties with the truth, and I have certainly taken them here. Having subsequently read more about the event in Leigh Montville's definitive biography *Evel* and the quickie paperback *Evel Knievel on Tour* by Sheldon Saltman (and viewed clips on YouTube and in the 2015 documentary *Being Evel*), it seems clear that Snake River was indeed a horrific shitshow, but the account in these pages is fictional. There is no Dynamite Dave Dixon, for example, and if there were any actual murders on the site, I'm unaware of them.

Hick Flicks was my overview of the hixploitation genre, primarily focused on drive-in movies of the '70s featuring good ol' boys, redneck sheriffs, CB radios, moonshine, gators, and plenty of automotive mayhem. *Lowdown Road* is the '70s drive-in movie playing in my mind, my own hick flick in novel form (beautifully visualized by artist Tony Stella in his note-perfect cover painting). First and foremost I need to thank Charles Ardai, Mr. Hard Case Crime himself and editor extraordinaire. After reading an early draft of *Lowdown Road*, he knew exactly where I'd gone off the rails and waved me back onto the track with good humor and boundless enthusiasm.

Lest you imagine crime fiction writers to be solitary sociopaths with warped minds who spend every waking hour conceiving all manner of dastardly deeds, I can assure you that's not the case. Sure, some of them are like that, but overall the crime fiction community is far more welcoming and supportive than I ever expected. My thanks to Eric Beetner, S.A. Cosby, May Cobb, Ted Flanagan, Paul J. Garth, Stephen J. Golds, Edwin Hill, Chris Holm, Gabino Iglesias, Scott Montgomery, Ron Earl Phillips, Rob Pierce, Clea Simon, and John Vercher. If I forgot to mention you, I owe you a beer at the next Bouchercon.

The first chapter of this book first appeared in slightly different form as a short story called "Late Pickup at Sonny's Icehouse" on the crime fiction site *Tough*. My thanks to publisher Rusty Barnes and editor Tim Hennessy.

Additional thanks to Pete Donaldson and Steve Fisher. Most of all, my eternal gratitude to Stephen King, writing idol of my youth growing up in Downeast Maine and a constant presence on my nightstand over four decades. His vocal support of my debut novel, *Charlesgate Confidential*, beginning with a cover blurb and extending to multiple shout-outs on Twitter, has truly been a dream come true. I can't imagine anyone I'd rather have in my corner. Maybe we can catch a Red Sox game someday.

Finally, loving thanks to my bride Robin Cuthbert. A writing career is rarely smooth sailing, and having a life partner who believes in you even when the waters are at their choppiest is pure gold.